Kate Mathieson is an Austr... memoir, *Ways to Come Home*, Finch Memoir Prize and debu... debut fiction novel, *Just As Y... ...*, was a warm-hearted and laugh-out-loud funny romantic comedy of 2020. Kate has lived in Scotland, England, New Zealand, Canada and Taiwan, places which are the inspiration for her books. She currently resides by the beach and canals of the most perfect place in the world, Sunshine Coast, Australia.

instagram.com/katieauthor

facebook.com/katerina.rose.555

Also by Kate Mathieson

Just As You Are

THE WEDDING DATE DISASTER

KATE MATHIESON

One More Chapter
a division of HarperCollins*Publishers* Ltd
1 London Bridge Street
London SE1 9GF
www.harpercollins.co.uk
HarperCollins*Publishers*
Macken House, 39/40 Mayor Street Upper,
Dublin 1, D01 C9W8, Ireland

This paperback edition 2025
1
First published in Great Britain in ebook format
by HarperCollins*Publishers* 2025
Copyright © Kate Mathieson 2025
Kate Mathieson asserts the moral right to be identified
as the author of this work

A catalogue record of this book is available from the British Library

ISBN: 978-0-00-860056-3

Printed and bound in the UK using 100% Renewable Electricity
by CPI Group (UK) Ltd

To all the fabulous women (yes, that includes you): always stay a little wild and unpredictable — like your hair on a humid day or your Wi-Fi signal.

Chapter One

Benjamin McDonald is already in the boardroom. Looking smug. *Of course.*

And I'm late. I hate being late. Especially today, when everything matters.

Shit, shit, shit.

Ben is in the corner chatting up a twenty-three-year-old intern. Predictable. He seems to be in his element; the girl appears fascinated by him, and so does he. He's probably telling her some long story, and she's getting all starry-eyed and putting her hand on his arm.

Ben's arrival at Peacock Publishing, just four months ago, basically came with its own parade. There were excitable whispers from every cubicle, group chats, and fervent discussions over lunch. Could someone this handsome possibly be single? The checks were done: no wedding ring; Facebook profile picture was solely him on a surfboard far out in some glistening water, and he never spoke about a significant other.

Within the first month, Ben had charmed the pants off almost everyone; guys and girls were all going gaga. Women started wearing higher heels and tighter dresses, men tighter pants and showing more calf. There were no Monday hangover looks anymore, and everyone seemed to be going to the hairdresser and the gym more often than usual. It seemed like our entire team was wondering who he was interested in, and how they could slip between his sheets for a stealth shagging session.

The thing about editors is that when we see a manuscript we really like, we're reckless about it, self-absorbed, we must have it, but all the people in the office became like that about Ben. Work wasn't getting done. Deadlines were missed. Which only made Ben look more like a star when he pulled in James McMahon, a best-selling author, whom Peacock had been trying to sign for almost a year.

I don't know what Ben did, but likely it involved lots of wine, beer and strip clubs, possibly chicken feathers and blood too. I expect this is how he signs most of his authors, given he's constantly out to long lunches full of expensive wine and fancy food, likely using his smooth looks to convince people to sign with him. He oozes city salesman to me. I feel that, if I were to look behind him when he walks by, I would see an oil slick in his wake.

Other colleagues, all wrapped up in their lives, aren't as clued up to his schmooze, and annoyingly seem to find him sweet. I file their delusions of Ben being kind under 'I'll Believe It When I See It'. And I have never seen it. In fact, Ben makes me break out in goosebumps in a bad way, the way you'd feel if you were swimming in a large ocean, and saw a big dark shadow beneath you. You're hoping *dolphin, dolphin, dolphin*, but you just *know* it's a great white shark, full of razor-pointed teeth.

There's just something about him that always suggests everything is a competition, and you are losing, and he has the upper hand. I've tried a few times to chat to him, but for some reason, he doesn't flirt with me, which is great – because I have a wonderful boyfriend, Adam – but also leaves me slightly confused. Why does he go out of his way to ignore me most of the time, only to then occasionally be a downright dick? On his first day he confused me with his secretary. Why? Because I'm a *woman*. Roll of eyes.

Am I the only one that can see right through him? I wonder this as I watch men and women making excuses to 'pass' by his office, and ask him loads of insane questions as if they were interested in his editing skills. *Please*. So what if he's won the genetic lottery?

Sure, Ben is a blond Adonis, handsome in that typical Aussie guy way, with glacial blue eyes, and perfect wavy hair. He looks rather like Simon Baker circa *The Mentalist* – tanned, chiselled and always wearing a three-piece suit, even when the rest of us are in jeans. You know the type: super expensive, dark navy, Gucci, and he looks pretty good in it. Which he knows. He also has a square jaw made to cut through steel.

But his personality is so unattractive that it always reminds me of that Edvard Munch image – you know the painting of that man on a bridge , howling in shrill existential pain: The Scream. Or maybe that's how I feel – screaming – whenever we are in the same room.

Like now. I stride as confidently as I can into the boardroom, where about forty people are milling around holding coffees and complaining about being up all night. I try not to yawn. I've barely slept a wink too and was up at five a.m. trying to pull together The Perfect Look. Have to hold my own with this editing crowd. The beauty of them. The elegant chicness. The way they could wear a garbage bag and call it *utilitarian exposé*, and everyone would nod and say '*mmmmm, wonderful*'. I'm not a good dresser, never have been, never cared that much. I would rather make room in my tiny flat for more books than for more clothes.

'Go as *you*,' my junior editor, Ruby, our best junior editor, and my favourite lunch date because of her hilarious dating stories, urged me last week, standing in front of me in high-waisted hot pink pants, and a matching almost-midriff-baring vest top. *Gen Z*. So full of confidence it's inspiring.

But go as me? I just can't. I'm happiest wearing tracksuit pants and a comfy singlet top, eating a fried chicken breast, whilst bingeing true crime or reading Jane Austen. At night, when normal people are sleeping, I'm hunched over a laptop in a darkened room at one a.m., in a sports bra, begging the creative gods to be good to me as I attempt to write my own book while eating corn chips. Tragic.

If only I were my half-sister, Lulu. Lulu who's in charge of curating six-page spreads in British *Vogue*. Lulu who could be on the cover. Lulu who makes everyone melt a little around her – the prettiness! The skinniness! The haunting beauty!

'Hey, Gemma, good luck today!' Claire, one of the new junior editors, crosses both fingers at me and I start to smile. I'll take all the luck I can get, especially if she's really rooting for me ... but then she turns around and says 'Bennie! Good luck today.'

Bennie?

Ben gives her a charming smile and does that thing where he tosses his head to the side, and looks at her from beneath a perfect curl of blond hair. I'm sure her knees wither a bit. *Damn, girl, don't fall for that.*

'Thanks, you,' he says in a smooth deep voice, and adjusts his navy blue three-piece suit, as I try not to smirk. I know that's rude, but he clearly doesn't know her name, and somehow, I manage to resist pointing that out.

As per usual, he manages to weasel his way out of any sticky situations with a lopsided smile and sometimes a wink (gross). Hence why I've nicknamed him Weasel: he just has a way of worming himself into any conversation, any book deal... Anything that is going well, you can be assured Ben (aka Weasel) is going to be there taking the glory.

Weasel surveys the room as if he were a celebrity about to make a speech, nodding a few times at people who wave at him – mostly women who suddenly have doe eyes. He seems determined to avoid me, despite the fact I'm standing two metres from him.

'Good morning, Ben,' I say between clenched teeth. Taking the high road, as I always do.

'Oh, Gemma, I didn't see you.'

Ugh. Ben. World's worst gift to *everyone*.

I wait for him to respond like a normal human.

This is the part where you say good morning too...

He doesn't.

Instead he flicks his eyes over my simple black dress. 'Heading to a finance meeting after this?'

I stiffen. What a dick. I know what he's doing: trying to psych me out. I take a deep breath; I don't need to be distracted by an asshole in Armani.

Elsa Liu, CEO extraordinaire, decked head to toe in a pink Dolce suit with sky-high Jimmy Choos, arrives with her usual flourish. How does someone who owns a publishing company end up owning a Lamborghini rather than a library? She's fantastically confident, and someone I look up to for her savviness, ambition, great taste in books and closet (except I'd have a very large library, instead of a fancy car). She looks stunning in her look-at-me pink.

I stare down at my dress, which suddenly feels like a drab black sack. This morning, I stood for an hour in my bra and undies looking around the room, because I literally had *nothing to wear*. After four wardrobe changes, I ended up in a simple French wool knit black dress with an asymmetrical neckline, which seemed to suit my pale English rose skin. It has been tailored to accentuate the hips I don't have, and finishes flatteringly just below my skinny knees, and at seven a.m. it felt perfect, paired with my killer red heels (patent leather, like a double plump lipgloss). I clipped my wavy brown hair into a soft bun at the nape of my neck, in the hope of looking librarian chic. Lastly, I donned my new tortoiseshell Versace reading glasses that emphasise the soft hazel of my eyes. Fashionable, yet focused. Nerdy, yet elegant.

I shouldn't worry about what I look like, but I do. Bad feminist? Hannah, my bestie, would have a fit. 'God sakes, Gemma, wear an old sack if you want, don't shave your underarm hair, show 'em your worth isn't tied up in how you look.'

That's Hannah, sticking it to the patriarchy one bullshit at a time. The thing is, it works for her. She's a social worker for LGBTQI, and she is known for being fierce and passionate, challenging politicians to change their policies and leading rallies up and down George Street. No one fucks with Han and we all love that about her. Jess, her partner, loves her so much, she recently got down on one knee and proposed, and really, they bring out the best in each other. Total couple goals.

Han's right about not worrying about what people think, I know that. Don't get me wrong, I'm all about women doing whatever the hell they want. But I can't help that little part inside of me that just wants to look really freakin' good doing whatever the hell I want.

Usually people wear casual clothes, but today they told us to dress up, and clearly I've totally missed the memo. I look around the boardroom, filled with gold skirts and pink shirts and bright splashes of blue and purple, mixed with Prada loafers or designer trainers, and a sinking doubt creeps in: I'm not a cool girl. I've never been a cool girl. I am nerdy and a book lover, and I've clearly misjudged today, dressing like I worked in a bank. I feel a sense of anxiety

7

and panic rise in my chest like a thousand tiny wasps stinging me.

Elsa strides by me in a flash of fuchsia, and beelines straight to Ben. I can't overhear what she's saying, but he's smiling the way he does, slightly lopsided and charming. I try not to panic. I won't be distracted by what seems just an innocent conversation.

Today is important and I have my eye on the prize. It isn't at all about what I'm wearing (although now I am questioning it); it's about who I am as an editor. I'm tenacious, and hopeful, and both of those traits got me an internship at a small publisher when I was twenty-one and no one else would hire me without experience. I worked hard, slogging it out making coffees and booking appointments, until I worked my way up to assistant, then junior editor, then editor by the time I was twenty-eight. There was a big party in my flat that night, as I got drunk and told everyone that I could now officially get my hands on the slush pile.

For the last six years, I've been a senior editor, but now the next step is on the table, and I want it, *badly*. Simply because I love books, and always had. I still turn to them when I need a rush of joy. I was hooked early; apparently, I gummied all over my father's favourite Michael Frayn. He used to have a scotch and read it most nights when he got home from his Fleet Street newspaper job. But that was before he moved out.

'Morning, Gemma.' Millie Powers, our newest intern, grins at me. 'I'm hoping you get it.'

Me too, Millie, me too.

I give her a big smile, nod thanks, and try not to let my anxiety show. Normally I'd let other people win and get the accolade, happy to stand in the shadows, but not today. This is something I've wanted my entire life. In fact, I want it so much I'm breaking out in a nervous sweat.

It all started a month ago, when Tony broke the news to the senior editors.

Tony, my boss and Head of Editing, was perpetually a designer-dressed grumpy-grump face, unless he was on the golf course or footy field (blissfully happy, and likely drunk), or muttering in rage about his ex-wife taking him to the cleaners. Last meeting he moaned that he only had one Porsche, not two. I cry for him at night. He's a terrible listener, but a really good editor, knows a hot book when he sees it, and, admittedly, I do have a soft spot for him, since he gave me many chances at editing books, including *Lovers Green*, which won a literary award several years back.

Tony had positioned himself at the front of the room with a slight scowl on his face, before he declared ceremoniously.

'There's going to be a new position created in the team: Chief Editor.'

Out of the people there, most had been recently promoted as the company grew, so it was clearly between three of us: me, Gavin and Ben.

Tony continued. 'It's a large step up. Think VIP. And, of course, more money.'

Ben's eyes lit up. Gavin cocked his head, as if weighing up the money versus the responsibility. He'd been a senior editor at Peacock for two years and could easily be in the running. But Ben? *No way,* I thought, *you've only been here four months, I've been here six years. SIX. Don't try and weasel your way in.* I tried to send telepathic thoughts his way.

And I'm pretty sure he was sending some thoughts too, because he looked pointedly at me, and narrowed his eyes, with that silly little smirk he does, as if he was telling me, *Watch out, Gemma, I'm hot on your tail. Didn't I bring in more books last quarter than you? What's happening? Dropping your game?*

Tony described the new role as key in the future of the company, and said it would take a lot of time and dedication. He basically said, 'Give me your blood, sweat and tears.'

Gavin said, 'Well, that's me out. My wife is already complaining that I spend too much time away from home.' He shrugged, looking a little defeated.

'That's what having three kids will do to you,' Ben said matter-of-factly.

Gavin looked crushed. My mouth dropped open. How could Tony think someone like this would be a good chief editor?

'Gavin, your *four* sons are adorable,' I tried to reassure him, and he gave me a weak smile.

Tony had continued. 'We're looking at breaking down the marketplace into luxury and traditional, rather than just verticals. Instead of looking after a certain genre, we want to be the first publishing house that makes the distinction for our VIP clients, that gives them the platinum level service, that understands them no matter what they write.'

I already wanted it so badly, more than I wanted most

things. I've been reading books since I was a little girl, and first fell in love with words. Words tell stories. Stories open hearts. And who doesn't want their hearts opened? To escape to another place for a little while? My childhood wasn't always the easiest, but I remember curling up with a book and letting it transport me into another world where anything was possible. As soon as I opened that book, BOOM, I could be anywhere else.

In fact, it was Judy White who taught me about love, when my mother couldn't. And Enid Blyton who taught me about magic and adventure. Books were everything to me. On the spot, right then, I would have given up my entire flat and my YSL imitation heels for that role, although I'm aware this is bribery, and generally frowned upon.

'This is such a great idea.' I nodded at Tony, trying to hide my total excitement.

'What about your romcoms? Who would look after the housewives who need to escape their routine lives?' Ben's lip was curled in what I can only describe as the beginning of a victorious sneer, as if he had me, in his mouth, like prey.

'Actually, Ben,' I said breezily, 'that's now Amy's niche.' *Talk about dropping your game; you don't even know what each of the editors manage.* I paused for a moment hoping he would look crestfallen, but he didn't. 'I look after non-fiction, though I am helping Amy out while she's on holiday.' Which is a very chief editor thing to do, I wanted to point out.

'You mean Gardening for the Elderly?' He laughed.

'It was one of the most successful books we've had here,

"Green", and was shortlisted for the Wallace Stegner Prize in Environmental Humanities. But maybe that was before you started? I'd be happy to go over the history of Peacock's success stories with you, when you have time.' I was surprised to hear the tone in my voice, but there's something about Ben that niggles at me.

'Wasn't that over two years ago?' Ben threw back the gauntlet, challenging me to keep going, right in front of Tony. But he knew I *couldn't;* it just wasn't me.

Gavin was staring at me as though I'd just grown another head. 'You okay?' he whispered, as though I'd lost my mind a bit. No one had ever seen me this fired up or frustrated, and it's because I'm great at keeping it hidden.

Han has a name for this alter ego of mine: Aunt Nelly Nicepants. She rolls her eyes at and tells me to just 'sod the lot of them and do whatever you want'. Thing I love about Han: her confidence. She's got this zest for life, and is like an ultra-cool devil on someone's shoulder, whispering in their ear, *Life's short, do it.* Apparently, I used to be a little devil too, but I've reformed. Or, as Han declares, lost my way.

I'm forever telling her I haven't completely lost my way. Firstly, I'm English, so I'm always going to be utterly polite even if I think you're a twat, and secondly, I've built my reputation based on being nice and warm and supporting people. Growing up, my mother basically personified the word *anxiety*. She was afraid of travel, of living, of life, of planes, of her dying, of all of us dying, of paying too much at the grocery store… Which has made me a life-long soother and pleaser of all people, especially authors and colleagues. Sometimes boyfriends too, for that matter. I can't help it. One of the reasons I'm as successful as I am is that I'm constantly helping, supporting, smiling – a shoulder to cry on, a place to moan, a cheerleader for anyone who is scared, happy to help wherever you want or need. I still have a little spice, but if I acted like Han I'd be fired in a second.

Tony chuckled. 'Okay, kids, I can see this has you both going. Which is great. Nothing wrong with a bit of healthy competition, but let's keep it clean. Best man wins.'

Gavin cleared his throat awkwardly. Quickly, Tony realised his mistake 'Best *person* wins. God, this political correctness shit. No offence, Gemma.'

'No offence taken.' I smiled warmly at Tony, even though that niggled me too. A part of me wanted to stand up and quote a cool feminist verse by Chimamanda Ngozi Adichie, followed by a mic drop mime, but somehow I thought it might not have the desired effect.

Ben winked at me like the sub-human he is.

I mean this utterly, and sincerely: I would pay the mafia to fix this situation. Since his arrival, every day has been excruciatingly painful whenever he's in sight. He's been the constant thorn in my side for the last four months. And it has been a *long* four months.

On his first day, he dropped off a folder that read *Appointments* at my desk and said, 'Can you book these in by five?' I looked at him quizzically, picking up the paper. 'Sorry?'

He said, 'Aren't you my *secretary*?'

I felt a wave of fury wash over me. Why, because I'm a

woman? Please. When I told him I was a senior editor, he seemed amused, and said, 'Oh, romcoms?'

I had to bite my tongue, fake a smile and say, 'Actually nature, food, non-fiction.' But he'd already left the room as if he couldn't even be bothered listening.

Did he enjoy annoying me a little too much? I could forgive a little mix-up, but then there was the time that he scheduled a 'boys' golf day' without batting an eyelid around Amy or myself. And then there were the excruciating occasions he thought it was okay to arrive at my desk with his line edits because people had mentioned I was wonderful at breathing life into badly written manuscripts, and he said I probably wouldn't mind doing his as well. I found myself trying to say no, but then I thought of those authors who were relying on Weasel – on Peacock – so I just did them, silent and seething.

Soon after that, he started sending his junior editors my way looking for 'pointers'. I wanted to say no, but I felt guilty, like I wasn't being a team player, and before I knew it, I had loads of other editors' work piling up on my desk, and I've never left the office before eight p.m., whilst Ben swans out at four p.m., without an excuse, saying loftily he was off to drinks with a new author.

For some insane reason, I think everyone deserves second or third chances so I tried again one day when I was feeling warm and in a particularly good mood. Perhaps we'd got off on the wrong foot with that secretary debacle, or the edit requests. Maybe I'd got it wrong?

So I approached him after an editors' meeting in the boardroom and suggested we get to know each other over a coffee, but he just said really loudly, 'I don't think we can date colleagues, Gemma, but thanks for the invitation.'

The entire team heard. I could feel my face turning beet red and I was so stunned I turned around so quickly that I teetered in my heels over a small bump in the carpet and knocked over a chair, which I then had to awkwardly pick up, hard to do in sky-high heels while wearing a pencil skirt. Of course, this made me *really* dislike him.

But in the weeks since that meeting, Gavin told me he's overheard Tony talking about me to some of the partners. Something about me being here for so long, knowing everything intricately, unlike anyone else. Tony has also started calling me 'sport', which he's never done before. People have told me it's in the bag, but still, that doesn't stop me worrying. I'm clear-eyed about the prospects of being the underdog, but behind Ben's bravado lurks something that suggests he can fail too.

It's been something the whole office has been wondering. Who will win the Grand Final of Editing. I hear people gossiping in the hallways, Team Me or Team Ben. I bet there's even a sweep like it's the Melbourne Cup. Because we all know, today one of us is going to be triumphant. One of us is going to be Chief.

It's either me, or it's Ben.

Chapter Two

About forty people are crammed in the board room. There's definitely a buzz. Coffee has kicked in and everyone is excitedly waiting for the big reveal.

My phone beeps. I notice my hand is shaking as I read the text from Adam, my boyfriend of eleven months.

Good Luck Baby, You Got This. Ambition means nothing without execution.

Adam Khan: dux of his school, thinks kitchens are overrated because Uber Eats is more efficient, and considers artificial intelligence superior to humans. He's actually *excited* about robots one day taking over the world.

We met on Hinge, and he was unlike the other guys I've dated: he's stable and consistent and calm. So what if he always has some saying on his fridge that he looks at every morning to prep himself for the day? It seems to have worked for him, because just last week, he was offered the role of Head of Digital Strategy (despite many conversations, I still have no idea what this means) at Lincoln, a new tech Artificial Intelligence company.

Adam is the type of person that has CEO dreams. Recently, he mapped out the rest of our lives: we'd both get promotions, then we'd have enough money for a house deposit somewhere we actually like; he'd get me a classy solitaire diamond; the wedding would be at the local country club with a band because DJs are just too loud nowadays, and we'd honeymoon in Italy, because I published Lucy Alder's book on long Italian lunches and I've always wanted to go. Florence. Positano. Places where lemons grow in pots, and the sea is a bright blue.

In a few years, we'd have two kids and start a property portfolio, or as he put it, 'an empire'.

I'm about to text him back, when someone grabs my arm.

'Gem! Are you feeling nervous? God, it's like everyone in the entire company is here.' Ruby scans the room. Before I can answer, she gives me a once over. 'I thought you were dressing … like *you*. You look like an accountant.'

'Yes, thank you for that.' I try to shake it off. Her rather large red dress is hard to miss. It falls to the floor like a theatre curtain, stitched in gold brocade. She looks like she's about to enact a Shakespeare soliloquy instead of attending a meeting. But she fits in, much more than I do.

'Anyway, Tony wanted to talk to you before the announcement.' She looks perplexed, worried.

'About?'

'He didn't say.' Ruby chews her lip.

For a second, my heart beats faster. I was late – the trains were delayed – and Tony wanted to talk to me. Was everything about this day *an omen*?

But no, that's insane. Of course it means *nothing*.

As if reading my thoughts, Ruby murmurs, 'Does something about today feel off to you?'

I try to swallow but my throat is dry. Her worried face makes me feel jittery. 'What do you mean, *off*?'

'Look.' She points out of the window. 'The sky suddenly has that weird grey-purple it gets before there's a massive storm. And I picked this tarot card this morning.' She digs inside the top of her long dress and pulls a tarot card from her bra. Her large, dark chocolate Filipino eyes widen even further as she flips the card into my hand and said in an ominous voice, 'The Tower.' On the card, there are people diving off a tower that is toppling over, and in flames. Across the entire image, the sky is full of lightning.

'God, what is this?' I hastily give it back to her. Not that I believe in that stuff, but I don't want any juju imprinting suicidal people or burning buildings on today.

'It's unexpected change, or…' Ruby explains.

'Or?' I ask quickly, but we are interrupted by the meeting starting, just as Ruby manages to say, 'Disaster.'

'Welcome, everyone!'

Tony enters the room and makes his way to the front of the room, quickly as if he's about to be tackled. He's not a fan of junior editors, feels that most of them are time wasters, and his main fear is to be locked in an elevator with an eager new editor who wants to tell him how much they're keen to 'change the world with words'. I know this because I was one of them (still am), but I learnt to shut up when he curtly responded, 'We're here to edit, not do brain surgery.'

Tony is wearing an open white Dolce shirt (we all know it's Dolce because it has a rather large gold crown in the upper left corner just below the pointed collar), perfectly pressed lime-green Italian pants and horsebit loafers without socks. They're probably Gucci or something. When we win literary awards or have a bestseller, that's where the money goes: not to authors, but to our management team and their extensive closets and McMansion houses on the north shore. He dismisses the podium and microphone Bec the receptionist has set up, and uses his distinct booming voice to welcome everyone, twice more.

I take a quick glance around the room and note Gavin at the back leaning against a wall (already looking defeated), and Ben standing up at the front next to Tony as if he's already won. *Jesus, this guy.* His hair perfectly in place. A small smirky smile. He turns his head and catches my eyes. Raises an eyebrow. I raise an eyebrow back at him.

So here we are, nemesis.

Tony booms. 'I want to move on quickly to why we're all here. There's been a lot of buzz about the direction of Peacock Publishing, and our plan to service VIP clients in a different way from that of any other publishing house.'

Elsa, standing next to Tony, like a prize everyone wants to win, beams. 'It's a wonderful, exciting time.' She adds a pause. 'I'm sure this person knows what they can do with this role, they're very capable.' She smiles somewhat in my direction. Or am I imagining that?

My throat feels dry, and my palms are immediately clammy. I resist the urge to rub them on my dress.

Tony pauses. 'So today we're here to announce that the new chief editor is…'

My heart is beating so loudly, my pulse throbs like a drum in my ears.

'Someone who is exuberant and shows a passion for editing and a unique approach to the entire game. So without further ado…'

The room is suddenly deathly silent. I can hear a collective holding of breath.

'Congratulations…'

My own brain repeats *Gemma Evans. Gemma Evans. Gemma*—

'Ben McDonald.'

The room erupts into applause. My stomach drops. All the blood in my face drains towards my feet, and for a second I feel dizzy, woozy. *This cannot be happening.*

Ben is grinning widely, a dazzling smile, as he turns to face everyone, and waving his hand like a royal.

I fight back the lump in my throat. I force myself to clap. Try to smile. But inside, I feel empty, shocked. *Don't cry.* Don't give him the satisfaction.

Tony is still talking. 'And of course we know that Ben moving up will leave a gaping hole, but we have another bit of special news. We have a very trustworthy and capable editor to fill in for us and take over Ben's portfolio, along with her own. Congratulations, Gemma Evans.'

I gasp. People are clapping for me now, but it's a slower clap, like it's lost some of its energy. We all know why: it's hardly a promotion. It's the runner-up prize. Ben's leftovers. Embarrassment flushes my cheeks, and my stomach knots. I nod *thank you*, but I just wish everyone would turn back around, so I could leave.

People are urging me to go and stand up the front, next to Weasel.

Hello, burning tower of hell.

Time slows as I move towards the front of the room. I turn around and face the crowd. My cheeks are burning red and I can feel tears starting behind my eyes, but I won't give him the satisfaction, though I could feel him gloating a foot away from me.

When the clapping dies down and people start heading towards the refreshment table for coffee and celebratory muffins, Ben turns his awful self to me, and *winks*. 'Does this mean I'm your boss now?'

I want to cut you into tiny pieces.

Thankfully Tony smiles and says, 'No, Ben, not yet', which feels like another gut punch right to the stomach.

Not yet.

'Aren't you going to congratulate me?' he says in such a sweet tone, but I knows he's mocking me.

And then they both stare at me, Tony and Ben. Waiting.

'Congrats,' I say then clamped my lips together. I need to keep my dignity and say nothing else, because *holy shit*, this day.

'Don't worry, Gemma, I'm happy to share with you some of my future plans.'

Tony nods, as if to say, *yes, teach her.*

And if it wasn't his annoying comments that bladed me in the stomach, something else gets me even deeper. *Future plans.*

Suddenly, I can feel the future Adam and I have planned crashing down. Like that bloody tower.

Chapter Three

S omehow, I manage to stick around in the boardroom for ten whole minutes, which is a very long time when you just want to curl up and cry. In a moment like this, you can't stride away like a sore loser, even though that's *exactly* what I want to do.

I retreat to the food table, which is the furthest place in the room from Ben as possible, where the sad little muffins that have a sign in front of them reading 'non-dairy, gluten-free, nut-free' are, given this day of political correctness and food allergies. *Fun-free,* I think, but I shove one in my mouth anyway.

Meanwhile, Ben is surrounded by a group of people, launching into a monologue, sharing his plans for the role – ad infinitum – to anyone who would listen. I roll my eyes. He thinks he's won an Oscar. I wish someone would play the 'wind up' music.

I glance up and saw Ruby has become part of his

adoring fan club (cult). She's listening to Ben and flicking her long dark hair over her shoulder. *Ugh.*

When no one is looking I slip out of the double doors and head straight to the bathrooms, lock myself in a stall, sit on the toilet lid, and think, *What the fuck just happened?*

For ten minutes I let myself cry silently into a wad of toilet paper. Tony's words keep repeating in my head. He's described Ben as exuberant and passionate – that's what you want in a star editor. And he's described me as trustworthy and capable. That's what you want in a toaster.

By the time I've cried myself out I feel slightly better, but I also now have a monumental headache. I flush the toilet, blot my mascara streaks away, and walk as quickly as I can down the hallway towards my office, wanting to just lose myself in a pile of work.

'Gem!'

Damnit.

Ruby calls to me from the end of the corridor, and I resist the urge of running into my office, locking myself in there, and telling everyone I have a highly contagious disease.

She hurries towards me looking flushed, a faraway look in her eyes. 'I didn't realise that Ben is actually quite smart. Besides being a hottie, he's got some great ideas for the Chief role.'

I grit my teeth. 'Great.'

She looks at me and her eyes mist over. 'Oh, sorry! I know you wanted that job, but you have autobiographies, which I think is much cooler.'

'Yeah, I guess.' Because we both know it isn't cooler.

She squeezes my arm. 'If you need to talk, just Teams me.'

'Thanks.' I don't want to talk. All I want is a gulp of someone's hip flask and maybe a really long holiday. To Italy. My ultimate destination.

I close my eyes. Lots of cocktails. Pasta. Cheese. Shopping. I hear Murano glass is quite fetching… Maybe I could learn to make gnocchi from scratch with someone's *nonna*. Maybe by the end she'll love me so much she'll be my *nonna* too. I'll master the language in a month, as if I'm some genius polyglot. I'll make bread from scratch.

I wonder what it'd be like, the Italian version of myself. Passionate. I'd learn to tell people no. I'd be feisty. Spicy. I'd yell, 'Piss off, little man whore' at Ben without feeling like I needed to apologise.

I like Italian Gemma so much I'm almost smiling and back to a happy place when Ruby says, 'Oh and be careful. I think that tarot card was for you. Nothing's happened to me today. And' – her voice lowers – 'bad things always come in threes.'

I give a little laugh but something in my stomach knots again. 'Ruby, this is one little bump in my life. I don't think it's written in the stars or anything.'

Despite wanting to lose myself under piles of work, for most of the morning I sit staring at the blinking cursor on my page, watching the emails pile up in my inbox. I scroll through them without responding: one from a distributor, one from the graphic designer with a potential new cover, one from a literary agent pitching her next amazing author.

For the rest of the day, I do exactly zero work, can't focus on anything. I consider putting a lock on my door and never exiting. But how would I eat? Can you eat paper and survive? I googled this. Turns out, no.

In the middle of imagining someone finding my skeleton with a wad of paper shoved in its gob, Tony knocks on the door. I take a deep breath. *I got this.*

'Hey, sport,' Tony says warmly, and immediately I know he wants something. 'Can you join us in the foyer for James McMahon's drinks?'

This is beginning to feel like the longest day of the year. I check the clock on my desk: five p.m.

I look up at him. 'Could I join the drinks?' I repeat, thinking, *Could I, or do I want to?* Because those answers are very different.

'Just for twenty minutes. Add your special Gemma magic touch.' He means my Nelly Nicepants self. Obviously a deal is on the line, or something has gone sour and he needs my help with making it right.

I hate the feeling of letting him down, even though I'm exhausted. What the fuck is wrong with me? Why can't I simply say, *No, I need to go home.*

When I don't say anything, he grins and says over his shoulder as he left, 'You're a lifesaver.'

Twenty minutes later I regret being a lifesaver. Unfortunately, James McMahon is a delight, in the same way that Hitler was kind and compassionate.

James has already approached me twice. The first time

he assumed I was the waitress and could I get him some more sandwiches, and patted his well-developed paunch. When I told him I was actually an editor, he put his meaty hand on my lower back, right where my black dress sucks me in the most, and rubbed me like a lamp holding a genie, and said, '*Oh, a career woman.*' For ten excruciating minutes, I made nice, flattering him, telling him I've read his manuscript (true) and loved it (half true) and he is a genius (utter horrible lie). Finally, I made some excuse to go and check the drinks.

The second time he approached me, his belly was overhanging his trousers as he pulled up his belt and I got a flash of pale white bulging stomach with downy grey hair. I cringed.

'Gemma!' He leaned towards me, spilled champagne on my shoe, didn't apologise, and then pulled me down to whisper in foul eggy sandwich breath into my ear, 'Where do we go after this?'

I wanted to tell him to do one, but I couldn't. I knew the game: I had to make nice with this creep.

Before I could answer, James made a final lunge towards the diagonal neckline of my dress, as though he was trying to whisper something, but wanted to whisper it to my breasts instead.

In a state of desperation, I tipped my almost full glass of red wine across my shoulder and winced as the blood-coloured coldness ran down my right side and dribbled into my heels. I exclaimed 'Oh, silly me!' and hurriedly left before he could offer to mop it up himself.

That's how I find myself in the disabled bathroom, in

my bra and undies, rinsing my black dress in the sink, then holding it under the dryer, praying it would not disintegrate. I'm not used to such fine knit stuff. It has been a splurge purchase and cost half a week's salary, because I thought a chief editor should wear semi-designer stuff at least. Except I'm not a chief editor.

I catch a glimpse of my reflection. Under the lights, my eyes are puffy, red, tired. My cheeks sunken and hollow. I feel overwhelmed and like the day just isn't stopping – hit after hit, they keep coming. I can barely take a breath between each round. And now I'm freezing in a tiny bathroom, walls paper-thin so I can hear a guy peeing in the next bathroom over. Great.

Outside, there's a murmur of voices as people walk down the hall.

'Great work, champ, hole in one today.' Tony and his never-ending sporting references.

'Thanks. But do you think she's on to it?' Weasel's voice.

My spidey senses bristled. Who's on to what? I have a feeling this is something I want to hear. I turn off the dryer and tiptoe closer to the locked door.

'No, she's too busy helping out everyone around the office. She can't say no.'

My face flames red. Could it... Are they talking about *me*?

'People-pleaser,' Weasel says, like someone would say *murderer*.

'Has to change ... otherwise ... we can't...' Tony's voice peters out. 'It's over.'

It's over. The words makes me freeze.

'Don't worry, I'll take care of it,' Weasel said, in his smug little voice.

The voices fade away as they walk down the corridor. I start shivering, and without thinking, I pull on my dress that's still damp and now completely crumpled. God, *were* they talking about me? I run through the other women in the office. Ruby? Amy? Tamara? The marketing team. But none of them really helps the rest of the team.

I feel my stomach churn, the way it does when you just *know*. They could have been talking about anyone, but it was *me*. I know it.

What am I not on to? My work? God, am I going to be *fired*? And 'people pleaser'. The way he said it. And Weasel going to 'take care of it', which sounds like a bad mafia plotline.

It's time to go home and end this hellish day. On the way out of the bathroom, I keep my eyes on the carpet, and hurry towards the lift before anyone can talk to me.

To make matters worse, when I finally get into the lift, utterly exhausted, and glance out through the closing doors, I see Weasel staring straight at me. He's seen the whole thing: me making a complete fool of myself, and now leaving in a damp, wrinkled dress.

Bloody wonderful.

Chapter Four

I'm clearly having one of the worst days of my life, but being outside in the soft winter evening makes me feel a tad better.

The stars are out. The sky is a black velvet. The storm has come and gone and everything is damp. The bushes are bristling with yellow wattle, which smells like honey. I can hear the marine roar from the traffic and bus brakes squealing, but if I concentrate, far off I can just hear the soft cackle of a kookaburra, which means it's going to rain again.

As I step onto the Harbour Bridge, the dazzling waters below, black and gold, all the lights reflecting the smooth curves of the Opera House, I look at the moon, glowing and full, and decide that, whatever happened today, it was just a day – a horrible day – and tomorrow I'll wake up feeling better.

I shove my earbuds in and flick through playlists

curated by emotion: happy; going out; infinite Sadness… I choose Feather Light, and Taylor Swift streams into my ears.

By habit I check my inbox while I wait at the next traffic lights in Kirribilli. Tony has emailed to say, *You left early, wanted to congratulate you on the new role.*

I flip him the bird – literally and figuratively – but write back, *Thanks, Tony, it's a great opportunity.*

One of our new writers, Tae Ng, has emailed, *I'm so excited about your suggested edits, but I have complete writer's block! Can you call and help?*

Not tonight, pal.

Adam has emailed too. *Hey babe, how did it go? Tell me all the details tomorrow, remember I'm out with the old work gang tonight, if you want to come along we're at The Ivy. I'll try not to get to yours too late.*

The wind picks up and starts to lash at my face, making me shiver. I scroll through my inbox, stopping abruptly on one name.

Patricia Evans. My mother.

It's an email, or rather what appears to be an eight-paragraph thesis from the middle of my parents' campervan trip, with the subject: Flights. *Flights? To where?*

For the last few months, my mum has been sending these long emails that I don't even bother reading because her anxiety turns my anxiety up and I always feel compelled to help. Eventually, I had the IT guys do something sneaky and move anything from my family straight into a Read Later file, but this one must have got through. Exhausted, I delete it.

I walk another few blocks, feeling the cold Sydney air,

which makes my cheeks flush. At the next set of lights, my thumb hovers over the trash folder, curiosity creeping up on me. But then I put my phone back in my bag and try not to think about my mum's email.

In fact, I try not to think about my family at all, especially about the time when it all started to go wrong.

That time in our family history is a bit like the Dark Ages, better not spoken about. Ever. Let's just say, it wasn't a good time for seven-year-old me, and worse for my mum, who hit the peak of her anxiety and became very close friends with Pinot Grigio and the psychic hotline.

I still remember those long, cold English winter nights, me hugging Mr Bunnikins in bed wondering when Daddy would be coming home, and Mum curled up at the end of the hallway, listening to the psychics tell her Dad would return and be very sorry for doing such a bad thing.

At the time I still didn't know what very bad thing Dad had done. But then a few months later, there was Dad at the front door. Behind him was a young woman holding a small, pink wriggling baby who cried really loudly all the time, and I knew immediately that shrieking thing was the bad thing.

Dad babbled an apology, saying over and over he had made a very big mistake (so psychics *can* get it right), and then confessed to my mum that he'd lost his job, and he and Marla had nowhere else to go. So Dad, Marla, Mum, me and crying Lulu became a strange family co-habiting in our home for the next seven years, with Dad in the basement and Marla and Lulu in the spare room.

My mother, instead of icing out Lulu (which would have

been normal behaviour), decided instead to show Marla
exactly who was *Mummy*. My mother, previously of 3am
psychic hotline addiction, suddenly became Mum-
Extraordinaire (read: driven by anxiety). She was up at 5am
every day. She wore rollers in her hair and then spent a
good hour styling herself into a perfect imitation of a
Stepford housewife. She wore actual lipstick – coral
coloured – and she reapplied it every hour. She bought an
apron. An actual 1950s frilly pink apron that she wore
around the house at all times, as if we were always catching
her just about to bake a plate of hot chocolate chip cookies.

And there *were* cookies, all types, on the bench for Lulu
and me each afternoon – oatmeal, and ginger snap and choc
chip. There were superb school lunches, with an array of
sandwiches she cut into shapes: frogs and ants and cows.
We had fresh fruit salad every morning. Gone were the days
of having a plain old ham sandwich on hard bread in a
brown paper bag; now I had fresh panini rolls with sliced
tomato, pastrami and mayo, fresh orange juice, a tub of
chocolate yoghurt, and a bag of potato crisps.

Mum, still in her pink apron, frenetically did the laundry
and most of the house cleaning before Marla even struggled
to get up. Mum suddenly became whiz of everything; there
was nothing too big or too small. She bought Lulu all kinds
of presents that Marla couldn't, and took her anywhere she
wanted to go. Marla decided the only way to deal with this
was to shower Lulu in the only thing she could afford:
affection. So if Lulu wasn't receiving presents from my
mother, she was being covered in hugs and kisses from
Marla, and I hated that she was still small enough to sit on

Dad's knee each night while he read the paper or his Michael Frayn.

Marla soon got bored with Dad (shocker), and Dad and Mum patched up the crisis, got back together, bought a campervan, and are now travelling around Europe as if it was their second honeymoon.

It's a time my mum still refers to as 'The Mid-Life Crisis', which is confusing because my mum also refers to Marla as 'The Mid-Life Crisis', even now. To Marla's face. And I almost feel bad for Marla, who is now well into her fifties, on her fourth husband, orange from self-tan and enjoying a lot of Botox, and still being referred to as a crisis. If someone referred to me as a crisis (like, to my face) it would send me into the corner weeping and requiring a thousand years of therapy. However, cheers to Marla and her healthy self-worth, because it seems to have done nothing to dint her self-esteem.

We're not one of *those* families that truthfully share feelings or work through stuff. We're British, very stiff upper lip and let's just talk about the weather, and give people directions for the A1, even if they didn't ask. We gladly sweep everything else under the rug and just drink a lot instead.

Since I left fifteen years ago, I've flown back to the UK for an obligatory Christmas visit every three years, but it's always a strained affair.

I'd stand on the driveway, arming myself with affirmations and hope. *This time will be different, I am a fully formed adult, for goodness' sake. I will let nothing irk me. Nothing will get me down!!*

Like clockwork, my mum would be already tipsy, and that means one thing: memories. Bang on ten minutes after arriving, ashen-faced and glum, she would pull me aside in the kitchen and whisper, 'He still hasn't said he loves me. Not really. After ... you know.' Bollocks. So we'd be already talking about the thing we weren't meant to be talking about.

Then she'd say, 'Does my right eye look bigger than the left? More bulge? Graves' disease is a big issue. Too many thyroid hormones.'

'Mum, you don't have Graves' disease,' I'd say, even though I've got no idea what that is.

Then Dad would come into the kitchen. 'Hello, love, you look good. Down under treating you well?' I'd nod, and he'd pull me aside later and say, 'Your mum seems a bit cranky, doesn't she?' And there it is, that awful feeling of being put in the middle of it all.

I've seen enough pseudo psychology YouTube clips to know not to get involved. And I know I shouldn't try to fix it because it isn't my fault, but if I didn't this would go on all day. So I'd do my best to appease the situation, going between them, telling Mum, 'Dad just said you look lovely.'

'Did he?' She'd look confused but would start glowing a bit. And then to Dad, 'Mum said it was the oven she was cranky with; she thinks you're a real help today.' And Dad's chest would puff up as he ran off to help set the table.

I would refill my glass of Sauv Blanc, and tell myself, *only four more hours*, then I'd be back in my hotel room, in a bathrobe, eating an overpriced Kit-Kat from the mini bar. Thank *God*. But those four hours stretched like four years because it wasn't just my parents making me go slowly insane – it was also Lulu.

Lulu, my half-sister, curled up on the couch like she is always about to be photographed for a British *Vogue* cover and appears bored by any topic that isn't about her. No matter what I wear I always feel dumpy in comparison.

Lulu is a petite, slim thing. Nothing sags. Nothing is puffy. She is eternally youthful with cherub lips, as if a thousand bees have stung them. Anyone who gets collagen lip-plumping injections is insanely jealous when they meet her. The thing about Lulu is that she has a way about her that makes her look sweet, even when she's pointing out your flaws, which is a favourite pastime. With her stunning, delicate features, she looks like one of those china dolls from horror movies: all innocent and sweet, until the haunting begins.

The last time I saw her, I hadn't even made it inside the hallway before she started staring at my forehead until I thought perhaps I'd suddenly grown a third eye.

'Gemma. Frown lines are a killer. Isn't it time for Botox? You know what they say when women *age prematurely*. Just be careful; go to someone who knows exactly where the needle should go.'

Typically I don't care where the fucking needle goes, as long as it isn't anywhere near me. I'm staunchly anti-Botox, mostly because I can't afford it, secondly because the idea of needles with paralytic ingredients going near my eyes makes me want to faint.

Over one Christmas lunch, while Lulu nibbled on a green leaf salad instead of turkey and cranberry like the rest of us, she wanted to talk about the latest Dior jacket, but how can someone spend thirty minutes discussing that? I ate three servings of Mum's trifle cake that lunch, as a reward for being there listening to Lulu prattle on about Vera Wang and the House of Gucci and small kitten heels, and who gives a shit?

So no, I don't want to read Mum's latest email asking if I'm sure Dad loves her or extolling Lulu and the latest wonderful thing she's done. I've put an ocean between us, isn't that enough?

Thankfully a phone call interrupts my thoughts. *Hannah.*

'Hey, how did it go?' Just hearing her voice makes me feel better.

'It was a disaster. Certifiable.'

'Which part?' I can hear her pouring a large glass of wine in the background.

'All of it.' I proceed to tell her everything: the promotion I didn't get, Weasel, Tony doubling my workload with no pay rise…

'Feck em all. The lot of them. You'll get a job somewhere else where they know you're amazing. Maybe you'll even get your own book published and in three years be sitting on Oprah's couch saying, "Well, Peacock Publishing couldn't see my talent." Pish. Total pish.'

See? Perfect friend. If anyone knows me, it's Hannah. We met in kindergarten aged five, after Han's family moved to London from Glasgow. Our teacher found us eating chewing gum we'd taken from another teacher's bag and we got put in time out. We tried to bust our way out of lockdown by attempting to balance on each other's shoulders to get out the window. We failed miserably, but from that day on we were inseparable.

We were so close we planned the move to Australia together, talking about it all through high school and university, planning it carefully, excited about our new life – better weather, cool jobs, and a chance to get away from our dysfunctional families. Hannah's mum still hasn't come to terms with the fact that her daughter is a lesbian, which makes me sad, but as Hannah says, *feck her*.

'How about a round of margaritas at Frankies? Jess will come too. And we can get a big plate of lime fish tacos too. You'll forget all about today.'

I waver a little. 'You know I love a salty rim.'

Hannah hoots. 'A salty rim! Sounds saucy, you dirty little minx.'

I laugh. 'I love the idea, Han. But right now, I'm terrible company. I think I just need to go to bed and pretend this day didn't happen.'

'Well, you know where we are if you change your mind. Call me anytime. Love you.'

'Love you too.'

It's eight p.m. by the time I walk up the cold pavement of 669 Military Road. *Finally home*.

I'm about to unlock my front door when I realise shoved under it is a cream-coloured, gold-embossed envelope, which now looks old and a bit frayed. I pick it up, noticing three large red stamps across the front manifesting the letter's displeasure at having been re-routed, once to my old

Sydney address in St Leonards, and then forwarded to this address but the wrong unit, to Mrs Gleeson, who must have shoved it under my door.

At the top right corner of the envelope, a large sticker proclaims, 'UK Air Mail.' *Oh, God.*

I can already hear Ruby saying, 'This is it. Bad thing number two.'

Chapter Five

The envelope could have a thousand great things in there. An offer of a house? Early retirement? A prince writing to tell me I'm his long-lost cousin and there's a spare Italian *palazzo* awaiting me.

But I know only one thing: it's from my *family*.

I've put an entire ocean's distance between us, but now the envelope is in my hands. Glossy and hideous. I can't tell what it's going to be. But it's something BIG.

My parents' wedding anniversary? A birthday? I could explain my way out of these ... or so I hope. I don't *have to* fly back to England, do I?

Before I can even get inside my apartment, curiosity and anxiety overwhelm me. I take the envelope and rip it open.

Miss Lulu Poppy Evans

&

Mr Charles 'Chip' Montague
request the pleasure of Gemma Evans and guest

at their marriage
from the fourth of July to the eighth of July
at Castello di Rosso, Tuscany, Italy

I take a deep breath in, hold it, and consider never breathing again. *Fuck. Fuck.*

She's getting married. And it's in Italy. *My* Italy. But instead of tasting the food, and writing my wonderful book, the first time I am going to Tuscany is to celebrate Lulu.

The universe is a savage bitch.

At the bottom of the invitation, it mentions an RSVP date, now very much been and gone. And now, *God*, Lulu's wedding is in less than two weeks.

Inside now, I sit down on the couch, and let out a sigh, feeling a hundred years old. This explained the strange emails Mum has been sending. I wonder momentarily why no one has called, but then remember I've recently upgraded my phone and it came with a new number and I've been so busy, I haven't got around to telling them.

I stare at the invite feeling sick. It states 'Gemma and guest'. Someone has handwritten next to it: *(only if you have a boyfriend, don't bring a friend).*

The nerve. The bloody nerve. Yes, thank you, I *do* have a boyfriend. And he is pretty lovely.

I immediately know I can't go alone; Adam simply has to come. He would be stable and calm and familiar. He would hold my hand and have my back. He would protect me from the craziness of my family. Yes, Adam will come, and everything will be fine.

Before I can change my mind, I log into the wedding

web portal – specially designed for Lulu and Chip – where it's raining geraniums and my cursor turns into a white dove as I attempt to find the RSVP box underneath a bunch of pink blooms. I take a deep breath and click the box.

Yes, *We* Will Attend.

I spend the rest of the night carefully crafting an email to Lulu apologising for the delay, congratulating her and checking (pleading) that it's still okay to bring a plus one, my *boyfriend*, Adam.

Marla (I try not to think of her as the floozy that bedded my dad all those years ago) responds almost immediately as it's midday in England.

Lulu is busy at a dress fitting. So gorgeous. Can't take our eyes off her. The wedding is packed. Donna Henry is coming! It's taken you a while to reply, we thought you'd died (she attempted a smiley thingy here) *but I guess we can make room for you and your guest.*

It's as though Marla can't bring herself to say boyfriend or partner. Or Adam. But she's managed to use the full name of someone – I think it's their local mayor? – whom I can guarantee Lulu doesn't know.

But the great news is this: Adam can come. Yes, I will be bringing a partner. I mean, he'll be more like a prisoner, but you know, whatever.

I can't sleep after that, and start to pace around my flat. Adam arrives to mine late after his drinks, about 2am, and I'm about to tell him about the dreaded envelope, but he's drunk. He curls his lean limbs around me and starts snoring in ten seconds.

Around dawn, I finally fall into a deep sleep only to wake up at nine. Adam, already dressed in jeans and a plaid shirt, is sitting at the end of the bed, scrolling through FX, his favourite stock exchange app.

I sit up, feeling tired and dishevelled. How do I tell him about yesterday? That I didn't get the job. My heart sinks.

Adam is the first man I've met that is ambitious, driven and consistent. He supports me doing long hours at work, and loves my independence and dedication to being a successful editor. We always joke that we're pretty similar: we're dedicated to our jobs and we want to be successful. We're also almost the same height and we could raid each other's wardrobes, although that would mean I'd be wearing preppy jumpers and chinos all the time. He wore that exact get-up the first time I met him. I still remember how over red wine and a wonderfully large cheese platter he asked me, genuinely, if I paid my credit card off on time. I laughed and thought, *Finally someone who is organised just like me.*

My ex, Richard (the Dick), a singer-songwriter whom I dated for three years, always had an excuse for why he couldn't pay for anything: he'd forgotten his wallet, his lease was up, his credit card was maxed. He moved in with me, and then proceeded to lie on the couch every day, pretending to be writing the next big song, when really I think he was just eating corn chips and watching *Friends* reruns. He never made it into the music industry, surprise,

surprise, and now I think he works at a local sandwich shop.

'So...?' Adam says, peering over his phone. 'How are we celebrating?'

For once, I have no words. Thankfully, Adam doesn't seem to notice.

'You're a chief editor! The Nikkei is up! I start my new job in a few weeks! It's a good day.' He stands up and yawns. 'How about eggs? Let me take you out.'

I get a glimpse of myself in the reflection and think I could really do with a Bloody Mary right now. Surely drinking in the morning isn't healthy if it's with tomato juice?

I nod. 'Sure.'

It's a perfect Sydney winter's day – blue skies, not a cloud, and warm enough that I only need a light wool cardigan and jeans for the walk to Café Soul. I fidget, trying to think of a good way to spring on the most planned man in the world that we are doing a quick trip to the other side of the world in just under two weeks. Even though we've only been dating a year, Adam gets a bit put out when things don't go like clockwork according to how he's planned them. Which makes me feel horribly worried about telling him about the wedding.

At the café, Adam orders a ham and cheese croissant and an extra-large coffee. I order poached eggs like the proper adult I am, rather than a cheese toastie, even though the children's menu calls to me.

'So?' he prompts me. 'How was yesterday, Miss Chief?' He pauses and waits for me to respond.

He tries again. 'Get it? You're a words person. Miss Chief. *Mischief*.'

I give a little laugh, but it comes out more like a sigh.

'Gemma?' He looks puzzled. 'I thought you'd be more excited?'

Ugh, I have to rip the Band-Aid off. 'Actually, it's just … I didn't get it. It went to that awful guy Ben.' I feel gutted as I remember Ben's smirk, still fresh in my mind.

I hope that Adam will just telepathically know how bad I feel, and give me a hug. I glance at him, waiting for a reassuring, *what a dick* or *I'm so sorry*. Neither comes.

Adam cocks his head to the side, with a look that says, *shit*. 'Oh babe. It's just… There's this really cute townhouse…'

This makes me feel a ton worse. Despite myself, I say 'And?'

'And we needed the extra salary, that's all.'

I try not to sigh. All I want is an extra-long hug, a forehead kiss – and a bloody cheese toastie – but picking up on signs, subtle or obvious, isn't Adam's forte.

'It's just a blip, Adam, that's all. We're fine. We'll get that townhouse. Or another one, a better one.' I babble for a bit before I realise *I* am comforting *him*.

'Yeah, course. I'm just disappointed for you.' He leans over and I think he's about to squeeze my hand, but instead he picks up a serviette and starts scribbling on it.

Absentmindedly he says, 'You're okay, right? We'll find you a new job. A better company. All we need is a good plan.'

Then Adam lifts the scrappy serviette he's been doodling on and in the middle is a number crunch of how much I need to make in order for us to get this new townhouse, but to the side he's drawn a cartoon of me at the top of a building, that says BEST PUBLISHING PLACE and I have a wonky crown on. I felt a whoosh of love for him.

'Adam...' I get teary just thinking about how sweet he is.

'Don't cry.' He looks petrified, thinking I'm going to start sobbing, something he hasn't done since he was ten.

'Sorry.' But there is a big fat blob of a tear on my cheek and I'm not really sorry. He's a sweetheart. 'I'm just touched.'

The waitress arrives with our breakfast then and we eat in silence for a while. Adam makes cooing noises over his croissant, which means it's a good one. And I think, *Okay, it's now or never, whilst he's in seventh heaven enjoying a mouthful of cheese, tell him about the wedding.*

'So there is something else I need to tell you...' I say cryptically. As soon as I start speaking, I feel a bit queasy. I mean, to some people this would be the best news – it is, after all, just a holiday, a little European holiday. But to Adam, who has already planned what to eat for breakfast for next month, it's going to be a bit of a shock.

I tread carefully. 'What are you doing in two weeks' time?'

His deep chocolate eyes flick over me. 'My taxes. Think this year is going to be a good return.'

He's not kidding. He likes to do his taxes just before the end of the financial year, and then consider what return he may get back to put towards his mortgage fund. Like I said, he's the prepared, calm and predictable type.

'Well, the thing is … Lulu is getting married. In two weeks.'

'Oh. Sounds nice,' he says looking relieved it isn't more serious.

'In *Italy*.'

'Wow.' Adam reaches for the newspaper and flips through to the stock market pages, scouring it for the latest on the Dow Jones or something. I want to say, *Can you look at me*? but I don't want to start an argument.

Instead, I say as upbeat as I can manage, 'In Tuscany, actually. They have great wine and coffee. It's beautiful, and it's *summer* over there.'

He looks at me with his large dark eyes. 'You're going?'

'Course. I have to.'

'Wow, cool. Italy. You'll have a great time.' He runs a hand through his hair and he looks so sweet I just want to kiss his cheeks and say, 'Please come.'

'I was hoping that maybe *we* … *we* will have a great time.' I cross my fingers on both hands as if pleading with the universe that he'll say yes. 'I RSVPed we would attend, since you have the time off before your new job. I just thought…'

He looks up at me slowly, perplexed, his eyebrows raised so high they almost meet his hairline.

I nervously send up a little prayer. 'We could go to Italy and be back before you know it. Plus, Tuscany is ultra-romantic. We could do some wine or cheese tasting. I know it's a long way, but it's *Tuscany*.'

'I can't go.'

I feel my stomach clench. 'I know this is totally last minute, but I was hoping, for me … you may consider it at least?'

He shakes his head. 'You know I can't. And, even if I could, I wouldn't be going to Italy. You can't start a new job as the Head of Digital Strategy jetlagged!'

'Right.' I feel deflated.

'I need to be at the top of my game. I'm sorry but I've got so much to do around my place before the new job starts. I need to get new suits, my ceiling cleaned.'

'Your ceiling *cleaned*?' Is that even a thing?

'Yes,' Adam says matter-of-factly. 'There's mildew gathering in the corner and I think it's bad for my respiratory health. For *ours*, when you stay over. Now come on, you, let's get another coffee and go for a walk.'

Damnit. Adam really isn't going to come. I'm picturing how it's going to play out and it isn't pretty. Me, alone, trying to explain why my boyfriend doesn't seem to exist. Adam, at home, with a weird sponge, cleaning his ceiling.

I sigh. This entire week feels like it's intent on destroying my life, a bit like the triffids did in that post-apocalyptic world coming in with their stinging stems and just killing people—

Adam taps me on the shoulder. 'Gemma, you're doing that thing you do. You're spacing out again.'

The walk back to my unit is pleasant, even though the sky has turned grey and it's a little windy. Adam holds my hand and warms it up by rubbing it between his. He jokes that for a Brit, I'm a weather wuss, and I'll enjoy going to Tuscany in the summer. The thought of warm weather, the sun beaming into my cold bones, makes me feel a little comforted.

The comfort doesn't last long though. As soon as Adam leaves, being home alone becomes a mind trap. How am I going to explain Adam isn't coming? I have RSVPed for a plus one. How am I going to explain *that*? My family aren't the type of people that say nothing, or think it's clearly something they shouldn't say anything about. Nope. Lulu would probably get on a microphone and ask, 'Why didn't you bring a plus one, Gem-man?' And I'd have to explain in front of the entire five-hundred-plus wedding guests that my boyfriend isn't here because of his ceiling.

I can't sleep or relax for the rest of the weekend because I know I'm going to have to go alone to Lulu's Italian Weddingpalooza.

I'm also trying to ignore the messages I have received from Mum:

Oh darling, I'm so glad to hear you can make it. Lulu was beside herself you hadn't RSVPed, but I kept telling her you'd be there to help out. You've always had such great organisational skills, and I can tell you, with the size of this wedding, Lulu needs all the help she can get!

And the ones from Lulu, which literally read as a list of demands:

Gemma – you're impossible. RSVPing two weeks out! This day is my day, four days actually, and I won't have it ruined! It's very important you know some things. Don't wear yellow because the bridesmaids are, and nothing that will clash with yellow – including scarlet and crimson red. Actually, all shades of orange and red, no green at all, and nothing electric blue. And of course, no black, but I think anyone knows that about weddings.

P.S. Do you think you can get to the second night's gala dinner early – someone needs to prep the goldfish. Eight p.m. at Crinitis.

As far as I'm concerned red and orange look great with yellow, so does green. Thankfully I have a powder lavender blue lace dress that will blend nicely into the background. And maybe I could sneak a black dress in and she won't notice. But 'prep the goldfish'? Whatever does that mean?

Thankfully, Tony approves me taking a week off work. 'Take two, Gemma, you have the time and HR are bugging me. You haven't had a holiday in two years apparently. But why is everyone going to Italy?'

'Everyone?' I ask him.

'Fraser's going to some lemon place and Amy's over there somewhere and—' Tony says before being interrupted by his mobile phone vibrating and leaving to take the call.

I was going to tell him Amy's in Greece not Italy, but I

leave him to the phone call and pop into the junior editors' room for a quick check-in to find Ruby by herself eating a slab of chocolate cake.

'Carve me a chunk,' I say sighing and falling into the chair opposite. 'A big one.'

'So, who are you going to take?' Ruby asks with big eyes when I tell her my predicament.

'God knows. I just know I can't go alone.'

I've done a solid hour of ringing people too. Even considered calling my ex, Richard, at the sandwich shop and inviting him to come, but then sanity washed over me. Hannah has jokingly suggested she could come as my surprise lover, and I loved that idea for a second. But springing on my parents I was a lesbian would have longer-term ramifications that I wouldn't really want to deal with.

A few hours later, over a few too many bottles of Sauv Blanc, I drunkenly tried to convince both Jess and Hannah to come. We could pretend we were a long-term wonderful throuple, and after the wedding, spend a week wine tasting in Tuscany. But Jess is turning thirty, and being a plus one to Lulu's wedding isn't exactly how she wants to ring in her new decade.

Desperate, I tried other friends – even guys I haven't spoken to in over a year – and everyone *wanted* to go, except no one actually could. I almost pulled out, but then I thought of Italy: delicious pasta, glittering oceans, stunning vineyards, sunshine and chilled wine.

'Well, have you thought about…' Ruby winks.

'What?' I raise my eyebrows.

'A bit of a … side piece?'

'You mean an *escort*?' I say, whipping my head around to check no one had heard. 'Absolutely not.'

Ruby laughs. 'Don't look shocked. Many people do it.'

Many desperate people. 'But don't escorts offer sex?'

Ruby shakes her head, 'They offer sex, but you don't have to. A guy I knew at university used to do it. He said it was like three hundred for dinner, and a thousand if you wanted to sleep with him. I think he was trying to break into movies, and was very good at characters so he could be the perfect businessman, or a personal trainer – apparently the girls loved that one – or a photographer, arty and complex.'

God, that sounds grim. I simply could not bring an escort.

'I'm just going to go by myself.' There, I've said it. The only possible answer to this predicament.

'Isn't that worse than a little pseudo boyfriend and some role playing?'

I think about it. Everyone would cluck and say, *Oh, poor Gemma, thirty-four and still hasn't found anyone.* They'd set me up with someone at the wedding. Likely someone probably my father's age, and they'd think, *Oh well, that's what you get at this time in your life, scraping the very bottom of the barrel.* I can almost hear Lulu now. *Well, at least he's rich,* she'd be saying about the balding, obese, handsy man in the corner. Damn it, Ruby was right.

Ruby chews the end of her pen. 'Why don't you let me see who I can find for you? No escorts. Promise. I have a wonderful little black book.' She winks at me, again.

'Hmmm, I don't know.'

She claps her hands. 'Please, let's do this! It's so fun! Maybe we could even write a book about it? It's kinda romantic if you think about it.'

I roll my eyes. 'We sell romcoms here; we don't live them. And besides, I have someone already – Adam.'

'Oh yeah.' Ruby looked a little flat when I reminded her of that. 'Does he mind that you're going to take someone else?'

'Um … not really.' In fact, when I mentioned that I could go with someone else, he told me that was a great idea, and even suggested a data scientist from his work, which I politely declined, since said scientist is twenty-two years old. 'Everyone else,' he said, 'is pretty much taken.' Then I said, 'So you wouldn't mind if someone pretended to be you?' and he looked at me with a calm, smooth face and said, 'Not at all.' Something about that bothered me at first, but then I sat with it, and after a few hours, I realised this is what secure, mature couples do. They trust each other.

Ruby is looking at me, concern all over her face. 'He's okay with it. That's weird, isn't it?'

'Is it? I think it's just Adam. He's very trusting. We're good. I trust him; he trusts me. Trustworthy. We both are.'

Ruby eyes me up and down suspiciously. 'I don't think I've ever heard someone use the word trust so many times in ten seconds. I mean, do you think he's the One?'

I laugh. 'The *One*? I'm going to file that under things that don't exist.'

'Maybe that means … you just haven't…'

I laugh again and shake my head. 'No, don't go all goo-goo on me. Next thing you'll start talking about twin flames and that butterfly feeling you get when you meet someone. Some elusive spark.'

That's the thing, when your entire world is books, you know all the tropes.

The workaholic city girl who goes to the country and finds the handsome man of her dreams.

The whodunit (the husband, always, or the jealous best friend).

The search for self (in a place like Bali or India).

And, of course, the elusive tracking down of the One.

After twenty-something years of dating and editing, I know it doesn't happen like it does in the movies, where a man sees you buying a croissant at your local bakery and he knows in an instant you are the One so he follows you (in a romantic non-stalkery way) up the street. Approaches you. You giggle. You are wearing a long floaty dress. You are a goddess infused with a feminine, ethereal beauty. You always smell like flowers, and don't leave sweat from your nether regions on gym equipment.

He is handsome, but more than that, he is kind. He doesn't stare at your breasts. Not until you want him to. Then he stares all the time like you are the Goddess of Perky Breasts, and they don't need constant underwire to remain north of the belt border.

He offers you a coffee, and when he does, his hand grazes yours. You feel butterflies. You manage to flip your hair in a carefree, rather than I-have-this-neck-pain way. He finds you enthralling, endearing. If some girl walked past in a slutty cowgirl outfit, or a bedazzled high-cut bikini, his eyes would never leave you. He walks you to where you are going, on the traffic side, of course. He is built to protect you. You both talk. He likes books! And good music! He likes sports, but only enough that it makes him manly. Not so much that he'll ditch you for a football game.

He takes your number. Calls straightaway. Takes you to coffee. To dinner. On road trips. He wants to hug you and watch stars with you. He brushes the hair out of your eyes, softly. It's easy with him. Different. He's your best friend *and* lover. He wants to talk. He doesn't sexualise you. But when he does sex you up, wow, just wow.

He hugs you when you cry. He fixes things around the house. He talks about how he feels and makes grand love gestures. Your house is full of flowers. He never ghosts you. If you have to wait even a moment for his call, for his message, you can be sure he is going to declare, '*You've been on my mind the entire time. The first thing I wanted to do was call you.*' He comes to your house one evening when it's raining because he was overcome with a thought and it had to be said aloud. He pulls you into the rain. You laugh (rather than telling him, '*Jesus, I just had my fucking hair straightened.*') He gets down on one knee and proclaims, '*I love you. Marry me.*'

Jesus, Mary and Jake, it does not go like that. Haven't we all watched enough of *The Bachelorette* to know how most things end up? With an ugly cry, and saying, 'I'll find someone who wants me' even though we all know it's not really going to happen.

At times like these, when I remember how badly love can go, I feel infinitely better about my own situation. So what if Adam can't come to a last-minute wedding on the other side of the world? He'll be here for me when I get back.

I say that aloud. 'Adam's great, and it's only a week, isn't it...'

Ruby picks up a pen and grabs a sheet of paper. 'Okay, so, are we actually doing this?'

I swallow hard. *What's the harm?*

Ruby's looking at me expectantly. With a sense of trepidation, I find myself nodding.

'Great! Tell me exactly what you want, and I'll help you find the perfect faux partner.'

Chapter Six

The brief reads a little like my old dating profile once did: an age-appropriate man (35–47). Could wear flip-flops and shorts just as easily as pull off a suit. Knows his way around wine and champagne. Enjoys food. Likes long walks. (Ruby rolls her eyes at that one and declares it boring and typical, but I know it's important that the man likes walking because I imagine he would have to keep following me and luring me back to the wedding, when I inevitably try to escape.) Likes books ('loves' would be a bonus), so we actually have things to talk about. Isn't a weirdo. Or a peeping Tom. Doesn't prey on the young. Doesn't have a sports car and a mid-life-crisis look. Is not an asshole (very important). Would be okay to go by the name 'Adam'.

'Do you want this partner to look like anything in particular? Height? Weight?' Ruby asks, her pen poised ready to take more notes.

'Good question.' I consider it. 'He should be taller than me … by quite a bit,' I muse aloud. 'Built, but not gym-junkie built.'

'So not at all like Adam?' Ruby asks.

I feel shocked. 'Oh no! No, nothing like that. I love Adam.' I pause. 'It's just … I'm describing the kind of guy that my family would expect. And it's that quintessentially typical Australian look.' I shrug.

'So your family don't know anything about Adam?' Ruby asks. 'We're narrowing the pool if we have to find a dark-haired, small, slim Clark Kent lookalike in about … um, four days, and I don't know how easy that would be.'

'No,' I answer honestly. 'My family and I haven't caught up in a while.'

Ruby sighs in relief and writes that down. 'Phew.' She chews her pen again. 'And are you offering … *something*?'

Finally realising what she might be alluding to, I said, 'God, no!'

'No, Gem, I mean cash.'

'Oh, should I? Or just pay for the flights and hotel?' Thankfully I have savings, given I haven't had a proper holiday in years, plus my annual leave was at an obscene level. And I'd be using all my credit card turned magically into frequent flyer points. Business class since I never get the chance to fly anywhere. 'I guess both.'

Ruby shrugs.

'Fine, make it five hundred dollars. That should be enough for them to undergo this pain,' I mutter, trying not to think about how extortionate this is going to be. 'But make it clear that they must act like they love me. But no kissing. And no sex – make that explicitly clear.'

This plus one must not, under any circumstance, think this is in any way a romantic trip. This is business only.

Chapter Seven

Sydney airport is crowded, and I'm nervously standing in the middle of the lounge waiting to board. Thanks to Ruby, I'm looking out for Mr Plus One, otherwise known on his passport as Thomas.

Except I have no idea what Thomas looks like. My stomach flips.

A glance out of the airport window shows blackness, cold, winter. I know if I cancelled now and stayed in Sydney with Adam, I'd be freezing in my little flat, and I'd never hear the end of it from my family.

God, this is actually happening. I'm going to this wedding with a *blind date*. I remember the phone conversation with Ruby, and I feel a little worried.

It started off so well.

'He likes books. Actually he loves them,' Ruby garbled excitedly. 'He was a last-minute contender, really last-minute. I was thinking Craig would be perfect, but Craig couldn't get time off, and I was beside myself thinking I was going to let you down. But I consulted the cards, and they said Ace of Cups and King of Pentacles!'

'I have no idea what that means,' I said, bewildered.

'Ace of Cups is the start of something new emotionally, and King of Pentacles means someone who is established with work and money!'

My heart started to beat a little faster. 'Okay, so what does he do for work?'

Ruby ignored me. 'So he is very, very cute. Bonus points. I asked if he owned a pair of flip-flops, which he thought was a strange thing to ask. But he does. And dress shoes.'

That was a great reaction, I like that he thought it a strange request; it shows this guy is somewhat normal. Except for the fact that he's agreed to travel to Tuscany with an absolute stranger.

'Do you know this guy well?' I said, slight trepidation leaking into my voice. 'He's not an axe murderer? He's not going to roofie my drink? He hasn't been arrested or spent time in jail, right? He won't be attempting to smuggle drugs on board by shoving them up his back passage?' It was starting to dawn on me just how bad this could go. Really bad. Really fucking bad.

'Hmmmm,' Ruby teased. 'No. I asked him that, and he told me there were absolutely no drugs or axes in his apartment. It's a penthouse apartment, I may add.'

I narrowed my eyes. 'Have you been there? Is this an ex?'

Ruby exclaimed, 'Not at all, I've never gotten close to this man on that level. In fact, he remained rather mysterious about his previous girlfriends, although he did mention he does know a few models.'

I sighed. 'He sounds like a douche.'

'Well, yes,' Ruby admitted, 'I can see how you could say that, but I think he has a lot of things going for him. And remember, he likes books – loves them. In fact, he's in the business.'

'He is?' My heart stopped for a second. 'God, it's not one of our authors, is it?' I would literally die of embarrassment if they thought have-it-all-together-Gemma was suddenly desperate for a date.

'Noooo,' Ruby said in a weird, drawn-out way.

'Do I know him?' I tried to go back over everyone that I know in the book world. Is it Tim from Hawkings Publishers? He's in his fifties, but looks great, still plays tennis, is a bachelor, has a large ego, and I could see him wining and dining supermodels. Not Tom, but maybe Ruby had been mistaken, swapping an i for an o?

Ruby gave a little laugh and ignored my question. 'I want you to know he's already taken the time off. He seemed pretty excited by a holiday in Italy, said he needed to do some work over there at the same time. Oh and he bought his own plane ticket too, so we didn't even need to use your points! So it's kinda a no-going-back thing.'

I narrowed my eyes once again. 'Ruby, who is it?'

Ruby refused to give any more away, but told me to trust in the universe, and that her cards are never wrong.

So now, standing in the business class lounge (thank you, points), I have no idea who I'm looking for, or who is looking for me.

And I'm frustrated at Adam because he's not coming, and I don't want to have to pretend to be all loved up with a stranger. The tension must have been simmering between us because we got into a heated discussion last night. Well, I got angry, and he got silent. And he wasn't thrilled. Told me to take some time out, which clearly I am because I'm going to Italy, with a stranger. And I'm really starting to question my decisions of the last few weeks because they've led me to meeting a strange man and pretending to be in love.

Thomas. I've quickly gone through the list of all the authors, publishers, literary agents I know, and no one I could think of is called Thomas or Tom.

A middle-aged man in too tight jeans and a rugby shirt, slightly rotund, with dark short hair – perhaps handsome if I squinted or got really drunk – walks past me slowly. Does he look familiar? I'm about to say quietly, *Thomas*? but he joins a woman with long blonde hair on the white couch and they look cosy.

I look at my watch to find it's just after 7am. It's getting close to boarding time now, but we've planned to meet in the business class lounge, rather than at the gate. I hear the flight announcement to prepare for boarding so I bend over to pick up my bags, and check my phone again. No calls.

'Gemma,' a voice from behind me says. I prepare myself to say hello to my faux escort. I take a quick breath, then turn around, a large smile on my face…

Which drops immediately.

In front of me, dear God, is the last person I want to see while waiting for a blind date.

'Fancy bumping into you here.'

'Weasel,' I hiss without thinking. 'What are you doing here?'

He laughs. 'Is that what you call me? Oh Gemma, you can come up with something better than that, can't you? Aren't you meant to be a word wrangler?'

I'll wrangle you in a second. 'What are you doing here?' I want to inch away from him, so he doesn't see me meet my blind date in the middle of an airport.

'I'm going on holiday. Now I'm chief editor, I can kinda go where and do what I want.'

'Nice,' I mutter, taking a step back and looking over his shoulder for Thomas.

'Yes, it is rather. Well, I hope it is,' Weasel is saying.

'So, where are you going?' *Please don't say Italy, please don't.*

'Actually, you should be asking me with who.'

'Actually, it's with whom,' I smugly point out, not giving a shit who he is going to meet or where he's going, as long as it isn't on my plane. I need at least one hundred miles between me and Weasel at all times.

'Are you asking me then, with *whom*?'

'Cut to the chase, McDonald. Spit it out. With whom are you going?' He's going to name drop someone, I just know it, some D-lister, I bet. Someone with big boobs. Or a Lolita type. Yes, I can absolutely see him with some nineteen-year-old. Or some new fancy author he wants to sign. Probably both.

Just then an announcement comes over the loudspeaker 'Qantas flight QF323 to Hong Kong has now finished boarding. Looking for two passengers. Gemma

Evans and Thomas McDonald, please come to the gate immediately.'

My brain takes a second. Thomas McDonald. As in Ben McDonald. It couldn't be ... could it? My plus one.

OH. MY. GOD.

My stomach clenches. My legs feel shaky. My mouth drops open. I can't seem to catch my breath. I close my eyes. My jumper feels tight around my neck, I can't swallow.

When I open my eyes, he smirked. 'Oh, Gemma, are you only figuring this out now?'

Thomas Ben McDonald. It's the third very bad thing.

Chapter Eight

By the time we land in Tuscany, three flights, thirty hours, ten wines and four chocolate puddings later, I still haven't managed to get my head around what has happened.

Ben, or *Thomas*, as he's suddenly calling himself (what a douche), has slept easily on each of the flights, like a devil who creates shit storms for his own happiness, then sleeps like a log.

I, on the other hand, have regressed dramatically. With everything that happened in the past two weeks, I was not feeling in a good place, and my motto of *keep it together, Gemma* wasn't working. While flying somewhere over Darwin with Weasel sleeping peacefully, I felt my anxiety rise and it has stayed there ever since.

I didn't get the job of my dreams. My boyfriend is at home cleaning his ceiling. And the guy who did get the job of my dreams and who makes my skin crawl is now pretending to be my boyfriend at Lulu's wedding.

To make matters worse, I'm about to lie to my family, which makes me feel insanely guilty, and I'm about to have to touch that cretin, after he has stolen my promotion, right out from under me. I'm prepared for any of this. And I can't even pretend to be okay about being in the same room as Weasel, let alone pretend to *like* him. Horrible. Horrid.

Weasel, freshly showered and perfect in his out-of-the-office attire, looks like a country club model. I could snap a photo of him in his white trainers and a simple white cotton T-shirt and blue shorts, and put it straight on the cover of *Vogue Italia*. He tosses back his beautiful blond locks like he's in a slow-mo movie, but still he says nothing, like he's just waiting for me to bust. But I won't.

This is a game of who cracks first, and I'm not going to lose.

In the long taxi ride from Florence airport to the wedding venue, I try to remember I'm in Italy. *Italy*. And I'm not going to let him spoil it.

Out the window, in the dusky pink evening, is a perfect view of Florence and off in the distance the rolling hills of Tuscany come closer and closer, our car bumping over cobbled stones as we turn this way and that.

We stop at a traffic light, next to a small café, where a beautiful lady sits by herself enjoying a sliver of lemon tart, her profile so strong and captivating she could be a bronze statue. I wind down the window and smell garlic and the woody scent of pizza crusts cooking in ancient stoves. There's something different about evening here. The summer glow runs over the stone buildings, green courtyards, dangling lines of fairy lights, the laughter, and everything feels easy. I start to unwind.

It's magical and perfect, and I vow to stay silent and pretend Weasel doesn't exist. But there he is, so calm and certain in that front seat, and I want to know why. *Why* did he come? It's eating me alive. Twenty minutes into the taxi ride, curiosity gets the better of me.

'I want to ask you a question, Ben.' I look at him. 'Or should I call you Thomas?'

'Oh, Gemma, have you been thinking about my name the entire time?'

No, I was too busy eating puddings and contemplating a return flight to Sydney.

'My middle name is Ben. But I guess even you have already figured that out.'

'Oh, Thomas Benjamin. TB. A virus that almost wiped out the world. How perfect.'

I think I catch a small smile playing across his full lips. 'Is that the question?' He turns slightly and looks at me.

'That's the first question.'

'Of how many?' He's clearly enjoying this, smelling like Christmas over there, whilst I just got a whiff of my own plane BO.

'Of however many I want.'

'I decline to participate in the Spanish Inquisition.'

'Don't worry, if I had a time machine, I wouldn't send you back to the Inquisition. I'd send you to 1347.'

'Oh how lovely, the bubonic plague.' He smiles. 'You know, darling, you really should get your rest. You get terribly grumpy when you don't get your sleepies.'

I want to kick his seat. I want to kick *him*. Instead, I wind down the window even more, letting the early evening Italian air stream in, taking in cool breaths. Somewhere far off it smells like jasmine and summer and wet earth.

Finally, I say, 'Why did you come?'

He pauses for a second and smiles. 'When Ruby told me about your situation, I thought, well … two birds, one stone. I want to sign an author over here, and I want to see what my junior editor gets up to.'

God, he riles me. *Junior* editor. But there's something even more alarming that makes me feel sick. 'Ruby told you about my *situation*?'

'Well, yes. She was in a state of desperation as she couldn't find anyone to come and help pretend that you're not single. It's not a great world for a woman of almost forty years of age, is it?'

I want to gut him. Gut him like a fish.

'I'm not single. I have a boyfriend, Adam.'

'Yes, and here I am. Adam, at your service,' Weasel says. 'But why this name? Will you be going by the name Eve?'

I roll my eyes. 'No, I have an actual boyfriend. Called Adam.'

'And he's not here because…'

I try not to react. 'Because of work.'

'Putting work above his girlfriend,' Weasel says, and the look he gives me over his shoulder is one hundred per cent smugness.

'Do you always say the meanest thing you can think of?'

'Do you always say the nicest thing to everyone else, even if it's a lie?' Weasel counters.

Ugh, I can't actually believe someone as offensive as this is allowed to exist in 2023.

'Well, Ben, or Thomas, whatever your name is, let's not forget that *you* wanted to come here and pretend to be my boyfriend.' I shake my head. 'That is another level of sadistic.'

'And inviting a stranger to be a plus one at your sister's wedding isn't masochistic?' Weasel raises his eyebrows at me.

'I was hoping for just one of the seven billion people on earth who isn't a wanker.'

He clenches his jaw slightly. And I feel a tad victorious. Must remember that one.

'You know, Gemma, I could be the most horrible boyfriend,' he taunts.

I resist the urge to whip my drawstring from my pyjama pants and clothesline him from behind. 'You *wouldn't.*'

'I could…'

'You're just *so* arrogant.' I shake my head. 'I mean, who says, "*I could be the most horrible boyfriend*"?'

He's still unfazed. 'Oh, are we doing observations? *Oh your kids are lovely, Charlie.*' His mimic is so off, it's laughable.

He runs a hand through his perfect hair. I hate his hands. I hate his hair.

I gasp. 'Oh God! Something's in your HAIR!'

He quickly pulls down the visor, urgently searching every strand. I snigger.

Weasel snaps the visor up. '*So* funny.'

'I rather think so,' I say smugly.

The driver looks at us strangely, like *what is happening?*

I should be embarrassed, and I slightly am. But also, I've won this round, and victory feels sweet. I hardly ever have the upper hand, so I'm not going to say another word. It looks like Weasel isn't going to either, but he keeps running his hands through his hair as if to check there isn't really something in there. As he does, light reflects off his watch. Large, chunky titanium. *Expensive*. He never wears that at work.

Suddenly, I realise this is the first time I've ever seen him outside the office and I know nothing about him. Not where he lives, not what he likes (probably voodoo dolls), not what he looks like out of work clothes. Underneath his shirt, he could be a couch potato, be sporting a dad bod, or be a muscular god. I hope it's the first, because then he'll have one less thing to be smug about.

I must have closed my eyes thinking about Weasel because when the driver wakes me, we are in the middle of a large, circular driveway complete with a beautiful old fountain idyllically trickling water and a thick row of roses, bright white, making the air smell so sweet. In front of me stands the tallest, most amazing hotel I've ever seen. Everything seems perfect, particularly because Weasel has disappeared without a trace.

This'll turn out to be what was otherwise known as the calm before the shit storm.

Chapter Nine

Lulu is getting married in a castle. An actual castle where knights and kings used to live hundreds of years ago.

Now, thanks to the pamphlet I briefly read at reception, it's been refurbished into a three-hundred-bedroom luxury hotel overlooking olive trees, rolling hills and perfect rows of cypress planted along roadside.

The foyer itself is extremely large and beautiful, with high ceilings and exposed dark timber beams. Thick carved stone walls allow a layer of coolness on this sticky summer night. The carpet is red, as if always waiting for royalty to tread upon its expensive threads, and all the staff wear white gloves. The smell of lavender wafts in from the nearby gardens.

I'm suddenly extremely embarrassed that I've turned up in a luxurious castle hotel in airline pyjamas. What started off as a mini coup against Weasel has mutated into a great fashion faux pas. I can see some of the hotel guests looking

at me as though I shouldn't have been let in. To make it
worse, I'm wearing the slippers they give you on the plane
too. The ones that show off your gnarly toes and should
only be worn shuffling around the shower room. And I
haven't had time for a pedicure, so my nails are long and
jagged. I scrunch my toes under, and hope to get to my
room without anyone I know seeing me.

I give the man behind the counter a big smile. 'I don't
normally dress like this. Long plane trip.'

'Rrrright,' he says in heavily accented English without
looking at me, making it clear he doesn't buy a word I'm
saying.

I shrug and give up, but then notice an old man next to
me and I say, 'I'm about to put on a ball gown. You'd never
guess though!'.

He sniffs the air a bit, as if that's his way of
acknowledging me, and once again I pray I can hightail it to
my room without the family seeing me. Lulu would
probably kill me with a bobby pin, slowly jabbing it in my
eye until I keel over, rather than let me walk around the
hotel dressed like this and sharing her surname.

'All done. The key to room thirty-six, and your uh …
companion is already checked in, room twenty-eight.' He
sniffs too, as though he can smell a couple fight.

The nightmare begins.

I nod in a way I hope is both graceful and demure, and
then catch the lift alone, thank goodness, and make it to my
room, absolutely exhausted. It's a standard room, but still
incredibly expensive. And I can see why. It has terracotta
floors, a winged white armchair, a small wrought-iron table,

which gives me writing vibes, and a matching wrought-iron bed with a clean Italian-style white bedspread and a series of purple, gold and green throw cushions that look like Versace designed them. Total comfort.

I push my cheek against the bathrobe hanging in the corner and it feels so plush, I want to wear it for ever. Except I only have two hours until the party. Outside it's dark, but still I lean against the window trying to catch a glimpse of the vineyard, but everything is just rolling black with tiny stars. Not even the light of another house, or a street lamp. I type a quick text to Ruby.

RUBY, literally like wtf??? Did I kill your mother in a past life? Of all people BEN MCDONALD.

I manage to crawl onto my bed and fall asleep for thirty minutes, before being woken by the screeching of the alarm.

I shove myself under the hot water of the shower, and try to let the tension go. Wrapped in the softest bathrobe, I make a strong black coffee to keep me going. I try calling Adam and Ruby but my phone just makes those strange beeping noises and says *call could not be connected.* I try connecting to the hotel Wi-Fi and sending emails but that doesn't work either. *Stupid phone,* I think, putting it on my bedside table. I really want to speak to Adam. I pick up the hotel phone to dial him, and glance at the clock. Damn. It's almost drinks time and I have to get ready.

What am I going to wear? I unzip my suitcase and start pulling out the dresses I've packed so carefully. I try on a maroon dress that was floor-length, but suddenly I look too much like a librarian. I hold up the black dress, but I remember Lulu specifically saying, NO BLACK. Finally, I try on the floating chiffon peach dress with spaghetti straps and an asymmetrical cut hemline, so one side comes all the way up to my lower thigh, and the other is grazing my ankle. It looks light and fashionable and seems to say, *Hello, Italian Summer.*

I pull it on, smear some coconut balm onto my legs, use the hotel's complimentary nail file to file down my horrific talons, noting I should indulge in a pedicure while I'm here, and pull on strappy white sandals with a low heel.

Junior editor, I scoff to myself. No wonder he's willing to spend an entire four days with me; he's trying to put me off my game. Maybe he's hoping I quit. He'll probably try and get one over Tony next, considering that's what people without souls do.

But I can't think about work now. Tonight is going to be make or break. I'm about to go into a ballroom of a hundred wedding guests for the welcome drinks, with a fake boyfriend, and I *have* to be on my game.

Chapter Ten

Dressed and with a hint of foundation and soft peach lipstick, I walk down to Weasel's room, where I knock loudly.

No answer.

I knock again.

Weasel finally answers, a towel slung around his tanned hips and an open white shirt on top. *Lord.* His body is the furthest thing from a dad bod that ever existed. He's all muscle. A muscular extravaganza. Large biceps, nicely rounded shoulders, the perfect six-pack, all of which could easily be featured on the front cover of *Men's Health.*

'Would you like to put on some clothes?' I say, trying not to look at his smooth, muscular chest, with a hint of dark chest hair. 'No one needs to see that when they're attempting to eat dinner.'

'Good morning to you too, muffin bear.' He winks. 'It looks like you slept well. How was the back of the cab?'

I decide to ignore his comments and push into the room

without being invited (who am I?). Suddenly the smell of pine wafts across everything. His room is immaculately clean, his clothes hung up in the wardrobe already, his bed untouched. I knew it, he's a vampire and sleeps upside down in the closet.

'Like what you see?' Weasel grins and leans against the bedroom wall, and I can tell he means his own mostly topless body, and yes, he's clearly a regular at the gym, but those things don't work on me.

'If you mean your thoracic region and your supposedly perfect rectus abdominal muscles, not really. Actually, I prefer what a person's heart is like, and you appear to be missing that vital organ.'

'Actually, I meant the view.' He nods out of the window, where you can see the long strands of the hotel's fairy lights reflecting and shimmering across a beautiful lake, and the rolling shadows of the Tuscan hills in the distance. 'But it's nice to know you think I'm perfect.'

'Unsubscribe,' I retort, perching on the edge of the desk.

It's time to prep him about what we're about to enter, a bit like the seven levels of hell. I feel the need to do so, so that we can at least get through it unscathed. He's already ruined my career; I don't need him ruining the rest of my life. 'Right, so I want to have a quick chat.'

'Oh, so *now* you want to speak?'

Ugh, this guy. How am I ever going to pretend to like him, to *love* him? 'You're too much,' I declare.

'*Et tu, Brute*,' he replies, grinning.

'If only I had swords,' I mutter, thinking of how Caesar was killed with forty jabs of a sword and how I wouldn't mind doing exactly that to Weasel right now. And then I can't help myself. 'Besides, that's factually incorrect. He never said that in Latin, apparently he said *And you, child* in Greek, and Shakespeare—'

'Made it into *Et tu, Brute* because it was more dramatic.'
Damn him.

'Now, Gemma, did you come in here to chat about Shakespeare, or was there an actual point to your visit?'

'I came here to prep you about my family.' But I don't want to tell him all about Lulu, my mum, my dad, Marla, and everything that has happened. I don't want him knowing anything about my personal life. 'Lulu's my half-sister; she's getting married to Chip, and she's um...'

I try again. 'My family haven't seen me in a while, and they don't know much about my life. It's kinda complicated. And they're, um, they're different from what other families may be like. To yours. They're ... uh...'

Just then a loud shrill voice rings out from outside the door Weasel has forgotten to close.

I look at Weasel with wide eyes. 'They're here.'

Chapter Eleven

M arla, Lulu's mother, totters into the room in a cloud of spice perfume. 'Oh, Gemma, hello darling.'

The waft is so thick, I start coughing.

'Oh Gemm-air, reeeaaaaally. Gosh, that better not be contagious. You can't be around Lulu if you're sick. She looks divine and we caaaaan't have *any* hiccups.'

I remember why I dislike being these people. For starters, we don't sound like that. We're all from Essex so I don't know why she suddenly speaks as if she were auditioning for the new *Made in Chelsea*. Lulu's the worst though, you'd think she was an actual member of the Royal Family. I resist calling Marla 'babes' to remind her where we're from, but I'm highly tempted.

Marla turns around to look at Weasel. 'And who do we have here?' Her eyes almost boggle staring at his smooth chest. 'In … not much at all.' Marla winks like the cougar of cougars and it makes me feel a tad ill. 'I'm Marla, mother of the gorgeous bride.' Her hair is bleached blonde, hairsprayed within an inch of its life so it looks more like a fortress set across her head in a curled bob that wouldn't move even in a tornado. She's wearing a French lace top and skirt in a soft nougat cream colour that's close enough to white that she could pass for the bride.

'This is uh, Wea—, Be—' I start to say, before Weasel steps forward offering his hand and says, 'I'm Adam.'

'Well, what a fine young specimen,' Marla coos, not shaking his hand, but instead offering, for him to kiss, a hand which is covered in gold and diamond rings, and to my disbelief, Ben doesn't even hesitate – he bends his head and gives the back of Marla's hand a quick kiss.

'You're from Australia?' she twitters, looking at where he's just kissed her. 'They doooo make them loveleh down there.'

Ben smiles and says, 'It seems they do the same in England, too.'

I want to die, right then and there. My half-sister's mother is about to do a soft porn with my pretend boyfriend.

'Well, I do hope that youuu have a loveleh time in Italeh.' Marla is now putting on an even posher English accent than The Queen. 'Now, I must be ooooff, but Gemma, you're needed downstairs by your mother.' She turns back and winks at Weasel. 'And Adam, I'll seeh you at the welcome drinks. Sorreh I can't stay longer.'

Marla turns to go, but before she reaches the door, she spins around. 'And do get changed out of your nightie, Gemma, no one wants to see that from the corridor.' And with that she leaves.

I take a deep breath. 'Well, that was ... horrible.' I'm regretting all the decisions I've made that have brought me here to this moment.

Weasel smirks a bit, watching me bite my cuticles, a nervous habit that makes an appearance when my anxiety rockets sky high.

I sigh. 'This is never going to work, you know, pretending we're together. I honestly do think it's best if you just left. Or stay here, in the room, but not be part of this wedding business.'

'So you can be matched with other single, older men at the wedding for the next few days? And have to confess Adam didn't turn up and then look like you made him up?'

I narrow my eyes. '*Ruby.*'

'She's quite the informant if you give her a bit of coffee and chocolate.' His eyes twinkle because he knows his jibes are getting to me.

'And what do you get out of this?'

'A bit of entertainment.' He winks.

I fight the wave of fury that rises in me. 'You're heinous. Truly.'

'You know, Gemma, this other side to you is actually quite intriguing. I didn't know you had it in you. It's far more interesting than the version of you that's just being nice to everyone all the time.'

I'm about to protest and say I'm not always nice, but it's not true and he knows it. I *am* always nice. But not right now. Right now, I'm seething and he can tell. This is what Ben does to me. Sends me into fits of anger.

'We can't do this. We can't pretend to even *like* each

other. We'll fight and it will be over in seconds. What the hell was Ruby thinking? What were *you* thinking? This is rubbish.'

'Now, Gemma, don't get mad, you're not very good at it. Out of practice?'

I hate him.

'Actually, if you stopped pretending to hate me, you'll be surprised at how wonderful a boyfriend I can be.'

'What makes you think I'm pretending?' *Every bone in my body detests you.*

He gives me a lopsided, charming smile. 'Well, let's see how you feel a few days from now, Gemmies.'

'That's. Not. My. Name.' My blood boils.

'Shall we do our couple names? Gadam. Ademma. Oh, that's terrible, isn't it? Oh well, at least I'll save you from all those relatives asking why you're single.'

He has me and he knows it. But it feels like everything is spiralling out of control. 'You're enjoying this, aren't you?'

The edges of his lips turn up. 'Yes, a little.'

I spin around and head for the corridor. 'I'm going to my room. I'll meet you downstairs for drinks.'

'Yes, darling, you better get out of your nightie.' He winks and I can see the corners of his mouth fighting a laugh.

Chapter Twelve

I change into my French LBD – long black dress. I apply thick red lipstick, and wear my hair down in soft waves. *There*, I think, looking at the mirror, *not bad for someone who's jetlagged and a prisoner.* And there's no way anyone could confuse this bad boy with a *nightgown*.

Downstairs, the foyer entrance is full of perfume and long chiffon gowns, and men in tuxedos. There are more selfie sticks with that O light around them then I could count. I have to duck several times so I don't get hit in the head, weaving my way around the line-up of gorgeous people intent on looking at themselves on their phone screens. I take a deep breath and wipe my sweaty hands on my dress, and then glance at myself in the long ballroom mirrors. *No awkwardness.* I'm attending tonight as the woman I am: happy, successful, confident.

I look around the entrance for Weasel. It's imperative that we prep a little. Get our story sorted, like how did we meet? How long have we been together? I have to prepare him for the onslaught that's my family. But he's nowhere to be found. I'm just about to call his room when a voice calls out, 'Gemma!'

'Mum.' She trots across the foyer, wearing a spearmint-coloured suit with a diamond necklace and a giant smile.

'It's so lovely to see you.' She reaches her arms around me for a hug, her blonde bob, straight-edged and glossy, tickling my neck. 'It's been too long, Gemma.' She looks like she's going to get emotional, the way she does after a Sauv Blanc. 'Has it really been two years already?' Her eyes get teary.

'I think so.' I find myself getting a little teary too, so I swallow hard and say, 'Fancy necklace. You look nice.' I grin; it feels nice to see her again.

'Oh thank you, darling. Have you seen Lulu though? She's stunning, of course.' Mum nods. 'The perfect bride. And Chip, he's a darling. Have you met him? Have you seen Dad?'

'I haven't yet.' I brace myself.

Mum steps back and looks at me. 'You know, Gemma, I have to say this. Really. I've been emailing you and I just don't hear from you at all. You have to be better at communicating, especially for a writer!'

'*Editor*, Mum. I edit books.'

'But I... Haven't you've always wanted to write too?' She looks confused. Mum has always been a bit absent-minded when it comes to what I actually do for a living.

'Well, I did write something about six months ago, about food and community. I gave it to Tony, my boss. But,' I shrug, 'I guess not.'

'Oh darling, that's a shame.' She picks a piece of non-existent lint off my dress. 'Now I hear you brought someone with you. Is it serious?' She smiles with hope.

'Uh…' I think of Adam back at home; is it serious? Yes, I suppose it is. He wants us to move in together, have babies, get married, and that's exactly what I want too. But then I think about Weasel here, which is the complete opposite, to the point that it's practically comical. 'Kinda, I guess.'

'So, where is he?' she says, looking over my shoulder. 'Didn't you come down together?'

God, my first lie. 'Yeah. He's just a bit held up.'

'Well, let's go in, he can find you inside.'

She pushes open the ballroom doors. The only word I can use to describe the entire place is 'spectacle'. Everything is silver and sparkly: silver sparkles on the tables, silver sparkle somethings hanging from the ceiling, silver adornments on all the walls, and a wall of white flowers, where people are instagramming themselves against the floral backdrop.

A flower wall is one of those things you go to order online and click 'put in basket'; you get to the checkout and it costs like a thousand pounds, and you think, *Do I really need this?* and most people would say, *Oh, not really.* But Lulu would think, *Give me two.* And here they were, two very large flower walls, and they were gorgeous. Simply stunning.

I look around and spot Lulu at the other end of the room in a silver sparkly dress. At her side is obviously Chip, a man who looks identical to a Ken doll, holding her blush-coloured drink in a coupe.

Across the ballroom I catch sight of my Aunty Janice, who can talk the ear off anyone, and her husband, my Uncle Jonathon, who's deaf. Also a few cousins – Harry, and David – who both look older but still familiar. But still no Weasel.

Maybe he's done a runner. Maybe, and more likely, he's found a bridesmaid to flirt with, possibly bed. Yes, for Mister I-Love-Supermodels, that seems entirely more plausible. Knowing Lulu, all her friends will probably be perfect model types, and Weasel will love it.

'Where's your man?' Aunty Janice joins Mum and me. She's short and stout in a floor-length gown that makes her look like she's dressed in the hotel's heavy drapes. When she opens her mouth, her jowls flaps around a bit, and she holds her hands over her very portly stomach.

'Hello, Aunty Janice,' I say sweetly. 'You look lovely in purple.'

'So what about this chap? Is it serious?' Aunty Janice says with a look like a bulldog; she's clamped her jaws around this subject and she's not letting go.

This is so painful. 'I … um…' I start to say, wishing the floor would open up and swallow me. I was pleading for Weasel to stay away, because this is not the kind of conversation I want him to be part of – at all. He'd blow my cover easily. And then I'd be the laughing stock of the entire wedding.

'Gemma Bear!'

I turn around. 'Dad!' He gives me a large hug and kiss on the cheek, his grey beard scuffling my face. I know he's the one who almost single-handedly tore the family apart, but I have a soft spot for my dad, always had.

'I heard the commotion, what's happening without me?' Lulu and her silver sparkles appear in the centre of the circle. 'Really, Gemma, didn't I say no black?'

She's followed by Chip, who close up looks even more like he's stepped off the pages of *Town and Country*. He's medium build, tall, and with light brown hair that has a cowlick at the front. He has a sweet smile, and a slight swagger to his walk that seems to say, *I got this*, but in quite an English debonair way, as if he was always walking around with a rifle perched on his shoulder for shooting clay pigeons, and saying things like 'jolly good' without a hint of irony. I imagine he looks very at home in tweed. He seems nice enough as he shakes my hand and says, 'Welcome, Gemma', as if he was welcoming me into my own family.

'Oh, thanks, Chip, lovely to meet you,' I say. 'Everything looks perfect. Congratulations both of you. Marvellous.'

Marvellous? Who did I think I was meeting, The Queen? I've never used the word 'marvellous' before. Next thing you know I'll probably be saluting or saying things like, 'Ohh old chap, mind pouring me a loveleh tea in that bone china.'

'Now, where is that morsel of yours?' Marla appears out of nowhere in another musky cloud. She's changed into a red caftan, and enough jewels that if I threw her off a boat, she'd sink in a second. Each of her Botoxed hands (yes, I heard she had filler in each finger to 'plump' them out, then Botox to avoid any knuckle wrinkles) is bedazzled in chunky gold (twenty-four carat, I bet) rings. She almost steals the show from Lulu in her layers of vibrant red. 'What's his name again?'

'Adam,' Lulu responds, then looks at Chip. 'Drink, baby, I need a drink. This is warm.' She smiles sweetly and holds up her coupe, as Chip nods already striding towards the bar.

'Is that him?' Aunty Janice points to a large overweight man who must be over fifty.

'Um no!' Is that who they thought I was with?

Lulu interrupts. 'Adam is lovely and very chivalrous and very handsome. All the girls think so. We bumped into him in the hotel hallway earlier, and he said he knew straightaway who I was, because I have that a bridal glow.'

She gleams. 'He was kind enough to escort me down here, where he got me and all the bridesmaids drinks before saying he had something very important to do. He's gorgeous, and very sure of himself.' She turns to look at me and tilts her head to the side as if pondering something. 'And he doesn't seem Gemma's usual type.'

'He doesn't?' I try to look nonchalant. Of course he was buying girls drinks. So far, so predictable.

'So, sweetie, where is this man? I would like to meet him, make sure he's a fine gentleman, even if he is Australian.' That's Dad, ever the gentleman himself, except when he was putting his penis in other women's vaginas, cheating on Mum, I want to point out, but don't.

'I … uh…' I'm not sure what to say. He's late, and maybe he isn't coming at all. I can't say he's working as my family wouldn't take too kindly to a guest not attending drinks because of some office thing. Finally I say, 'I think he's a bit sick.'

'Sick?' Lulu looks worried and her voice goes up a notch. 'I *touched* him earlier, briefly ... do you think ... I can't be sick on my wedding day!'

'Oh dear!' My mum and her hypochondria flare up, as she grabs her throat and does a quick swallow. 'With what?'

'I think it's a ... a...' I try to think of something not gross, and not contagious. 'An autoimmune thing, like um, rheumatoid arthritis.'

Mum is still clutching her neck, but Lulu looks relieved. 'Oh, an old person's disease.'

I take the moment to change the subject. 'So Lulu, tell me about tomorrow?'

'You *should* have already read the *full itinerary*, Gemma,' she says pointedly.

I feel a bit disappointed in myself, and try to think fast, but just being around my family seems to make me regress to my unsure, uncertain seventeen-year-old self. 'Oh, I did, I just wanted to hear your ... um, take on it. The afternoon tea, right?'

'Well, in the morning the bridal party will be getting massages, then there's the afternoon tea, followed by the gala dinner. You're still coming early for the goldfish, right?'

I nodded quickly. 'Course.'

'And most importantly, there's the dawn photo shoot tomorrow. I have to go and do some last-minute preparation.' She leans in and whispers to me, 'Beauty things,' then steps back. 'And the photographers need a stand-in, so they can check the light and white balance, and set up for the actual shoot on the morning of the wedding. Will you do it?'

I'm nodding, relieved the attention is off Weasel and me. 'Yes, of course I'll do it.'

'Great, that's perfect. You and Adam can meet the photographer Emily in the foyer at six a.m.'

'Adam?' I repeat. 'Six a.m.?'

'Yes, silly, it's a dawn shoot, and we need both of you there, to be me and Chip. And that allows me a sleep in – got to get my beauty sleep! I can't have wrinkles or puffy eyes on my wedding day.'

'Yes, of course.'

Just when I think I've avoided the Adam conversation, Mum says, 'So tell us a little about Adam before we meet him.'

Lulu rolls her eyes, and I think she even stamps her feet a bit. She hates the attention not being on her, and I hate the attention being on me. But the rest of my family leans in, as though I'm about to give them the winning lottery numbers. Oh God. My stomach is in knots. My heart is beating so fast. I'm about to lie, to my family, and I feel *terrible*.

I take a deep breath, and decide it's best to just describe the real Adam, at home. 'Well, he's very sensible, and practical and grounded,' I start, and I can see my dad nodding in approval. 'And he's successful, and ambitious, and he just got a new job, which is why he couldn't be—' I stop myself. 'Which is why he can't be in Italy for more than a few days.'

'What's his new job?' Lulu suddenly looks interested.

My mum looks worried. 'Can he do it if he's sick?'

'Head of...'

'Chief editor. And I'm not sick, unless you mean I'm sick of waiting for a drink and a dance,' a smooth voice says behind me.

I whirl around and there is Weasel, wearing a crisp white shirt open slightly at the neck to reveal his chest, along with navy pants and cufflinks in the shape of books. He's carrying two champagnes and two whiskeys. His hair is slightly wet, as though he'd just stepped out of the shower, and he smells again like pine and mint, like a cold Christmas forest. Mum and Marla twitter like teenagers. *Damn*, I can't help thinking as my eyes follow the strong curve of his jawline. *He really is good-looking.*

He gives me one champagne, my mum another, and a whiskey to my dad. When he sees Lulu about to pout, he says, 'I've got something a little more special coming for you. With fairy floss.' And she gleams, walking right into his ninja trap. So *that's* how he gets some of the girls to flush at work.

'Well. This is ... uh, Adam,' I say, trying to smile happily, imagining that the actual Adam was standing next to me. I try not to look at anyone directly, in case they can tell I'm lying. I was always such an awful liar.

Weasel looks down at me with soft adoring eyes, as if I were the most important person in the world to him. His acting is ... brilliant. He lightly rests his hand on my back. The shock of his body touching mine makes every single cell in my body twang. I do a weird cough to cover up the strange, jittery feeling clanging through my body.

And then the questions start.

Where did you grow up? What do you do? How old are you? Do you believe in this feminist bullshit or are you a man? (That was from Aunty Janice, God bless her, cos I might clock her with a heavy magnum of champagne before the night is over.)

Everyone seems taken by him. Weasel laughs easily and answers every question without a hint of impatience or stubbornness, whilst I try to keep my mouth from falling open at his instantaneous transformation.

'Well, you're exactly as Gemma described you.'

My eyebrows shoot up in fear. My stomach is in knots. This would be the perfect time for him to just lay me in it. Right now. And walk out and leave me to a giant mess. I brace for the worst.

'Everyone is absolutely lovely and lively and welcoming. I'm so happy to be here.' He raises his glass and everyone follows suit, and just on time Lulu's pink fairy floss cocktail arrives and it's fancy, instead of tacky, and she practically swoons at him. I take a quick glance at him, to see if he's being facetious or sarcastic, but nothing on his face registers as anything other than genuine. God, I have to give it to him, he is good.

Chip comes back from the bar with two champagnes then and I can see he's a little downcast at having been outdone by the sugar snap drink, so I smile and say, 'I'd love another one of those, Chip, if you don't mind?' And Chip gratefully hands it to me, and I down half of it out of sheer nerves.

Thank goodness, Lulu starts telling Weasel about all the

people at the wedding, and about her dress being couture, from a designer I'm sure he's never heard of, but he manages to look raptured. He's a better actor than Tom Hanks and for a second I feel relieved. Could we pull this off? If we keep the attention off us, and on Lulu, perhaps we'll be okay.

'So you're an editor too, Adam?' My mum nods enthusiastically. 'Chief, did you say?' She looks impressed.

'I am, but your daughter is one hell of an editor.' I look up to see Weasel's sarcasm, but he has hidden it very well, because I can't see anything other than earnestness.

'Well, come on, tell us the story of how you got together,' Aunty Janice jabbers.

'Shouldn't we be focusing on Lulu and Chip?' I almost squeak.

Lulu purses her lips and tilts her head to the side. 'Yes, but I want to hear this too,' she says as if she finds it hard to believe suave Weasel is with me.

'I'm going to let Adam tell that,' I say quickly. 'Go ahead.'

'No, after you, *honey*. I know you like telling the story. Especially how romantic it was. Like one of your romcoms.'

There it is, the dig. I knew he couldn't help it. I grit my teeth and try not to say, *I don't edit romcoms.*

Lulu raises her eyebrows. '*Really*?' She hates romcoms; she think they're cheap and tacky, clichéd like red roses, candlelight, and teddy bears on Valentine's Day, finds them too middle-class, or, as she puts it, bougie and basic. It isn't her *Vogue* style. She looks at me. 'You edit romcoms?' As if this very act would see me disowned from the family, and right about now, I would take that exit gratefully to run off into the dark night.

'I uh … edited some for a colleague… I was covering for her.' I seem to have lost the power of words because I'm rambling, unable to make a full sentence.

'Don't worry, how we met was very chic, rather than cliché,' Weasel says and for a second I'm struck that Lulu looks like she's agreeing with him.

'Was it romantic?' my mum asks.

'Well, Patricia, you could say that.'

I cringe as Weasel says this, because I know what he's doing, leading her on. I almost feel sorry for my mum and Lulu, because he and I both know *exactly* how he feels about romance. I don't think he has a romantic bone in his body.

'Actually Adam hates all that,' I declare. 'He's not into that romantic stuff at *all*.'

I glance at Weasel, who tries not to smile as he says, 'Well, *actually*, Gemma doesn't remember, but we met a long time ago. A perfect meet-cute, which is always romantic.'

I raise my eyebrows, wondering what bullshit he's about to make up.

'It was at an awards night for the Finch Memoir prize. She doesn't remember me trying to talk to her.'

'I'm sure I would have remembered,' I say, willing myself to play along. I have gone to the Finch night, most years actually, and I definitely don't remember Weasel ever being there.

'I tried to talk to her, several times in fact, but she didn't give a damn.' Oh, he's good. He definitely could have been an actor. 'In fact, she actually asked if I was someone's secretary.'

'Really?' Mum says, her eyebrows raised. 'That doesn't sound like you, Gemma. She's usually keen to chat to any guy who's willing.' She looks at Weasel. 'Unfortunately she's normally into guys that just aren't that into her. Unrequited love, poor poppet.'

I grimace. 'That was when I was younger, Mum, just after uni, and … well, we don't need to revisit that, do we?'

Mum, not taking the hint, keeps on talking to Weasel. 'She had a string of those artsy types. You know – poets, musicians, writers that couldn't get a deal. I mean, she tried to get them published, but her work wouldn't do it. Commitment phobia, isn't that how you explained it, Gemma?'

'Something like that,' I say, staring at the floor, feeling my face start to burn.

'Come on, Gemma, you can tell the story of how we met for the second time at the office,' Weasel insists, and I'm almost grateful he's changed the subject.

I say quickly, 'We met at work. In a meeting. We both like coffee, and it just clicked. Straightaway. And then *voila*. Here we are. One year later.'

'Oh, that's not exactly true, is it?' Weasel's eyes are glinting. 'You missed out the best part.'

'Did I?' I'm telling Weasel with my eyes that this is enough. *Stop talking.*

'Yes, the bit where I asked you if you were my secretary, teasing you about our first meeting.'

My confused face says it all. 'That's why…' Is it *true*?

'Then, a few weeks later, you asked me out for coffee.'

'Right. I did.' Because that bit is unfortunately true.

'But you got a bit nervous, didn't you? You tripped over the carpet, and landed awkwardly in your very tall red heels. I asked if you were okay, and you looked up at me as if to say, *Well, aren't you charming?*'

I want to kill him.

'Oh yes,' I say through gritted teeth, because I did trip on some uneven carpet, and he did ask if I was okay, but it was in a righteous tone, not a helpful one. 'That bit.'

'Oh, that does sound more like Gemma.' Mum nods. 'Especially the falling over part. Never was light on her feet, not like me, or Lulu. Takes after her father. Two left feet.'

Before anyone can ask any more questions, or give background information about my lack of coordination, I give Lulu a bright smile. 'You know, I'd like to hear about Chip and Lulu. It is their day after all.'

'Days,' Lulu corrects me. 'So Chip and I,' Lulu addresses the group, 'we just knew it the first time we saw each other in Harrods.'

Lulu says Harrods as if trying to make it clear that she's marrying into *money*. Which is good, because I'm pretty sure this wedding would bankrupt our entire family, who are used to shopping in Asda's special aisles. It's likely we now have massive debts that I'll be paying off in my old age, whilst Lulu and Chip play golf.

Lulu gushes. 'And of course Daddy had to meet him next, and loved Chip. And both Mummy and Mum.' She looks at Marla and then at my mum, and I feel like a child of some weird polyamorous cult. I can see Weasel raise his eyebrows just slightly, and I'm looking at him telepathically telling him not to react.

'After that, Chip took me out to go clay-pigeon shooting in his wonderful vintage MG, and ... well, the next weekend he whisked me away to his cottage in the Cotswolds. The rest is history!' She waves her massive sparkler in the air, and it's so large I can't believe she's able to lift her hand. It almost covers half of her finger, from knuckle to joint. I'm surprised that the three wise men didn't turn up offering gold, frankincense and myrrh with that thing glinting in the air.

But Chip looks in awe at being with Lulu, and Lulu looks smitten with Chip and her incredibly huge ring. They are actually both very sweet. Them and their clay-pigeon, Harrods type of life. It's easy to see that they actually do truly love each other.

'Well, that was a lovely story!' I say, genuinely smiling. 'How about a toast to the newlyweds-to-be?' I raise my glass.

Everyone clinks and says, 'To Lulu and Chip.' I take a big sip, thinking I've expertly negotiated the way out of my story, and I'm just about to ask Lulu which caterer and flowers she has chosen, when Aunty Janice says, 'So Gemma, are you two going up the aisle next?'

The woman just won't give up.

'Not anytime soon.'

'But you're in love?'

'I think love happens over time.' I give her my most brilliant smile and hope that will shut this shit down.

Lulu looks at Chip. 'I think love is instant, the moment you meet someone. When you know you just know.'

I clear my throat. God, does everyone still believe in this elusive, fictitious The One?

'I don't think that always happens. Sometimes absolutely, and you guys are lucky that was the case for you. But sometimes it's a much slower burn that ends up feeling warm and comfortable,' I say, thinking about the real Adam at home.

'It sounds like you're talking about an old shoe, Gemma! Not love.' Lulu gives an airy laugh.

Mum nods. 'I have to agree with Lulu. I felt the same when I saw your father.' She's looking over at him with a funny soft expression on her face.

Marla says, 'And me too, when I saw your father,' which breaks the Mum–Dad love spell immediately. Mum suddenly looks uncomfortable and Dad's eyes are shifting between Mum and Marla, looking equally chuffed and scared. I can see Weasel staring at me, and I know he's busting to know this story.

'Yes, well, crisis averted,' Mum says haughtily, taking a sip of champagne.

Marla, unscathed by the crisis comment, tilts her head, narrows her eyes and stares at us. I can tell she and her Botoxed hands smell something fake.

'I think love is about the smaller things,' Weasel says, looking at me. 'What about the time you couldn't find that marketing proposal and you were looking everywhere for it, and you thought you'd thrown it out, and then it miraculously it appeared on your desk?'

It takes me a second, but then I remember. It was a few months ago, and I was desperate to find it for fear Tony would have me bound and gagged. 'Sean found it.'

'Did he?' Weasel turns to address the group. 'Or did I find it in the kitchen, and put it on your desk?'

I feel confused and uncertain. How did he find out about that? And what a low blow to use it to his advantage.

'And the time that you told everyone you weren't having coffee, but then you started getting headaches, and a little box of headache pills found its way to your desk.'

Now I'm extremely confused, because I was sure Bec had found a box of ibuprofen and left them for me.

'I may not do grand gestures of love, but it's the small things that carry you through a relationship.' He looks directly at me with his sharp blue eyes. 'And I notice.'

'Hear, hear!' my dad says, clinking his glass with Weasel's.

'Sounds like a keeper to me.' Aunty Janice nods then adds under her breath, 'Hope you hate the feminists too.'

God, she's insane.

Lulu and Chip lean over and kiss each other. My dad ducks his head and kisses my mum. And then everyone looks at us.

'Well, now what are you waiting for? Give each other a kiss!' Aunty Janice says, wetting her own lips as though she's the one about to be kissed.

I feel my body stiffen. Everyone goes silent. My mouth goes dry.

Just at that moment, thankfully, a bell rings out. 'Can

everyone please gather for the speeches?' the MC says into the microphone.

I breathe a sigh of relief as everyone moves closer to the front podium. When I'm close enough to Weasel, against my will, I say in a low voice, 'What was that stuff about the painkillers and the marketing proposal? I mean it was quite ... good.' I hate complimenting Weasel, but it's true. 'I'm a terrible liar.'

'You don't say,' he whispers.

'I'm not as practised as some people who appear to have been born without a conscience.'

'Shush, Gemma, the speeches have started.' Weasel nods to the front of the hall where my dad is standing awkwardly and fumbling with the microphone that's already on before saying three times, 'Welcome, everyone. It's a lovely evening, isn't it? Glad you could all come.'

The speeches are excruciatingly long and painful. First Marla makes a lot of 'loveleh' comments about what everyone is wearing, and how Lulu is amazing, and how Chip is just as amazing, and how they like to jaunt around the countryside, and this means they will be together for ever. After twenty minutes of that drivel, I can see people almost dozing off into their champagne.

Then the bridesmaids, who all look a bit like blonde, veneered influencer clones who had all visited the same Brazilian butt lift doctor, twitter about how life without Lulu would be the worst thing, like, ever. They do this as a rhyming poem and I'm sure E.E. Cummings turns in his grave.

Then my dad says more things about how precious Lulu

is, and everyone ooohs and ahhhs. And then Mum mentions how Lulu was a gift from heaven, which seems a little hyperbolic. And then Chip's father, who with his perfect grey hair looks like he belongs in a country club ad, makes a very long speech comparing love to a good golf match, which gets very intricate when he starts to liken different girls to different clubs. I just keep thinking, *Please don't say 'hole in one'.*

At the end of the night, we all toast Lulu and Chip, and as I take a quick sip of wine I try not to yawn.

'Where's Adam?' Marla has sidled over in a waft of musk, and looks pointedly at me. When I turn around to see if Weasel is still alive after those torturous hours – yes, hours – spent listening to people on microphones, I notice he's a few metres away, and has been cornered by two of the beaming blonde bridesmaids.

'Oh, he's very friendly.' I dismiss her with a wave of my hand, as though I'm very nonchalant. 'Likes to meet all the guests.'

'Careful, Gemma,' she warns me before leaving with a flick of her red caftan, like a villain in a film.

Careful of what? Does she mean that my pretend boyfriend is a Lothario? Well, yes, clearly. Or worse, has she smelled a rat?

Just in case I should look like the concerned girlfriend, I step a little closer, until I can overhear parts of Weasel's conversation.

'Are you from Australia?' one of them is saying in a very posh accent.

'Do you surf?' The other one giggles.

'Well, yes, and yes.' Weasel gives them a charming smile and I'm sure I can see one of them literally melting under his gaze. She starts flipping her hair like mad, and putting her finger on her lips, as if it's seductive and maybe it would be if they weren't asking about sharks, which are evidently part of his family ancestry as he's clearly very good at this: a hunter, a predator surrounded by blonde prey.

'Do you see them often? Do you get scared?' one of them exclaims excitedly.

Weasel winks. 'Nothing really scares me.'

He's a typical player, no doubt about it, like all the other men who smile charmingly, and know just how to tuck a piece of hair behind your ear in that way that makes your knees weak. Men who tell you exactly what you want to hear, just so they can hop into your bed and take your clothes off, and hug you fiercely in the morning as they take your number and then never call.

Thank God for men like Adam. Thank God for men who want commitment, and to make a home. I feel a sudden need to hear his voice.

I go back to my room for a second, grab my phone off the charger and check for messages from Adam. Annoyingly there are none, and I realise my phone says SOS only. I walk down to the foyer, with it in my hand. 'I'm sorry, my phone doesn't seem to be working, is there Wi-Fi?'

'We've had a request for no hotel Wi-Fi,' the apologetic desk clerk says in perfect English with the bare minimum of an Italian accent. 'Specifically for the wedding. It appears the frequency seems to uh, mess with the doves that are to be released.' He shrugs as if even saying those words is an abomination of embarrassment.

Lulu has organised to turn off Wi-Fi across the entire hotel? Of course she has. What a self-centred... I stop myself, and feel a tad guilty. It's her wedding after all, and if she wants to go all out, who am I to judge that?

'Oh, well, thank you,' I say, politely, and then decide to just switch on data roaming and accept the charges. Quickly I shoot off a message to Adam.

Arrived okay, plus one is doing my head in, you'll never guess who it is. Wish you were here! How are you?

Then I quickly check my work email account, which has nothing urgent except for Tony asking me if my phone is switched on and would I mind checking in with him tomorrow. I reply.

Sure thing, Tony.

'Gemma! It's time for the family dance. Lulu is beside herself that you're not in there,' Mum says, poking her head out of the large wooden ballroom doors.

'Oh, sorry.' I push my phone into my bra, so deep you can't see it, and then hurry to the door, for whatever this family dance is.

The entire room is dark and Lulu and Chip are positioned in the front and middle, bathed in a spotlight. An unfamiliar slow song is playing and both of them are moving to the music, lost in a tangle of arms and legs, and Lulu seems graceful even though dancing isn't her forte. They do a series of turns and little jumps and Chip looks like a stiff cardboard cut-out, bless his soul.

Towards the end of the song, the bridesmaids and groomsmen all come out and do a choreographed number and bridesmaid Mia is by far the best dancer. I could see her and Lulu trying to outdo each other.

When the soundtrack changes to 'My Endless Love', Mum says, 'Come on, Gemma, it's our turn.' Mum takes up with Dad, and Marla is swanning about with a fake-tanned fellow I guess must be her latest husband (he looks twenty years older than anyone in a coffin).

Weasel steps onto the dance floor first, then turns around and holds out his hand. I don't want to touch it. That hand has probably been up some bridesmaid's skirt in the bathroom, not twenty minutes ago. Instead I smile and wave him over to a corner, far away from the limelight. In the publishing world, I want the attention. On the dance floor, not on your life.

I gingerly put my left hand on his right shoulder, and make sure there's a lot of distance between us, so it's almost impossible for anything but our hands to touch.

He ducks his head and leans towards me. 'You want this to look real, don't you?'

'Oh, it does.' I look directly at him. 'It looks like we've had a massive fight because you've been chatting up bridesmaids all night, and I'm pissed off. Super real.' I give him a killer smile. 'Should I be disinfecting my hands?'

'Well, you know what they say, Gemma, we may be fighting, but make-up sex is the best.'

I roll my eyes as he guides me across the dance floor like we are suddenly doing an Argentinian tango.

'Stop showing off,' I tell him. 'This is Lulu's night.'

'I think she's enjoying herself perfectly.'

I look over and he's right: Lulu's head is resting on Chip's shoulder and they both look happy.

Weasel pulls me back into the corner, and as I turn, he pulls me towards him slightly. 'Don't twirl away from me, Gemma, you have to stay close. Haven't you danced with a partner before?'

'Not really, no. I'm too busy doing things like working.'

'I could teach you.' He twirls me around. 'You'd be rather good after I'm done with you. You could be a natural.'

I throw my head back and laugh. 'Does that actually work on people? Is that the kind of line you feed your supermodels, instead of food?'

'Supermodels?' His brow furrows.

'Yes, Ruby told me all about them.'

'I don't know what you mean.'

'Oh, are they hush-hush? Can't pick up the bridesmaids when they're worried about supermodel competition. Got it.' I lay my finger against my nose as if to say, your secret is safe with me.

'I think you've had one too many wines, Gemma. Got to watch that. Now stop behaving like an angry little hamster. We're meant to be in love, remember?'

He pulls me towards him and puts his hand on my

lower back. I want to wriggle away, but I see Mum looking over at us, and she seems so happy that I smile and pretend I'm happy too.

My lips are close to his ear now and I can't help myself. 'Why did you really come here? This seems a lot of work, to be listening to my family's marathon speeches simply because you want to be, what did you call it? *Entertained*.'

'Oh, well, you know.' Weasel shrugs. 'I love Italy. The finger food we had before was delicious. Prosciutto and melon. Plus, I told you I'm here to sign an author.'

'Who?'

'Now, now, Gemma, don't go prying. The deal isn't done yet.'

'Fine, but you could have just come to Italy to sign them; you didn't need to come with me. Here.' I want to blow his cover right off; I want him to know I'm on his trail, that somehow I know about him trying to take down my career. He won't succeed. I'll make sure of that. In fact, I'll even log on over here and work. That would show Tony exactly how much of a dedicated employee I am.

'Being here with you...' He peters off. 'Well, now you kinda owe me.'

My eyes widen and I stop dancing and step backwards. 'I *owe* you?'

'Shush, Gemma, got to keep up the façade.' He grabs me and spins me to the side and before I know it he's dipping me, leaning on top of me. I can feel the warmth of his body, the wall of muscle beneath his expensive white shirt. 'You never know when I may need a favour. I've done you one, so you could do me one...'

'Let. Me. Up,' I say with gritted teeth.

He lifts me up and whispers, 'And before you get all wifey and worried, I can tell you there are no supermodels, and the bridesmaids are harmless and boring. They wanted to talk about surfing and beaches, and how easily they could get a tan in Bondi. It almost put me to sleep.'

'You could have a threesome with them for all I care.' I shrug, wishing the song was over.

'Threesomes are overrated.' He winks at me.

'You are dis-gust-ing.' I roll my eyes. 'And for the record, I don't owe you a thing.'

Then just as my mum looks over, Weasel sticks his cheek to mine, and all I can smell is pine, and all I can feel is his slight stubble. He looks at me and traces his fingers on my lips, and I suddenly think, *Oh God, he's going to kiss me. And that's disgusting. And where has that finger been?* Out of the corner of my eye, I can see Aunty Janice elbowing poor Uncle Jonathon and looking over at us as if they were watching a romantic movie.

Thankfully the music stops, and I step as far away from Weasel as I can, before I'm tempted to hit him.

Chapter Thirteen

F ive a.m. is an ugly time of day. Not outside. Outside it's an ashy dawn, ready for the first summer streaks of sun, and looks rather beautiful. In the early morning light, I can just make out the stone- and terracotta-coloured rooftops dotted on the nearby hills. Being here makes my heart happy. It's truly beautiful.

Inside is a different story. I'm exhausted. After the family dance, I went straight to my room. But I didn't sleep well. I tried calling Adam, but it wouldn't go through, and I fell asleep in my clothes with my phone in my hand.

When I wake up there are no texts. But then I calculate my five a.m. is his two p.m., and hurriedly dial his number.

He answers on the third ring.

'Adam! Hello! How are you?'

'I'm great, Gemma.' Just hearing his voice, so familiar and calm, I feel a sense of relaxation spread across me.

'How's things at home?' I lie back in the large lounge

chair and stare out the window, watching Tuscany wake up and the sky become a grey, milky white. I put my hand on the window and it's warmish already.

'Good, really good. Prepping for the big role. I got a Hugo Boss suit, dark navy; it's great, Gemma. And new aftershave. I've just popped some things in the washing machine and really, I'm all ready to go.'

'Sounds great, babe. So, it's crazy over here.' I tell him quickly everything, from Weasel to the beautiful hotel we're staying in, to the drinks and dancing last night. 'He's into supermodels and bridesmaids and threesomes, and he probably has a thousand STDs, so I feel like disinfecting myself.'

He gives a quick laugh. 'I'm sure you've got this, Gemma. I have no doubt.' He pauses. 'I found some new apartments I think you're going to love.'

'Really?'

'Yeah, I can send them to you.'

'I don't think my phone's working over here. I didn't get any texts from you, so maybe Messenger isn't working properly.'

'I didn't send any texts.'

'You didn't?' I ask, surprised.

'No, you were sad, and it wasn't great the way we left things, was it?'

I remember me asking him to come to Italy with me, and him saying no, and me feeling a bit upset, and Adam saying he couldn't talk when things got too emotional because that never goes well.

'I guess not.'

'I wanted you to calm down a little before we spoke again, and so I left you to it. And you sound great now, Gemma, really good. And I'm so glad.'

'Yeah... okay.' Adam is the most rational man I've ever met, and whilst his calmness usually sooths me, sometimes – like now – I feel a deep twinge of dismay that he needed time away until things calmed down. Well, really, until *I* calmed down.

'I'll send you that townhouse information. There's a block of them for sale. Tell me which one you like and we'll book in an inspection when you get home. Love you.'

'Love you too.' I stare at my phone after he hangs up, feeling something I can't place. Anyway, now isn't the time to analyse; I have a photo shoot to attend.

I pull on my sweatpants, a singlet and the bathrobe over the top. Something white, I giggle, and make my way down to the foyer.

'Well, don't you look...' Weasel's eyes take me in as he sits on the couch wearing low-slung black sweatpants and a tight white T-shirt.

'Lovely?' I offer. 'Fetching?'

'Like a terry-towelling meringue.'

'Perfect. All brides should look like a meringue, even stand-in ones.'

'I got you a coffee.' Weasel holds up a takeaway cup. Inside is a milky cappuccino.

'Oh, I don't drink normal milk,' I say, handing the cup back. 'I only drink...'

'Soy.' He hands the cup back to me. 'With extra froth. By

the way, the barista looked at me like ordering soy was a murderous act in Italy.'

I squint at the coffee, trying to figure it out. Has he put laxatives in there? 'How did you know?'

'Gemma, I'm your *loving* boyfriend, I know these things.'

I still can't puzzle it out, but then realise Ruby must have given him a list of pointers.

I take a grateful sip of coffee, and the warmth slides down my throat. 'Ahhh, the elixir of the gods.'

Weasel laughs. 'I agree. Especially at this early hour.' He lifts his drink and before I can pull away, he puts his coffee lid to mine, and cheers.

I pull mine away and take a long sip. I can't trust this guy, not for a second. It's all just an act. And I feel confident I've built a pretty accurate version of Weasel in my head as a charming, cut-throat liar.

'You know, you're actually quite interesting, Gemma.'

Ahhh, so this is how he does it. The charm offensive so many girls fall for. He must think I'm completely naïve, or stupid. I roll my eyes.

'Really? Does that actually work? Coffee and a one-line compliment?'

He holds a poker face for a few seconds before he breaks out in a grin. 'Actually, yes, it kind of does.'

'They must be *very* easy targets.'

'Perhaps...' His tone is slightly bashful but still confident. 'Maybe I just need more of a challenge.'

'Maybe you need a soul.'

He tilts his head, staring at me, his face going slightly

red as if he's fighting something, or struggling to breathe. Then he puts his head back and laughs loudly, his perfect teeth making him look like he's in a toothpaste commercial. When he's finished, he grins at me.

I realise I've never heard him laugh like that, and it almost makes me smile. *Almost*. But only because he's practically heaved up a lung.

'You sound like a walrus.' I can't help slipping the boot in, just in case he thought we were getting friendly. We aren't.

'You're so different outside of work.' Then he puts his hands up. 'Not a line, I promise.'

'Thank God. Save them for the bridesmaids.'

'No, I'm spoken for.'

'You are?' Not that I care.

'With you.'

'*Right*, of course.'

I can feel him looking at me, his head tilted to the side taking me in. God, he's cocky.

'You know, Miss Meringue, I think for this whole charade to be a bit easier, maybe you could start being civil, and stop calling me Weasel?'

I'm about to protest when he says, 'Even in your head.'

I shrug. 'Only if you can stop chatting up bridesmaids. I don't want to find my *perfect* boyfriend is doing bits in a broom closet.'

'Not my style.'

'Really though? Isn't it?' I say. When I heard he was into supermodels, I googled him. Of course I did. And Ruby was kinda right: there are lots of photos of sunsets and sunrises, and him watching the sunsets and sunrises with a model blonde, and then a stunning brunette. Too many to count.

He's about to say something when Emily the photographer bursts through the doors, profusely apologising for being late. She has a fearful look and seems to think I'm about to go bridezilla by proxy like Lulu would have, but I just say it's okay, and she immediately relaxes.

It's still a little pre-dawn chilly outside, despite it being summer. We walk through the damp grass, past the herb garden, the rose garden, the large stone-statue fountain. Geraniums spill over the hotel balconies, bright blood red and fuchsia pink, and a shy soft white.

My breath is hot and foggy in the fresh air as we walk between large cypress trees, and the cool air smells like earth. I notice Weasel's chest seems to harden, not that I'm looking, but it's difficult not to with his thin white T-shirt, especially when Emily positions us against the hills, facing the hotel, where behind us the sun is about to rise. We stand about two feet apart and I feel a bit awkward, so I undo and re-tighten my bathrobe for no reason.

'Can you get a bit closer together?' she's yelling from thirty feet away, disturbing all the poor summer crickets who are just trying to have a sleep in. I'm pretty sure Emily is thinking we deserve all the WORST EVER awards as a couple.

'Put an arm around each other.'

I hesitate. I don't want to touch him. It's only then that I really come face-to-face with this whole charade. Everyone here thinks we are in love. They would be expecting a lot more than touching arms. What the fuck am I doing?

Weasel steps closer, and I try not to inhale the pleasant woodsy smell of him. His muscles distract me momentarily but then he slides one arm around me, and it feels like a snake that initially you're not worried about because it's not venomous, but then you realise it's giving you a really tight hug, and you're like, *Oh, it's a bone crusher and I'm gonna die because I wasn't on my game.*

Weasel is looking at me. 'What are you thinking about?'

'Why?'

'It's the same expression you sometimes get at work too, in the pitch meetings.'

'You stare at me in meetings? Stalker.'

'Only when I think you're about to have a seizure. So?'

'I'm thinking about snakes.' I shrug matter-of-factly. 'That bone-crush you.'

He laughs loudly, again. He tips his head back and almost cackles, and it's so catching that I can't help but giggle too.

'I like this side of you.'

'The right side?' I ask because that's the cheek that was shoved in his direction.

'The truthful side.'

I raise my eyebrows so high they almost hide in my hairline. 'I *am* truthful,' I say proudly, like I'm a two-year-old about to provide a list of points as to why I should be chosen for the kindergarten relay team, but thankfully stop myself. Who cares what he thinks.

Weasel challenges me. 'Do you *really* think Gavin's three children are lovely? Have you even met them?'

Annoyance bubbles in my chest. '*Four.* Four children. I

have seen many photos,' I respond, looking into his annoying blue eyes. 'And listened to many stories. And this is what *caring* about other humans feels like.'

'I'm an honest guy and upfront—'

'Direct. Rude. Inconsiderate. There are so many better synonyms.'

'And *honestly*, you could have spent your time a lot better than chatting in the kitchen. You could have been chasing and signing new authors, finding ways to increase sales, and—'

My blood boils. 'Stepping over people to climb to the top? Such wonderful leadership qualities.'

'SORRY, CAN WE LOSE THE BATHROBE?' Emily shouts like we're on the set of a bad porn, interrupting our little spat.

Begrudgingly, I loosen it and throw it to the side, and am left standing in a singlet that has been accidentally couldn't-be-bothered-to-do-separate-loads washed with colours so is now off-white, and grey sweat pants.

'Are those from the plane? Or is your entire wardrobe grey?' Weasel smirks.

'I like to be comfortable and not force myself into little dresses. People don't have to look amazing all the time.'

He smirks. 'Mission accomplished.'

Ugh, I detest this lump pretending to be human.

Emily orders us into more faux romantic positions. Leaning back towards each other, separated by rose bushes. I like that one, extra distance. Him walking ahead of me, towards the sunrise – separately thank goodness – both of us looking back over our shoulders. I feel ridiculous doing something so delicate in grey sweats.

'This feels...' I say, struggling to find the words. Awkward? Weird? Horrible?

'Like you've always dreamt.' Weasel winks.

I'm sure if he keeps speaking like this, I'll just start yelling, 'YOU'RE A DICKHEAD', which isn't something you want to yell at the person you're supposedly madly in love with.

'My dreams definitely wouldn't have you in them.'

When Emily asks him to get down on one knee and look up at me with adoration, the absurdity of what is happening suddenly dawns on me: I'm with my archnemesis in a field in Italy pretending I love him while he looks like he's proposing.

He shrugs as if it's something he's done before, and I realise he's probably dated so many people he's proposed multiple times, not because he actually wanted to get married, but because he's a player that has a charade to hold up, lying to keep girls around. I take delight in thinking they said no, or that they ended things wretchedly, because I dislike him so much. In any case, I like that for once he's down on the ground.

I can't help myself. 'You look at home down there.'

He winks. 'I have many talents, including on my knees.'

'Oh God. Disgust— I can't even. I mean, how did we even get *here*?'

'By plane.'

'OKAY, HOLD HANDS NOW, SIDE BY SIDE AND FACE ME.'

He stands up and holds out a hand, and for a few seconds I wonder how it will feel to touch it. I hesitate.

'Seriously, I must have committed some atrocity in a past life...'

'How about lying by niceness? In this life.'

I hate him, I hate him, I hate him.

He reaches over to hold my hand, and I expect it to be horrible. But as soon as we touch, a zing goes up and down my spine. I look away and pretend it didn't just give me a little shiver that's still reverberating across my chest and giving me tingles.

'KEEP HOLDING HANDS BUT A LITTLE CLOSER.'

Emily is now on my hit list. I think about taking her out with a three-day-old Italian pastry, throwing it right at her camera or at her head, anything, so we can just stop this nightmare.

'Look at us holding hands, who would have thought?'

'Honestly, holding hands with you is worse than the worst torture.' This of course isn't true. His hand is quite perfect actually – largish and muscular, like he's from the country and has spent years planting trees or something, but with fingernails that are manicured – but he doesn't need to know that.

'Breaking bones on a rack?'

'Child's play compared to this.'

'Water infinitely dripping on your head?'

'Like a fun water park.'

He thinks carefully. 'Hmmm, how about solitary confinement and sleep deprivation?'

'I am experiencing all those things right now.' Then I

can't help myself. I want to take him down a peg or two; something about him brings out the worst in me. 'Actually … being here with you is like the worst torture of all, for which I'm paying with a pound of flesh.'

When he doesn't say anything, I think, *Ha, got him.* Not the English major he pretends to be. Finally, I roll my eyes for extra effect and say triumphantly, 'Shakespeare.'

'Yes, Shylock, I got the reference. The human heart weighs about a pound, so basically you're saying that you would pay with your heart for me to come to this wedding. Awww, Gemma, that's so sweet.'

I really hate him.

'OKAY, TURN AND FACE EACH OTHER. GEMMA, PUT YOUR ARMS AROUND HIS NECK.'

I want to shout NO, but I can't. Instead I turn my body to face his, put my arms around his muscular neck, and stare intently at his cheek, not his eyes. But I can see his stubble making him look more masculine, and the line of his square jaw, his lips, so I look over his shoulder towards a hilltop that is just becoming golden with the sunlight and it's beautiful, and that's the only reason I can stand here so close to this guy. The cicadas start to pulse from beneath every bush as the world wakes up.

'So now we're stuck here do you want to tell me the story of your family?'

'Not really.'

'But you probably should. Especially if I'm going to be the son-in-law.'

'Please, I would never marry you.'

'But you'd marry Adam?'

KATE MATHIESON

'Of course. In fact, we will.' And it gives me great satisfaction to say that. You can have your supermodels, Weasel, and I'll have Adam.

He shrugs. 'So you're not going to tell me about Marla and your father?'

'I am not.'

He looks over at me. 'Are you going to tell me *anything* about *any* of your family?'

'I am not.' Weasel can never know about how deep the wounds run in my family. I could never trust him with one bit of information about myself.

'What about the weird tension between you and your sister?'

'Half-sister.'

He raises his eyebrows as if to make a point.

'It's fine.' I shrug, giving my usual answer.

Weasel gazes at me. 'Is it though? It's okay if you're not fine.'

My eyes quickly flick over his face, looking for signs of sarcasm, but there are none. I'm distracted slightly, because although I don't go for looks, he really is a very handsome human up this close. It's distracting. Pity he has no soul.

'GREAT, JUST A BIT CLOSER.'

Weasel takes a half step confidently towards me. I mean to give him a stern look that says, *Stay in your space*, but I'm distracted by the way his neck is strong with muscles, and I can see the deep tan on his chest, making him a smooth olive colour. For some reason, I'd expected he'd be pale, but, quite frankly, he's got a great tan, and I hate myself that I can't seem to find anything out of place. My

126

eyes take him in, up and down, looking for a flaw, any flaw.

'What are you looking for?' He's watching me watch him.

The one thing about me, I'm quick-witted with words. 'A pulse. Seems reptiles can get down to one beat per minute, so I'm just checking.'

He laughs. 'Am I really that cold-blooded to you?'

'Yes.'

He takes his hand and puts it on my cheek, softly, and I try not to feel the heat as my skin buzzes slightly. 'See. Warm.'

I blink. My heartbeat quickens. This is weird.

'BIT CLOSER.'

He leans in. My whole body stiffens. He's so close now. I refuse to look at him, but I can feel his face is only inches from mine. He is broad, broader than I expected, and I can feel the strength of his muscles. And I don't want to look at him because I don't know what is happening. Instead, I look back at the sunrise, which is now streams of pink and orange, and the sun poking its head above the hills, until I think my retinas may permanently burn. I keep myself occupied by trying to name what I can see. *Cerulean sky. Um... Tuscan yellow sun. Lemon yellow. Canary yellow. Butter. Marigold. Corn.* Now I'm just listing things that are yellow and I feel ridiculous. I lean away slightly, and he wraps his hands tighter, pressing into my lower back. Warm and strong.

In spite of myself, I shiver. 'Cold?' he murmurs. 'Or something else?'

I frown. 'Cold.'

'Really? I mean I could have guessed otherwise…'

My eyes flick to his for a second, and it's a mistake I can't undo. His piercing blue eyes are so intense, they burn into my soul.

'Are you lying to me, Gemma Evans?' His voice is smooth, deep; I feel it down to my toes. I smell him everywhere around me. Pine. Cedar. Woods and earth.

I narrow my eyes and am about to spitfire a response when Emily yells, 'CAN YOU GUYS KISS? NOW THE SUN'S ALMOST UP, I NEED TO CHECK THE WHITE BALANCE.'

'Well then…' He sounds so cocky.

I narrow my eyes. 'One hundred per cent never going to happen.'

'Course not.'

'Never.'

'So then…' He leaves it open, as if he'd kiss me, and now the ball's in my court.

'So then … nothing.'

'*Gemma*.'

'*Weasel*.'

He smirks. 'Our photographer is waiting.'

I feel totally out of my depth right now. 'We can pretend.'

'How? You want me to put my hand on your mouth and then kiss that, like we're back in school?' He has the audacity to wink, because he knows it's going to wind me up even more. And he's a jerk because it works.

'Are you high? Not at all.' I sigh as if he's completely

dumb. 'If you put your head forward, and I do too, but we're inches apart, it will look the same from where she's standing. As if we're...' I can't bring myself to say it.

'Kissing.' He gives a short laugh. 'You can't even say it.'

'Whatever.' I just want this to be over. He's still holding me, and we're close, and my stomach is feeling jittery, and I tell myself it's just the coffee. His entire charm assault, all the winking and smooth voice, is something I've seen him use with every girl in the office, but I'm different. I see his ways and I refuse to let them overwhelm me.

He leans in slightly, putting his lips right before mine. If I move a fraction they'll touch. I try not to react like someone's holding a dead rat near my mouth.

We stay there in silence for a second, until Emily, who is now a plague on my house, shouts, 'BIT CLOSER.'

He pulls me towards him, his hands warm on my lower back. I feel my breathing get faster. He seems to watch my chest as it begins to rise and fall quicker.

'You know, we may have to kiss sometime these next few days.'

'No, we won't,' I squeak, even as my heart sinks. He's probably right. What couple go four days without touching each other, or kissing? Jesus, I haven't thought this plan through well at all.

'We probably will.'

'No, we *won't*.'

'Most definitely, even if it's a cheek kiss.'

This gives me an idea. I look over at Emily, who has her hand on her hip, and seems to be waiting for us. I'm going to put myself out of this misery. Take matters into my own hands.

I lean forward quickly, aiming for his right cheek, the lower bit, close to his mouth, so it looks as though it's on the lips to anyone far enough away. And I kiss him. My lips on his soft, stubbly cheek. For two long, horrible seconds. But he's unprepared, so his eyes are open, and he looks surprised. I can feel my own body stiffen even more, and I realise my eyes are open too. I lean back and resist the urge to wipe my lips.

Weasel looks disgusted. 'What was that?'

'Quite like how I expect kissing Lucifer would feel.'

I mean awful and shite, but he raises his eyebrows and says, 'Hot?' then shakes his head as if I have a lot to learn if I think that's a great kiss.

That's the last thing I need, a kissing tutorial from this wanker who clearly thinks he is a gift to all women. Because I personally would like a refund.

'CAN YOU KISS AGAIN? LONGER, SO I CAN CHECK THE FRAMING.'

In the background I see the doors to the hotel foyer open, and Lulu and Chip, and a small entourage including the bridesmaids, step into the courtyard. Lulu has large sunglasses on and is holding a giant coffee, and I can tell that from behind those fly eyes she is scrutinising everything we're doing. The last thing I need is her seeing me in this position. She'd know in a heartbeat that it was off. A first kiss. A kiss I don't want. She has a sense about these things.

'Does your boyfriend kiss well? Just imagine him.'

Ugh. What a jerk. Still, I think back to Adam. His kisses are nice. Dependable. Warm.

'Yes, he kisses just fine, thank you.'

'Good, so do I. When I kiss someone, I want you to know, I mean it.'

I want to roll my eyes. This is like a B-grade romance film. I'm about to say something snarky in reply when I see Lulu walking closer, and staring at us. She lifts her sunglasses as if this is about to be an inspection. I can just imagine her yelling out, 'Why aren't you guys kissing?'

Weasel's eyes flicker over, and I know he sees her too. Before I can say anything, he leans in, holds my face with one hand and pulls me into him, staring at my mouth.

We're *this close*.

Without warning, his mouth finds mine. Easily. An electric jolt runs up my spine. His lips are soft. His warm mouth pressing against mine. God, he really knows what he's doing. He holds me behind my neck, tugs my hair, and his mouth opens a little more. He kisses me softly, then slightly more passionately, trailing his finger across my cheek. The graze of his finger makes my skin tingle. He tastes like coffee and mint. My heart is pounding. My knees are buzzing. When he finally steps back, I can see his chest is rising and falling quickly too.

'Like that.' His voice is lower, rougher.

What the actual fuck?

'Why did you do *that*?' Disentangling myself and stepping back, I want to scrape my tongue but Lulu is still watching. I want to tell him off, but also I can't get my breath. I can feel the coolness of the early morning float over my arms, now his warmth isn't near me. I try to hate him, but I'm stirred. Like every part of me is alive, my skin, my hair, tingling. My body is a traitor.

'People were watching.' He gives a brief wave towards Lulu and Chip. Chip returns the wave, but Lulu just tilts her head as if she's trying to work something out.

'You didn't need to do *that*.' What a monster. Trying to show off his kissing techniques.

'You know I did. Lulu needed to be convinced.'

I scoff at that, but he's right. If we hadn't kissed there would have been questions. He picks up my bathrobe with surprising care and offers it to me. I tighten it around myself, well aware I look even frumpier now Lulu is fifty metres away in a matching crop top and long pants that are mocha latte coloured.

'Besides, I don't know where *those* have been either.' I motioned to his lips.

'Well, on a coffee. A toothbrush. Maybe a water bottle too.'

I was going to say something else, something I wanted to be scathing, to stop this horrible guy from perfectly kissing people, but Emily shouts, 'GREAT, THANKS, GUYS, WE'RE DONE.'

I start walking back towards the grand hotel entry, trying to tell myself it wasn't a giant mistake bringing a blind date to Lulu's wedding. Even though it was, clearly, the biggest mistake I could have ever made.

I briefly wave at Chip and Lulu and stop for some excruciating small talk, asking how they slept, even though all I desperately want is a shower and to wipe my lips.

Weasel is off chatting to some other groomsmen I haven't met, so I gratefully make a quick exit, mumbling something about a long, hot shower.

I'm halfway across the foyer, and I can still smell his telltale scent, mint, around me. *Lingering like a bad smell*. I feel annoyed, and irritable, and something else I can't put my finger on.

It isn't until I get into the lift that I recognise the feeling … *wobbly*. Must be low blood sugar.

Chapter Fourteen

'That's not how I want it,' Lulu complains. I'm almost sure she's going to stomp her foot. 'It's just not right.'

We're both staring at the hanging bunting, which looks a little sad and withered, the individual triangles curling on themselves. We are inside the old oil mill, which has been elaborately set up for Lulu's dinner. Looking around I can tell Dad has spared no expense. There are tea light candles on top of tea light candles, and everything is lace and pink, with a soft pink runner lying down the middle of the long table, topped with large blush pink peonies held in intricate white vases, and looked over by ancient candelabras that had been shipped in from Rome – or so Lulu told me – along with some bird cages with real doves.

'Hmm, well … I'm not sure what we can do? Blanket the sun? Put up blackout curtains?' I was joking but Lulu stares at me as though it was an actual option, so I quickly add, 'Kidding.'

Outside is hellishly hot already. The Tuscan sun is

streaming down in yellow blazes across the terracotta rooftops, and standing outside feels like a blast furnace, or a hair dryer on high aimed at my face, it's a sucking dry heat, making my skin feel zapped of moisture. The fountain outside gurgles, and the pool where half the wedding party are splashing around sounds like a party with a backing track of loud music and the delight of guests gorging morning mimosas. I imagine myself sliding into the cool water, lying on a lilo with a never-ending glass of bubbles, maybe even having a nap. My idea of heaven.

My stomach growls, bringing me out of my daydream. At breakfast, I'd only eaten one bite of a delicious brioche before she dragged me into the tea room, pointed at the ceiling and almost started howling. I was already zonked from being jetlagged, so it took me a while to figure out she meant the bunting.

'Honestly, I don't think anyone will notice,' I say gently. 'They'll all be looking at how beautiful you are.'

'Oh Gemma.' Lulu turns to look at me, her eyes misting up. 'Do you think so?' She pauses. 'Were you always so nice?'

There, bunting crisis averted. Was this a moment? I'm not sure because we've never been close and this feels strange. I give her a hopeful smile.

'So, will you go and get more bunting from the store?' Lulu is saying in her innocent voice, reaching into her bag and pulling out a piece of paper. 'Here's the address. And here are the keys to a rental. Chip organised it, just in case. He's so *thoughtful*. I think it needs some petrol. Would you mind?'

I quickly realise we weren't having a moment; this is just Lulu trying to get what she wants.

'I don't know how to drive in Italy,' I say, staring at the keys in my hand. Don't they drive on the other side here? And fast? The entire idea is farcical.

Lulu almost starts whimpering and I swallow back my uncertainty. 'But I guess I could figure it out.'

'Perfect!' Lulu quicky smiles. 'I knew you wouldn't mind missing out on the silly girlie stuff like manis and pedis. You never liked that stuff anyway. You'd better get going.' Lulu taps her rose-gold watch before waving for Chip, who seems to just be waiting in the hall ready to be called on, and they descend down the stairs, probably back to hell – their hot, burning home.

Honestly, I could do with someone tending to my nails, and massaging my calves – it sounds like bliss after thirty-something hours on a plane. Plus, I'm overdue for a buff and polish; after too many long nights at work my nails are sad and jagged. And how does she know what I like?

But maybe this was better. This way I can explore my Italy, my way. A little road trip down some cute Italian farm laneways. Maybe I could stop off and try some cheese? A little vino? Maybe I could meet a wonderful, delicious Italian man, who would happily take over as Adam, and Weasel could pack his bags, and leave Italy for good.

It isn't like I imagined at all. Firstly, the little yellow car is about a quarter the size of a regular car. Literally, my push bike would have been bigger. I'm practically sitting in the back seat and on top of the steering wheel all at once. My knees are so cramped they hit the steering wheel, and I need to move them every time I turned the wheel, which was a lot. The streets here – if you can call them streets – are more like gravel pits with large potholes, and constantly winding. I have the perfect view, what you think of when you imagine quintessential Tuscany: undulating hills, groves of olive trees, and the tell-tale row of cypresses marking the road like a guide. I roll down the window and breathe in the heat, the dust, the scent of roses somewhere, soft and sweet. I can't help but smile; Tuscany *is* for lovers. If only I was with Adam. If only we had a glass of Chianti, if only we could just park somewhere and sit under a tree, and listen to the cicadas pulse.

Within the next few minutes my mood dramatically changes. Squished into this car my back starts aching, and then my knees grind into my own bones. Everything hurts when you're so low to the ground, you're practically Fred Flintstone-ing it, and using your feet to move about.

Using my feet might have been quicker, because when Lulu said there was no petrol, she really wasn't joking. About two kilometres down a very thin, curvy road, the car chugs a little, coughs and then dies. Panicked, I pull on the handbrake in the middle of the road. My fear is of rolling off the hill and into the valley below. I take a deep breath, and think, *Well, Gemma, let's get out of this situation and quickly*, because if another car comes along I'm blocking most of the narrow road.

My phone, with zero signal, is of utterly no help. Time for old school. I get out the map shoved under the passenger seat, and unfold it along the bonnet of the car, trying to figure out where I am, and in which direction I should walk to get petrol. It's extremely hot, and I can feel the sweat running off my face and making little pools of water under my arms and in my bra. Thankfully the map is in English, but I still can't quite figure where I am.

A small car zips around the curve towards me, and breaks heavily. *No, no, no. Shit.*

The man at the wheel starts yelling at me. I have no idea what he's saying, but I suppose he wants me to move.

'*Signor. Ciao! Anglaise?*' I ask him. 'I've run out of petrol. Can you help me?'

'*Non anglaise!*' he yells and starts beeping his horn, which makes the old man from a nearby farm come out to watch what's happening. I try to ask him too, but he just scoffs and tuts and makes a sound like 'pfffft' and continues to watch the irate man beep at me, which is making me hot and flustered.

The guy in the car just seems to like pressing the horn, which is making me feel like a nuisance, but there's was nothing I can do. I decide that the car is small enough I can probably move it myself, so gingerly I take the handbrake off, and start to try and push it, but it won't budge a bit. For a small car, it's not light.

Now the guy is starting to yell some things which sound very much like, *cazzo*, and some other swear words, and I turn around to him, mortified, and yell out, 'I'M REALLY SORRY.' Which is probably the most English thing I've ever done because I really should have just told him to do one.

Thankfully, an old three-wheeled truck arrives a few

minutes later, dusty and dirty from a nearby farm. When they speak English and have enough petrol to get me to the city, I feel indebted to them, and give them twenty euro, and almost kiss their dirty, sweaty cheeks. *Thank goodness*. I drive to the nearest petrol station and fill up again, just in case, and then take a breath as I hit the city traffic, my knuckles grabbing the wheel so hard they turn white. *Please let me get through this*, I pray.

By now, Lulu would have her creamy feet deep in warm suds, but I'm driving around and around a city, trying desperately to find a parking spot that isn't fit just for an ant. Gosh, the way they park in Italy is crazy, literally on top of one another. And I don't think I could do that without scraping either my car or someone else's.

In the end, to be safe, I park at one end of the city and decide to walk the three kilometres to the bunting store marked on my map, which is closing in a few hours, of course, for siesta. Just in case, I jog to the store, enter sweaty and red-faced, grab the yellow bunting, pay an exorbitant price for those little lemon and white plastic triangles, and then trudge the three kilometres back to the car.

By midday I make it back to the hotel, sweaty, hot, exhausted and completely jet-lagged. My black skirt and white T-shirt have streaks of dirt on them from where I attempted to move that damn car. All I want is a hot shower and a quick lie down to decompress and to call Ruby and Adam. I really need to hear a comforting voice. I enter the hotel foyer, praying that no one I know sees me like this. I make it to the lift, where I'm gratefully thinking, *Thank you, thank you, thank you,* when the lift doors open and Lulu walks out, arm in arm with Weasel.

What are these two doing together? I think, *Planning world domination?*

'Oh goodness, Gemma, what's happened?' Lulu looks shocked. 'Have you been robbed?'

Weasel eyes me up and down and tries not to laugh.

'The car didn't have much petrol, so it broke down, I had to push it, and then find the bunting.' I hold up the shopping bags in my hands, expecting Lulu to say a big thank you.

She peers into the bag. 'No, this is the wrong yellow!' she exclaims dismally. 'This is sunshine yellow, and I wanted powdered yellow.' Her bottom lip almost pouts.

'This is the only yellow they had,' I say apologetically.

'I feel like I'm going to cry,' she say pouting again and her bottom lip quivers. 'It feels like this is a bad sign. It's a curse. It means Chip and I, the wedding…' Her entire face looks crushed. 'Are we doomed?'

I can't help it. As if I were on autopilot, I reach out to her and say, 'It's okay, Lulu,' and before I know it Nelly Nicepants pops out, and I'm opening my mouth and saying, 'Should I go back and see if they have powder yellow?'

And then Lulu is suddenly clapping her hands and smiling, 'Oh would you? That would be darling. But please make sure you're back and ready for the ladies' afternoon tea. And remember, don't wear yellow.'

I can feel Weasel's eyes widen, his stupid little face, eyebrows so high they're almost catching a ride on his perfect hairline. He stares incredulously at me, then Lulu, then back at me, and I catch the edge of a smirk playing on his lips. I want to bop him on the head and tell him to go away. *This*, I want to tell him, *is what you do for family and friends.* Yes, it's tiring sometimes, but you support people, you help them, you make them feel better, and just hope one day they'll do the same for you.

'Right, well, I'd better be going,' I say, trying to pep myself to take another step forward and not fall asleep right in the middle of the foyer.

'Do you like my nails?' She shoves a pink pearly nail in my face.

'They're lovely.' I nod, and reach out for them, but she gives a little snort of disgust looking down at mine, which are covered in Tuscan dirt.

'You really should shower.'

'I'd love to,' I say wryly, thinking that's exactly what I would be doing if I wasn't bunting hunting.

'Oh and this guy is delightful, Gemma,' Lulu calls out to me as I trudge back towards that little shit of a car, nodding at Weasel. 'Wherever did you find him?'

'In a dumpster,' I mutter.

As I left, I hear Lulu twitter, and say to Weasel, 'How strange she is sometimes.'

Chapter Fifteen

'Wait, Gemma!' Weasel is calling out to me and running across the driveway.

I think about ignoring him but just in case there's anyone from my family watching, I force myself to turn around.

'I'm coming with you. I tried to say that but you just exploded out of there like you were part of a bunting storm-out.' He grins at me as he arrives at the car. 'Boyfriend duties.'

'You *really* don't have to.'

'I do.' He turns and nods towards the foyer, where Lulu is staring at us through the window, as though she could sense something. 'Maybe we should hug? Even if you look a bit homeless.'

God, he's enjoying this.

'Not a chance.'

'Fine, but at least look like you're happy to be spending time with me, your loving boyfriend.'

'You can drive then,' I say, throwing him the keys. '*Loving* boyfriend.'

He walks towards the carpark, but I nod at the tiny little car. 'Your chariot awaits.'

'You have to be joking,' he says, eyeing it up.

'Well, you can always go back to the hotel...' I plead with the universe.

He shakes his head and shrugs. 'Nah, I got this. Easy.'

I've never laughed so much as when Weasel tries to stuff himself in that driver's seat. He wiggles around a bit, but not a part of him can move. 'Well, this is ... tight.'

Laughing, I settle into the passenger seat, finally finding a great reason to be small.

'I see you find this funny.' He is hunched forward in the driver's seat, so his long legs are bent like a spider's and his knees could almost be earrings.

'Too ... funny,' I manage to splutter, in between those hiccupping laughs you get when you can't catch your breath.

The car, with the added weight and height of Weasel, almost stalls as we turn onto the gravel road, and I hold on to the sides of the seat as it suddenly lurches forward under his heavy foot. I'm sure he's used to a convertible sports car, zooming around with supermodels cooing at him, not a matchbox car.

'This car is a shit,' Weasel mutters under his breath.

'You know, if *you* were a car, you'd be one of these.'

'Well, Gemma I'm not really that small at all—'

Ew. 'Don't even start...'

'I meant my *height*. I'm six foot three. And, while we're on the subject, you'd be a Mini Cooper.'

'Oh they're quite savvy. Vintage. I'll take it.' I sit back with a satisfied nod.

'No, like a three-wheeler one. Like the one Mr Bean drives around London and it keeps tipping over.'

He wants to get under my skin, but I won't let him. 'A-ha, so one that requires great driving skills, and doesn't just go for anyone.' I felt quite chuffed with my witty response.

'For no one actually.'

His comment doesn't even sting. I feel proud of myself. 'Actually, on second thought, Thomas Benjamin, you'd be a tank that plods over everyone, but one of those ones that have run out of petrol and have been lost in the desert.'

He can't help but crack a small mile. 'With just a nozzle sticking up?'

'Rusted.' I poke my arm up as though it was a sad little rusted tank nozzle. 'Forgotten.' And I can't help but laugh at the idea of Weasel as a rusted tank.

'I don't know why I helped you out.' He shakes his head, trying to ignore my laughing, which has become weird little snorts as I struggle to breathe. I start laughing harder, and he looks at me like he wants to throw me out of the car. This feels different ... and suddenly, I realise, I'm *enjoying* this.

Sighing, he shifts the gears as we near a hairpin turn, and the car makes a weird clunking sound. He looks at me and says, 'By the way, you sound like a walrus when you laugh.'

And I take pleasure in that too because I can tell I've

hassled him enough that he's lost his charm for a second, and is trying to get under my skin, and it isn't working.

On the way to Florence, we have to stop multiple times as Weasel has lost feeling in his foot, which makes me laugh even harder. At one point he has to lift his left onto the car bonnet to stretch out a cramp and I try not to look at how muscular and tanned his legs are in navy shorts, like he's a regular rower.

The memory of the kiss this morning – Weasel's lips on mine – flashes in my head. I think about it for two seconds before I put on a layer of lip balm to try and cover the sensation. I try not to think about, or look at, his inviting lips from then on.

My intent is to keep everything completely PG, so when he gets back into the car, I say quickly, 'Do you bottle tan?'

He smirks. 'Staring at my legs, Gemma?'

'Only out of pity. I heard you're meant to exfoliate first, otherwise it streaks.'

He looks down at his legs quickly, and I feel a pang of happiness. Got him again! The look on his face tells me I've won round two. I kinda like this less charming version of Weasel; he seems almost … *human*.

When we get close to the store, he turns into a small avenue next to the famous street Via Maggio, and drives past a small Bar Tabacchi. A little further on he manages to expertly park the car right outside a little trattoria, with one hand on the wheel like a race car driver, which even I have to admit is a little impressive. Inside the shop, we buy the entire stock of powered yellow bunting. All of it, just in case. I think it cost about a hundred euros.

On the way out, I stand on the side of the narrow cobbled roadway, looking around this big, beautiful city, and thinking about the history of such a place. I've been in such a rush before I haven't had time to take it all in: the curved narrow streets, so many beautiful big doorways, some heavy bronze, lavishly decorated, with high archways, some tiny and in between ancient stone archways and walls. I run my hand over the cool stone, gaining some respite from the heat, and I imagine what living here hundreds of years ago would have been like.

As I walk towards the car, I trail a finger across a red wooden door, and wonder who I would have been if I'd lived during the Renaissance. A peasant woman? Likely a girl that dresses as a boy and poses as a writer all her life just for the chance of being published—

'Come on, Michelangelo, before you decide you need to start painting it,' he says, grabbing my hand and pulling me away. I give him a withering look, and try not to notice that his hand is large and warm, and my hand feels small and delicate in his. Because being nice to each other isn't something we do, I pull my hand away and say defensively, 'I *can* walk, you know.'

He shrugs, his blue eyes becoming a bit cloudy, and says, 'Suit yourself'.

And instead of thinking *strike three*! I feel … almost guilty.

Back in the little yellow car we zoom out of the city. On the way, we take the famous Lungarno Torrigiani freeway, which stretches along the south bank of the Arno River. Across the water, on the shoreline, are historic buildings with bright yellow façades, the brilliant green hills of Tuscany behind. It's glorious and for a second I forget that I hate Weasel, because I can't help but feel extremely happy.

I sigh contentedly. 'I love Italy.'

Weasel glances at me. 'Yeah, it's beautiful. Have you been to Pienza?'

I shakes my head.

'It has beautiful cobbled streets.'

'And little piazzas?'

'Yep, most of them honey-coloured. And an ancient well.'

I nod enthusiastically and wonder who he went there with, but I can't bring myself to ask.

'You'd love it there, I bet. It's one of the most romantic places.' He says this without a hint of cynicism. Is this man a *romantic?* Surely not.

'It does sound wonderful.'

We share a look and it makes me feel … unusual. I sense his eyes running across my face and when I take a quick side-eye glance at him, he smiles. He is being at least twenty per cent nicer than he's ever been in his life. Shocked that neither of us is being snarky or haughty for once, I'm caught off guard. I try to remember that I hate him, but I can't summon the feeling.

'We could go now, take a little road trip.'

'We couldn't.'

'It would just take an hour. No one would miss us.'

A little road trip to a romantic city? Weasel and I? What madness is this? And why do I feel slightly tempted?

'No, we can't.' I try to say it firmly, sticking to my guns. I stare down at the map unfolded near my feet and try not to watch his large hand as it shifts the gear stick with an authority that makes me sweat a bit. 'Are you hot? I'm hot.' I wind down the window, but the air is steamy and sticky outside, so I wind it back up.

'How about that newly found invention – the air-conditioning?' He gives me a puzzled glance and turns up the dial, and a stream of slightly cooler air huffs into the small car.

I'm thankful he changed the subject. 'Do you think Lulu would even have noticed the sunshine yellow bunting if we'd just hung it up?' he asks.

'Without a doubt. Don't let her innocent looks fool you. Lulu's like a shark: she can sniff out a drop of bad colour anywhere. She works for British *Vogue*.'

'Oh what a paragon of the world,' he says with a hint of sarcasm.

For the next ten minutes we chat about Lulu's job, and interiors, and then he asks if I could design the interior of any house what my style would be.

Him: industrial glass and steel.

Me: Tuscan country cottage.

'Yours sounds like a fortress.'

'Yours sounds like it's full of the colour peach, from the 1980s.'

I shrug. 'You and I are so different. I don't think we'd ever agree on one thing in this entire universe.'

Just as I say that, Weasel turns the car onto a lovely stretch of winding road, to the right of which is an old millhouse entirely made of stone, and a cute little wooden sign out the front that says *formaggio*.

'Let's stop and try some,' Weasel suggests.

I have images of Lulu losing her shit over the bunting. It's been three hours since she originally sent me out and it would be siesta soon, and then afternoon tea.

'I don't have time.'

He's already slowing down near the turn and I can feel myself waning. 'C'mon, just twenty minutes.'

I look at my watch. 'We can't be late. Lulu would kill me, skin me alive and probably keep my head on a stick outside her house as a warning to everyone else. Bunting is a very serious matter.'

'She'd have to go through me first.' He winks, turning into the gravel driveway. 'And if it's got to do with a wheel of brie, I'm going to come out swinging.'

I feel myself relenting. Cheese in any form is most definitely my kryptonite. It would be nice to have some soft delicate brie, even if it was with Satan. 'Fine. Five minutes.'

'And who knows, they may not have a dress code and will be fine letting a homeless person in.' He smirks.

As a reflex, I lean over to hit him, but I have terrible aim, and manage instead of getting his arm, to swat at his chest, where his white shirt is open and I touch his wall of muscle and feel his chest hair. Instantaneously I snatch my hand back as though it's been burned. Yikes.

'Gemma.' He leans over and looks me deeply in the eyes. *Close. Very close.* 'If you want to touch me, you just have to ask.'

'You're revolting,' I say, but it seems to lack the sting it had just a day ago. I busy myself getting out of the car and making sure I walk at least a metre away from him, keeping a distance so he knows I didn't want to *touch* him.

The old stone building is gorgeous. On the outside it looks like a little church, inside is the cutest little cheesemonger's, with beautiful soft pecorinos. There's a hard cheese that's aged in mountain caves, and a creamy goats log. And my favourite: melt-in-your-mouth creamy mozzarella. There's a wheel of parmigiano, about a metre wide, and the man behind the counter shaves off slice after slice, with the sharpest of knives.

Weasel orders for both of us, and I'm surprised, because he selects exactly what I was hoping he would: a sample platter of five different cheeses, with a cluster of tiny round tomatoes that burst against the roof of our mouths.

The waiter offers us a rosé, the colour of soft pink petals. Weasel orders a bottle, and out of spite, I decide not to drink it, but it smells like soft, blushing honey, and is called *bacio al lampone* – raspberry kiss – so I can't help myself.

It's cool and flowery. Slightly sweet. Delicious.

The waiter arrives with olives, handpicked he assures us, from the nearby grove. They've been covered by a dash of olive oil and a sprinkle of salt. I close my eyes and eat one. It makes my lips slippery and taste so salty, I don't know how to describe it, other than to say that it's a thousand times better than the bottled ones I usually buy at Coles.

'It's like sea air and deep earth,' I murmure.

Weasel laughs. 'Have *you* ever thought of being a writer?'

My eyes snaps open. Does he know? Has Tony let on? I try not to look at his mesmerisingly full lips, slippery with oil too. I ignore him and drink the cool honeyed wine.

'So? Have you?'

'Can I get some more of that rosé?' I try to keep my voice steady, and act as if he's not said something that travels straight from his smooth, deep voice to my heart. That's the most vulnerable part of me. The soft squishy starfish underbelly. Not a chance I' ever let on to him – even Adam doesn't know I want to be a writer. He'd want to map out a series of best-selling books for me to write, and I know he'd ask me how much a writer makes and I'd have to admit: not much at all. Unless you're one of the two per cent of authors that sell a million books, but most writers aren't; they do it for the love of writing, not for the paycheck.

Back in the car, the two glasses of wine have softened me. Italy has softened me. I don't even hate Weasel anymore. Suddenly, I'm not even worried about getting back, or Lulu, and I roll down the window and let my hand ride the breeze. It feels it hot on my skin. Still hungry, I eat camembert straight from the shopping bag of cheese Weasel insisted we purchase, using my fingers as a knife.

'Can I have some? Or are you also a cheese hoarder? Should I know this about you?' he asks.

'I am a cheese hoarder. Also biscuits,' I say, carving him out a piece. 'Mind my fingers.'

'Should I disinfect myself?' he teased. 'Don't know where those fingers have been.'

'Well, I can tell you where: on a dirty bonnet, on a map, in a bunting store, all across the city of Florence, and worse still, I had to touch this guy last night during a dance, and I have no idea what he gets up to.' I plunk the piece of cheese into his outstretched hand.

'You're telling me you haven't showered since then?'

I try not to smile, but I'm sure he catches me quickly before I look out the window. 'I *have*.'

On the way back, we're held up on a tiny, narrow road behind an English tourist in a slightly bigger vehicle than ours, with a flat tyre, and Weasel gets out to help him. I think he's taking the 'I'm a nice guy' act way too far because I'm sure the real Weasel would just sit back and beep like the other asshole did to me earlier.

At first, I find myself watching Weasel and his muscular arms pump away as he jacks the car into the air and I'm surprised at how easily he does it.

Back at the hotel, late and anxious, the glow of the wine has worn off and a headache looms across my temples.

Weasel grabs my left hand as we walked into the foyer, and when I look down in surprise, he says, 'Just in case.' He seems to be taking these pretend boyfriend duties even more seriously than I am.

I try to ignore the warmth of his hand as I quickly walk, almost jog, across the foyer, dragging him with me, and hand the bunting to the concierge like I'm suddenly on *The Amazing Race*. 'Please make sure these go up in the oil mill immediately. It's for the afternoon tea, and' – I lower my voice – 'the bride will have a fit if they're not there like, um, pronto.'

The concierge nods, and I turn around and breathe a quick sigh of relief. We've made it, relatively unscathed.

'Can I have my hand back now?' I say, detangling myself and walking purposefully towards the lift. My mind is already back in wedding planning mode, racing as I think about what colour I'm allowed to wear, and whether I need to check on Lulu.

Weasel swaggers next to me. 'Now how about a wine to celebrate Buntinggate? Go upstairs, have a shower, get dressed and come back down in ten minutes.'

'Stop ordering me around like this is the 1950s. How about *you* go upstairs, have a shower, get dressed and come down in ten minutes.'

'How about we both do it?'

I check his face for a hint of mockery, but he seems sincere.

Inside the lift, he presses the button for the second floor.

'I'm cutting it fine as it is, and I need to check on Lulu, and do all those other sisterly pre-wedding things, before I even consider getting changed for the ladies' afternoon tea. Which I'm already probably late for. And you have the boys' golf afternoon.'

'Since you're busy, I could bring a wine to you.'

I stare at him, and then look around. 'You don't need to pretend to be nice. No one's even in earshot. This is a lift.'

He gives me one of those earth-shattering smiles, which I expect makes the pants of unsuspecting women fly off – not mine – but I have to admit, something in me jolts a little. The lift door opens and we step out, and I'm half expecting some witty one-liner, but instead, he glances at me with those blue sapphire eyes as he walks towards his room, and says without a trace of sarcasm, 'Who says I'm pretending?'

Chapter Sixteen

I make it a few more steps to my hotel door before I stop, utterly confused. The Weasel I knew from Peacock was cutthroat and arrogant. Weasel in the taxi from the airport was positively diabolical and made me want to scream. But Weasel the fake boyfriend is annoyingly charming, the perfect coffee-buying, bunting-helping, cheese-eating stand-in.

I thought it was a giant act this whole time, but now … he isn't pretending. *Apparently.*

The entire thing is disorientating. Resisting the urge to look at him, I dig deep into my bag for my room key. Finally, I give in and glance up, expecting him to be smirking like it was a hilarious prank. But Weasel just gives me that inviting grin before he disappears inside his hotel room. My heart beats quickly.

What in the world?

For the first time I contemplate the possibility of Weasel

being a man, instead of my enemy. A very handsome man. I feel gratified and weirded out by all that wine talk. Was he *flirting*?

But then the memory of his overheard words sears through me. *It's over.* Words said so seriously, and sounding so ... *calculated.* The last few months come back to me with a jolt. And suddenly my brain gratefully exits the frothy bubble and says, *HELL, NO.*

Of course, this is his way in. Probably just a giant ruse to make me relaxed around him.

Like a judge, I stare at the cold, hard facts and come to a decision. He's playing with me. Him, cat. Me, string. And honestly, I realise, that's just the kind of despicable person he is. This entire helpful faux boyfriend act is just that: an act.

My brain rights itself. The giddiness disappears. I take a solemn vow not to think of his inviting lips, or his tanned legs, or his chest hair or his tempting warm, large hands ever again.

Instead, I march straight to my room, grab a pen and paper, and write down:

THINGS THAT MATTER.

1. *I have someone. A good someone. Even if he is not at the wedding with me.*
2. *This someone wants to look after me, thinks cheating is an insidious pox, and is dedicated to us and our future. HE WANTS TO BUY A HOUSE.*

3. *For the first time in a decade, I have a plus one that I can proudly bring to any event (except this wedding) who is genuinely interested in my ambition and success.*

4. *We talk about interesting topics (climate change, love, my favourite poetry, his AI, how to be calm and rational) and I am learning to be patient and try and listen when he talks about politics or sports (note – this is a skill I still haven't mastered).*

5. *I'm not on those horrible dating apps anymore. (Thank God I'm not seeing another fifty-something man, looking for his 'soulmate' between the ages of eighteen and twenty-two. PLEASE.)*

6. *He is an IT geek – Sheldon style, wears glasses and I find all of this rather CUTE.*

7. *When we're not tired, there can be good chemistry between us. Kissing is nice.*

8. *He is the hugger after sex. Yes. HIM.*

9. *He doesn't see the grey hairs that are busy multiplying on my head and have amassed so that there are too many to pluck individually, and now I'm about to be one of those women who have to trot off to the hairdresser's every five weeks to get my roots done. Same, same for wrinkles, which, no matter how much Clinique under-eye thingy I wear, does not make me glow like promised. He thinks I'm cute, even though I'm a bit saggy, and creased.*

10. *He doesn't play around, nice one minute, horrible the next. Not a mind fuck. IMPORTANT!*

11. *He's teaching me how to keep all my emotions in check.*

I stick this up on my bathroom mirror, and vow to look at the ADAM LIST every chance I get.

Chapter Seventeen

Lulu's ladies' afternoon tea is a short walk through the lovely rose gardens and labyrinth grass maze, past a large fountain adjacent to the hotel.

From outside, the oil mill feels both charmingly rustic and very sophisticated, with a modern glass and wrought-iron terrace looking over the surrounding countryside. Inside, all the ladies have gathered alongside the long tables of peonies, and it smells like rose and vanilla and jasmine. Arched perfectly across the ceiling is the powder yellow bunting, and I have to admit, it looks stunning.

We start out with some lovely pastries and cupcakes, and fresh pots of coffee, scones and cream (you can take the girl out of England, but...), and a game of Where Were We? Around the room there are ten or so numbered pictures of Lulu and Chip on various trips, and we each have to guess and write down where we think each picture was taken. Turns out they enjoyed trips to Monaco, and Rome, and Tuscany, and even Lapland. I come fifth out of twenty, which isn't so bad considering I hadn't really spoken to Lulu in a while. Mum won. And for a moment I think Marla is going to have a conniption that Mum won, because she says, sounding miffed, 'Well, that looked like Cyprus to me. It's where I went on my honeymoon.'

To which Mum replies, 'Which one?'

Good to see that the rivalry is still going strong.

There are musical chairs after that; who can make the best cocktail (Mia, a skinny something with shitloads of vodka); who knows the most Italian wedding words (hint: no one), and then teams of four dressing Lulu up in a bridal dress made of ivy and paper, which left a disaster site for the poor waitresses to clean up.

A delicious set of finger foods is set up on three tiers. Before we can eat though, there are photos of the food to be taken for Instagram, and photos of the girls, and selfies, both portrait and landscape, and pouts and smiles, and head tilts. And filters, lots of filters.

After another glass of wine, I can feel my eyes almost droop a little, jetlag in full force. I check my watch and see that it's almost midnight at home. I definitely need a nap before tonight.

'Gemma?' Lulu is peering at my head, breaking me out of my spell.

'Yes?'

'Do you *pluck* your grey hairs?' she says loudly in front of Mia and Amie, who probably have never had a grey hair in their lives. They have perfect flawless skin and glossy hair and they are all looking at me.

'Uh, no.' I shrug as if to say, *What are you talking about?*

She gets up out of her seat opposite me, and comes around the table, leaning in close and peering at my hair. I feel a whoosh of embarrassment. Where's Mum? Or Aunty Janice? Or anyone else over fifty that could help me explain my way out of this one.

'You do!' Lulu demands getting even closer.

'I don't,' I say, fibbing.

'No, I can see them! I can see them growing back; they're sticking up. Little wiry baby greys.' She points at my head. 'Want me to take a photo?' She pulls out her phone.

My neck flushes crimson. 'Definitely not.' I lean back and put both hands over my head protectively, and wish I had the confidence to tell her – *politely, of course* – to feck off. I say quickly, 'It must be a stray blonde hair.'

'But your hair is dark brown.' Lulu looks at me as if I was mental.

I know I can't say a thing, otherwise I'll be accused of spoiling the day. I clutch both hands into fists, and just keep pushing my nails into my palms, trying not to feel a tad exhausted and over it, which is hard after not enough sleep and too many afternoon rosés.

'Lucky I'm blonde, because I don't think this will ever be an issue for me, no matter how old I get!' Lulu says.

'Yes, lucky for you.' I nod, reaching out to the waitress and taking another wine and gulping half of it down in one go.

Then Lulu suddenly bursts out laughing. 'Oh goodness, this reminds me of my tenth birthday. Do you remember? When we found you had dark hairs on your upper lip? Gem-man!'

'*What*?' Mia asks, leaning in, intrigued. 'Tell me.'

My headache immediately starts thumping harder. I shoot a look at Lulu, a warning, and telepathically tell her, *Enough, shut up right now*. To make it clearer I won't tolerate this, I say breezily, 'There's nothing to tell,' and excuse myself to the loo.

Inside, the bathrooms are decadent with white marble floors and walls and I let my forehead rest on the coolness of the wall next to the sink.

How the hell did that just happen? I already know. Because besides being beautiful, Lulu seems to have a mean streak. Like a scorpion tail, it can flash and strike you before you even notice.

Case in point, Lulu's fateful tenth birthday. I turned up to Marla's new house (husband number two by that time), expecting I was going to be the older one, the cooler one. In all my seventeen-year-old glory I was wearing large black Kepper jeans, a black midriff-baring top and black cap, slightly turned sideways and up. I thought I looked very Lisa Left Eye Lopes circa TLC, very cool.

But upon seeing me, Lulu declared I looked exactly like a man. She also then leaned in, and asked if I was growing a moustache because there was hair on my lip, and didn't that only happen to boys? The other girls exploded into laughter and I made some feeble excuse and left the party before bursting into tears down the street. And from then on, I was known as Gem-man to Lulu and her posse.

Is it any coincidence that the moment I turned eighteen, I left for university in Leeds? And after graduating, decided to put an entire ocean between us, leaving England and taking a job halfway across the world?

I close my eyes and wish I were anywhere else – back in my apartment with Adam hugging me, while we do something simple, like making coffee or watching a movie. Or having a salty marg with Hannah. I give a half-smile. The idea of Han being here, telling people they're shitheads and to fuck right off cheers me up a bit.

Just in case they are still talking about me, I hang out in the bathroom for a while, giving them enough time to lose interest and find something else to gossip about.

As I come back from the bathroom, hoping to slide unseen back into my chair, I see that – thankfully – they've moved on.

'So Gemma, I wanted to talk to you.' Mia pulls her chair closer to mine and checks Lulu is busy talking about silk dresses with Amie. 'I have this idea for a book.'

This happens a *lot*. I feel a bit like sticking one of the forks in my eye, but instead, I put on a smile and say, 'Oh, do you?'

'I wanted to write about this girl who's looking for her next big break in modelling. But then she decides to take up Instagram instead and she becomes famous that way, meeting the who's who.'

I want to say, *So a memoir, then?* but instead I nod and lean forward, cupping my chin in my hands as if I were spellbound by the idea, and ask in Nelly Nicepants voice, 'And how much have you written?'

'I haven't started.'

I sat back. 'Okay, so when you have started, send me some chapters. And I'll let you know what I think.'

'Well, I was thinking I'm not that good at the writing part, but the idea is great. So could you help me out?'

'With what? Oh, you mean ... the writing part?'

Mia nods. Everything in me screamed, *You want to be a writer, but you can't write?* But instead I say, 'Well maybe I could give you some tips to get started. Here's my card, we can go from there.' I scramble around in my bag for a business card and slide it across to her.

Lulu sees my card and immediately says, 'No shop talk at my wedding!' She looks at both of us. 'This isn't about work.'

I nods. 'You're right. Sorry.'

Mia licks her lips. 'So tell me more about Adam; he's kinda hunky. Are you guys serious?' Her green eyes dance across my face.

Lulu gives a quick airy laugh. 'I think she means to say monogamous, not serious.'

'Oh, um...' Am I answering about Weasel or the real Adam? 'Kinda serious. And monogamous.'

Mia's face drops slightly and I swear she says, 'That's a shame' under her breath.

'You know, darling' – Mum arrives on the scene nursing a wine – 'that Adam. He's different from the rest of the guys you've gone for. He's not wishy-washy. Won't back down. Says what he thinks. I think he's good for you.'

'You can tell all that from meeting him once?' I asked wryly.

'One thing I do know, Gemma, is love. And heartache.'

She checks to make sure Lulu isn't listening, but Lulu is taking a selfie with Isabella. 'I have a good feeling about him, call it a mother's intuition. I had the same thing about Chip. And now look where we are.'

'Okay, ladies.' Amie clinks her spoon on her glass of champagne, until the chitchat dies down. 'Now we've all had a few champagnes, it's time to move on to the secret ladies' part of the day! Sexcapades. We're going to go around the circle and say the hottest place we've done it and who we've done it with.'

God, no.

I look at Mum, horrified, but she's was doing a little go-go-go dance with her fists as if this was actually fun. No, I don't want to hear about her doing it with Dad. Or, worse, with someone else.

Lulu goes first, something about yachts, Chip and a French marina. I try to drown out my mum talking about her latest caravan trip with Dad, and a small pond that was never the same again. Mia mentions a threesome in Ibiza – of course she did; she is Weasel's soulmate – and then it's my turn.

'So go on, Gemma,' Lulu says, her hand going around in circles as if I'm taking too long. 'Don't make it up, tell the truth.'

'It's got to be with Adam,' Mia says, a devilish glint in her eye.

My mind races and I think back to the hottest time Adam and I got down to it, and realise, we haven't really. Sex has been the one thing that we seem to not have totally mastered. Whilst it's nice, and close, it's never really ever earth-shattering. So instead, I take a vow of apology, and use an encounter with my ex, Richard, instead. 'It was on the bonnet of his car,' I say, flushed. 'At a park at sunset, because we couldn't wait until we got home.'

Mia raises an eyebrow, as if that's somehow too tame for him, and she's right, it probably is. 'Is that what he'd say too?'

And then I realise I have to text Weasel to tell him, *We've had hot sex on the bonnet of your car*, and hope that no one from work ever sees it.

Chapter Eighteen

After the afternoon tea, Lulu, having eaten not much and drunk a lot of champagne, is feeling tired, so I take her back to her hotel room, where she passes out on the bed. I take her shoes off, and try to wrangle her out of her dress, but give up and cover her with a blanket instead, setting a wake-up call in two hours, for seven p.m.

I want to call Adam but it's still before dawn in Australia. I have some time to kill, but not enough to sleep, so I quickly log in to check my work emails.

In my inbox are four emails, each asking me to look at manuscripts or authors' notes. One is from a new author, Zaneb, demanding a complete redo as apparently the latest edits from a junior editor, Charlie, were awful, and she wants me to fix them.

Tony has been CC'd on her email and he's sent me a direct email, saying he's fuming. I feel a rush of guilt run through my body, and quickly write back to him. *Don't worry. I'll fix this. Leave it with me.*

I don't have time to do the edits right now, but still I consider them in the back of my mind as I rush around getting ready, pulling on a light orange dress that hugs my figure and ends tightly mid-calf, and make sure I get to the ballroom just after seven p.m.

Inside the ballroom, the wait staff are finishing preparing for the soirée. Lulu has specifically asked for the scent of rose to be pumped into the room, and I don't know how they've done it, but it really does smell like a garden in there.

Exactly at eight, Lulu makes her entrance. It's about the ninth entrance she's made this weekend, but she nails it. She looks entirely refreshed, wearing a long beige silk dress that looks more like a slip, and makes her look young and innocent, despite the full, bold red lipstick. Very dramatic, and very eye-catching.

She floats across to me. 'How do I look?'

'Fabulous as always,' I reassure her, and when that doesn't seem to be enough I add, 'Like a young Marilyn, Ann-Margret or one of the great, classic beauties.'

She smiles without looking at me, and waves at someone across the the floor. 'Now will you please look out for the caterers? I want to make sure all the dinners go out on time. And make sure that Aunty Janice, who's still a little boozed from lunch, isn't falling off her chair. I don't want anything embarrassing to happen. Donna Henry is meant to be flying in later and everything needs to be *perfect*.'

As requested, I keep an eye on the caterers, the wait staff and Aunty Janice, to whom I keep bringing soda water and telling her there's vodka in it too. Marla natters on and on about how Donna Henry the *Mayor* is coming tonight, and asks everyone (even though no one is really listening), who else's wedding has such a VIP?

Mum is off drinking Sauv Blanc at the bar, and Dad is trying to smuggle a cigar out the back without Mum catching him. Weasel is the talk of the town, having won the boys' afternoon golf competition, and now all the men love him and can't stop clapping him on the back. Every time I pass, I have to pretend how overjoyed I am and how amazing my boyfriend is, and it feels like the chief editor job announcement day all over again, looking at Weasel and clapping with a fake smile on my face.

They serve the entrée of *pesce all'acqua pazza* – poached fish – but I'm too busy to eat. Lulu has specifically asked me to look out for the table decorations, which are goldfish in large bowls. 'Take out any floaters, would you?' she'd asked. 'No one wants to look at dead fish.' *When they're already eating dead fish*, I think, but refrain from saying anything. There are literally twenty fish per table, across ten tables. That's a lotta fish.

Table eight has the first casualty, and when no one is looking I shove my hand in the water and try to grab it. But fish are tricky and slippery little things, and it takes three times for me to actually get it. Then I'm standing there with a dead fish in my wet hand, and no pockets. I quickly grab someone's serviette and wrap it up and hightail it out of there into the kitchen where I dump it in the bin.

Next they serve the mains: *osso buco di vitellone in tegame con piselli e pancetta*, which basically means it's served from a hot pan with a side of peas or something.

I don't eat. Instead, I go back out for another round of Go Fish, but my feet are starting to ache and my head is starting to pound a little, so when everything looks fine, I slip outside onto the balcony for some fresh air.

Outside it's a perfect, still summer's evening, and all the stars are out. I can't see past a few metres, where the fairy lights stop. I gulp in a mouthful of fresh Italian air. The scent of jasmine bougainvillea is beautiful. I run my finger along the stone fence that looks out towards the lake and listen to the evening bees as they buzz around the terracotta pots.

Despite how gorgeous it is, I can't shake the beginning of a deep headache that looms in my temples, a constant throb. It feels like for ever since the last time I slept an entire night. I just want to lie under the covers and sleep for ever. I can't even make conversation anymore; I'm that tired. What I wouldn't do to just close my eyes. I do, for just a second, then hear the door open and footsteps coming towards where I'm standing.

'Hot sex on the car huh? I hope it wasn't the car from today.'

So that's why he's here, to gloat. I open one eye. 'You have to delete that text. Like yesterday.'

'Okay, okay.' He gets out his phone, selects the message, holds it up to show me and presses delete. 'But at least tell me, how good was I?'

'Thankfully they didn't ask for details. That's not a visual I think my brain could ever delete.'

But of course, now I've said it, I think about it for a second. His muscular legs, his strong hands on my thighs, me leaning back, arching on top of the bonnet, my white cotton undies pushed to the side, sexy and innocent all at once.

I should have felt revolted. But instead, I feel hot and sweaty. For some reason my heart does a thrilling pitter patter of fast beats. My face feels flushed, and even though the night sky is cooling down, I seem to be getting hotter.

His voice is low and deep. 'Gem, are you blushing? Thinking about us on a bonnet of a car?'

My eyes snap open. 'Absolutely not. You can go inside. I just need a minute, and then I'll be back inside to help Lulu.'

But instead, he cocks his perfect head to the side and says, 'Riddle me this. Why do you do everything for your sister?'

I raise an eyebrow. 'Define *everything*.'

'I saw you picking a dead goldfish out of a bowl; I'd say that's quite a lot. And the bunting. And her list of demands.'

I shrug. 'As screwed up as they are, they're still my family. And I like my friends and family. I love them. And I care about them. And that means putting them first.'

'Before yourself?'

'Of course,' I say. 'It's what any good person would do.'

'Is it though?' His eyes linger on my face. 'Who looks after you then?'

His question makes me feel uncomfortable. This is suddenly going way too deep. He's trying to get intel on me, obviously, and I'm not going there.

I clear my throat. 'Nope, we don't need to do this. This

gets in deep stuff. We are pretend partners, surface level only.'

I'm about to say something else, but my head starts throbbing. Suddenly, I feel a bit strange, like I'm floating outside my body. *Jetlag*. I close my eyes and take another breath of Italian air.

'You don't look right.' He narrows his eyes.

'Thanks for your excellent opinion, Doctor, but I am absolutely fine.' My head starts spinning.

'Are you sure? You look like you're going to pass out.'

'I've been looking after myself for thirty-something years, and I think I've got this.' I take a deep breath and feel a wave of heat and nausea flush through me.

He takes a step towards me and reaches out to my forehead with his palm but I tense at him coming towards me, especially after that kiss, so I duck and say, 'Can't tell where those bad boys have been.'

But as I duck, I feel a bit dizzy and reach out for the railing, but it's further away than I thought, and I start to lean into absolute air. In these heels that's a dangerous thing to do and I teeter for a second and can tell exactly what's going to happen: I'm going to trip and fall. Except Weasel steps in and suddenly his hands are catching my shoulders, holding me, stopping me from falling any further.

'You're hot,' he say, pretending to care.

'Oh God, this is how you do it.' I straighten up, refusing to buy into this terrible charade. *How predictable*, I think, trying to get girls to literally fall into his arms. I shake off his arms. 'With all these cheesy lines. You know, *you* should be the one editing romcoms.'

'No, Gemma, I mean really, you're hot. You're burning up.'

I step away from him, put my hand on my cheek, and it does feel a little warm. 'I'm tired, I'm jetlagged and I've got a deadline to meet. And it's hot in there. Out here too. And there are so many fish.' I'm not sure what I'm saying.

He stares at me. 'You know, you really don't look great.'

'Exactly what every girl wants to hear,' I say dryly. 'Anyway, I've got to get back in. More speeches,' I say, heading back towards the door before he can say anything else.

Inside, I retrieve three more dearly departed goldfish. As I'm dumping their poor bodies in the trash can, I text Adam.

Not feeling the best – so many things happening. Need a holiday from this holiday. Wish you were here to give me a big hug. How are you?

'Oh Gemma, there you are!' Lulu grabs me. 'I want some photos for Insta, will you take them?'

For the next twenty minutes, Lulu and Mia perfect their head tilt, and then pretend to walk towards me, and look straight into the camera in a provocative way that makes me feel almost uncomfortable. I hold the phone vertically, horizontally; I do slow-mo's and what feel like a thousand boomerangs or zoomies or something. By the end I can feel my legs shaking, and I'm sweating from places one shouldn't – feet, calves, neck and inner thighs.

Before I can sit down, Mum corners me at the table, 'Oh

wasn't today just splendid? Now Dad and I want to come out and do a caravan trip around Australia! Can you imagine? We think it will take about three months. Can we stay with you and Adam for a while, when we get there?' She peers at me. 'Gemma? Are you okay?'

'Fine, Mum, I'm great and yes, that sounds like a good idea.'

Thankfully everyone is shushed just then because it's speech time, which means I actually get to sit down. I didn't even know rehearsal dinner speeches were a thing, especially after yesterday's long torturous hours, but apparently they are.

I collapse into the chair, sticky and sweaty, with a throbbing head, and hope I can keep my eyes open for the next hour, or at least pretend to. Dessert has been served and in front of me is a sticky sweet dark chocolate dome. I take my spoon and dig into the centre. The middle is a river of chocolate lava, and I should like this. I should *love* it, but I don't want a bite. My mouth waters, but not in a good way. Miserably, I put down the spoon.

Weasel is staring at me from across the table with raised eyebrows, acting as if he's concerned. He's looking at me like he's a member of the Italian First Aid Army, like he's going to lay me down on the middle of the table and perform every type of examination to find what's ailing me. Like he's suffering because he's not showing everyone the wonderful boyfriend he is. And I know it's all for show. I want to growl at him, *I'm fine*, but I don't even have the energy. So I just shrug, close my eyes, and lean back in my chair.

The groomsmen get up and do a quick roast of Chip, but since he's a good Eton boy, there is barely a thing to say about him, with the exception of why everyone calls him Chip – because once he found one and ate it on the floor in the middle of a school assembly. Very mild. I'm disappointed. I'm also sweating from inside my elbows.

There's a quick break while the hotel sets up for the final speech, which apparently requires a projection screen. Of course it does. Perhaps there's also a cannon and a twelve-army salute. I know I'm being surly, but I can't help it, I feel like I'm at the wedding of European royalty.

Instead of sitting at the table, with Weasel shooting me pretend-to-care looks, I do another round of Go Fish, and thankfully, all remaining fish are surviving so far. Back at the table, I slide into my chair, and drink another glass of water. Perhaps I'm imagining it, but I do start to feel a little better.

Someone gets up to the mic. It's Amy and Mia, and I think, *Are we going to have a repeat of the other night? Another rhyming poem?* But this time they have a slide show that is going to go through a roast of Lulu. This will be interesting, I think, because what can you roast Lulu about?

It starts off with how she came into the world, and there are photos. So many photos. For the next twenty minutes, it's photos of her early birthdays. Photos of Lulu being the grinning centre of attention. Photos of Lulu as a baby. Photos of Lulu at four, and five and six. In some of the photos, I catch a glimpse of myself, off to the side wearing a balloon skirt and fluoro leg warmers. I hope no one notices.

Amy keeps repeating how Lulu has always been

amazing. And now Lulu is seven, and eight, and nine. I wonder if we're going to have to sit through the entire photo collection of Lulu's life, when Lulu's tenth birthday party photos fly across the screen. And Mia smiles and my stomach drops and I'm thinking, *No*, no, they won't. They *can't*.

This is a wedding, about Lulu and Chip. I don't feature; I don't factor. They can't possibly tell a story about me.

The slide show flips from an image of Lulu to another photo. Slightly grainy. I gulp. They've blown it up, but I know the photo. It's me in my Keppers, and Mia is laughing hilariously as she starts telling the entire story, ending with calling me 'Gem-man!'

I feel mortified. Everyone is roaring with laughter, and I'm pretending to laugh too, but my eyes are hot with tears. Mia and Amy go through another set of photos of Lulu as a teenager, then at university, but I can't see a thing. My face is burning red with shame. I am telling myself not to cry. I can't even imagine what Weasel is doing, laughing too, I bet. I refuse to look at him.

To sit there for another ten minutes while they finish their speech feels positively unbearable. But I do it. I do it because I am Gemma, and I will get through this, and because if I stand up I'll draw way more attention to myself. *Don't cry*, I keep reminding myself.

At the end of their speech, Amy and Mia get a roaring round of applause, and even though I can't feel my feet, I stand up to go and find anything, a wine, a bathroom, a place I can guillotine my own head.

Uncle Jonathon stops me on the way, and in his own deaf way, shouts, 'THAT WAS HILARIOUS. GEM-MAN!'

I nod and laugh it off. But really, why did I think this was going to go any other way than it does every time I'm with my family?

All I want is to hear is a familiar voice. *Adam.* I dig my phone out of my tiny silly bag, and dial his number. This time it rings – I have signal! But it rings out. I message him:

Everything going to shit. Please call me.

It says delivered, but unread. *Damn.*

I feel terrible, my head is pounding and I desperately want to leave but I can't; I'd never hear the end of it. My cheeks burn with shame.

I look for my mum. I need a big hug. But she's talking to someone I don't know, and when she catches my eye she just gives me a smile and a quick wave. I had hoped things had changed, but they haven't. My family are oblivious to me hurting; they are so used to me being fine – just as I am so used to saying I am – and we are all guilty of sweeping things like this under the carpet. If I said something I'd never hear the end of it. They'd all look at me perplexed and say, *But it was only a joke.* And then I'd be Gemma who can't take a joke, or Gemma who makes mountains out of molehills. Whatever way you look at it, I can't win.

It makes me want to cry – and this is why I wanted Adam here, the real Adam. Although he's slightly allergic to emotions, he would have hugged me, or squeezed my hand reassuringly and walked me back from the brink.

Because it felt bleak out here, being ridiculed in front of hundreds of people.

'*Fuck me,*' I mutter, as the night's events really hit me. I will cry about this later, when I'm alone. For now, I need a drink, stat.

Standing in line for a champagne, my stomach clenches. I swallow the lump in my throat. I feel the prickling of tears behind my eyes. *Look up.* I read somewhere if you look up you can't cry. But it's too late, one tear has escaped. A guy standing next to me notices, and steps away. That's the thing about the English: we're worried crying is like a contagious disease.

I wipe away the tear and blink more away. My cheeks feel very warm to the touch. When I think about it, my arms feel like a melted firepit. And why are the back of my knees so hot? The headache has returned with a throb.

Outside the window, besides a few fairy lights, the entire world is in total blackness. If I had the confidence to just walk outside and keep walking I wonder where I'd end up. Perhaps I'd sprain my ankle in a ditch. Or end up eaten by wolves in the woods. Or be kidnapped by thieves. I'd go willingly. *Anything* would be better than this.

The thought grabs me. *Over here, without Han and Adam, I'm really fucking alone. What idiot does this to themselves?*

The bartender looks at me. '*Sì?*'

I order a tequila shot – because why not – with a champagne chaser. May as well get fucked up and blot this night out as much as possible. I feel another tear trail down my cheek, and I quickly wipe it away.

'Gemma.'

Weasel. The *last* person I want to see. I can only imagine the ridicule, for the rest of eternity. *Remember that time you were called a man and it made you cry?*

But I won't let my guard down. This is the guy who wants my career to be over. This is perfect for him. I can't be weak, I have to be strong. So I do the most mature thing I can: I ignore him.

'Gemma.' Not a question or a sentence, just my name again, thick, on his tongue. When I don't respond, he adds, 'Are you okay?'

I swallow hard, and look down in my purse as if I need to scrounge up some money for the free drinks at the bar. 'I'm fine.'

'C'mon, you can't be fine.'

He steps forward, but I continue to look away. It's uncomfortable having him this close behind me. Despite trying to be strong, I can feel the lump in my throat. More tears gather in my eyes and if I blinked hard they'd run down my cheeks.

'That was pretty brutal.'

I refuse to look at him, and try to be nonchalant. 'Just another day in Evans heaven.'

'Those bridesmaids, even your sister … that was horrible.'

I feel a sudden instinct to leap to their defence, *They didn't know better, they thought it was funny, maybe I'm taking this to heart unnecessarily.* But my head is pounding, and my skin feels flushed, and the world is getting blurry and a bit topsy turvy, so I just shrug.

'Surely you're going to say something?'

'Mmm.' *No, actually, Weasel, I am not.*

'Do you want me to say something?'

Absolutely not, are you insane? Have you seen my family? I'll be crucified for spoiling Lulu's day.

I swallow the lump in my throat, still not looking at him. 'Nope. It's fine.'

He sighs. I can tell he's exasperated with me, the way cocky people who are confident and gorgeous get with mediocre-looking people who keep the peace and try to sweep things under the rug.

'Are you going to look at me?'

'I'm buying a drink.' I know it sounds petulant, but I'm buying time trying to compose myself, so he doesn't see me disappointed, insecure and vulnerable.

'I can see that, but conversations are usually face to face, not to the back of someone's head.'

I'm not in the mood for Weasel, but I can see he will follow me around until I give him what he wants, persistent little twat.

Finally, I brace myself and turn around. His eyes quickly flick over my tell-tale red cheeks. I thought his face would be predictable – laughing, or winking, or doing that lopsided grin – but now I see something I hadn't seen before. His jaw clenches as he takes in the state of me and it's impossible to tell what he's thinking but I'm sure it's not good. I can see him narrowing his eyes, and he obviously thinks that having your faux girlfriend teased and ridiculed is embarrassing. I bet this has never happened in his life, that he's always been the ridiculer, not the ridiculee. *Is that even a thing?*

'I'm tired. Headache too. So whatever smart comment you want to make, save it. Oh and apologies, your royal highness, for bringing you into the gutter with me.'

'Gutter?' He does a good job of looking like he has no idea what I'm talking about.

'Yes, your wagon is hitched to mine, so that makes you the not so proud boyfriend of...' I couldn't even bring myself to say it. *Gem-man.*

'Gemma, stop.'

He moves towards me, and for a second, in my silly shame stupor, I think, *He's going to hit me*, but then it dawns on me. There are two arms. Weasel is going to hug me.

'Don't.' I step away from him.

It's the last thing I need right now. If someone so much as touches me, I'll lose it. I'd crumble into a pile and sob. Just his attempt to be nice has tears already forming in my eyes, and my throat has that lump it gets when you're about to bawl. I'm right on the precipice of tears and any sort of kindness could push me right over.

'Are you okay?' He doesn't sound sarcastic or full of pity. He sounds *kind*. For a second our eyes meet, and I can swear he actually looks sorry.

Fuck.

I know it's going to happen before it does. As I close my eyes, a few tears slide down my cheek, without warning.

His eyes flicker with surprise. 'Gemma, I...'

Before he can say anything else, I hold up my hand as if to say, *Stop, please.* Thankfully he does. I step away from him, so I'm out of touching distance.

'It's just a headache ... makes me cry...' I mutter, grab

my tequila shot from the bar and knock it back quickly. But instead of it giving me a sense of relief, it burns incredibly badly. 'Ugh.' I feel a sudden urge to spit it out.

A hot wave comes over me. Then a mix of chills and hot flushes start in my toes, and run up and down my body. Parts are sweating, and other parts shivering. My head keeps spinning and my stomach is cramping.

'Uh-oh.' Suddenly a shiver goes up and down my body and not in a good way. I feel like vomiting and crying all at the same time. My head is pounding so much that I can't even position it in any way to make it stop. My throat feels thick and my tongue furry. Maybe I've picked up something on the plane. I step away from the bar, leaving my champagne there.

'You okay?' Weasel is saying, but it sounds far off, distant, and slow.

I swallow the saliva in my mouth. My feet are aching and almost without thinking I slip off my shoes and pick them up. If only I could tip toe out of here, head to my room for a quick lie down and have a cold shower.

I can see a group of people, including Aunty Janice and half the wedding party, are clustered around an older lady with a perfect grey bob by the gold-embossed ballroom entrance. It looks as though she's just arrived. Wearing a two-piece fuchsia suit, she's clearly left a trail behind of her perfume, which has a strong musk and spice. Normally that would be delicious, but any smell right now makes my stomach cramp more. I put a hand on my belly and warn it, *Not now.*

I walk quickly towards the large doors, determined to sneak away quietly, when a shadow steps across my path.

'Gemma.' Lulu gives me an accusing glance, as if I've already spoiled her night. She gives me a once-over, looking at my shoes in my hands. She whispers furtively. 'That,' she points to the fuchsia woman, 'is Donna Henry. The MAYOR. Do *not* embarrass me.'

'Yep.' I can't think of anything else to say. It's all lost to the cotton fluff that my brain has become.

Weasel appears next to me, like one of those annoying whack-a-moles just popping out from anywhere. 'You look weird.'

'I...'

'Gemma?'

'I...

I start to walk around Lulu because it feels urgent now. Something is going to come out, and I can't tell which end. I need the bathroom and I will myself to just run. But my stomach suddenly cramps. God. I won't make it. Just before the ballroom entrance I turn without warning and heave some horrible green bile into a poor pot full of pink pansies.

'Gemma, what are you *doing*?' Lulu hisses, absolutely horrified.

Many of the other guests have heard me too and they are standing with mouths like big Os as I wipe the spit from my mouth. Donna Henry pauses just a few metres away, looking over at the doorway, wondering whatever the commotion could be.

Lulu gives me a look of utter disgust, as if I were a diseased leper asking for a full body massage. 'Don't you know the *mayor* is right here,' she hisses. 'And you go and get so drunk you vomit in a ballroom pot plant at a five-star hotel. TAKE IT AWAY,' she yells at a waiter, who looks horrified at her demand, but starts pulling it away.

'I'm not drunk, I'm sick,' I manage to say as the entire world starts spinning.

'Sick?' Lulu gasps, looking me over. 'Well, keep your distance from me. I can't have a bug on my wedding day.'

It's coming again. This time, I push past Lulu and run through the open ballroom doors and into the foyer where the wedding party has moved. With urgency I turn right, and run towards the bathroom, trying to lock it behind me, and dash into the first cubicle. A whoosh of heat comes over me. Feeling dizzy, I turn around and vomit into the toilet. Finished, I press my hot forehead against the cool door.

I hear someone coming into the bathroom, which means I didn't lock it like I'd thought.

I try to say, 'Go away, I'm in here,' but the retching feeling comes over me again. The hot and cold chills. My stomach spasms. I lean over and vomit again, feeling like I can't breathe. When I finish I flush the toilet, feeling shaky.

A voice says, 'I knew you were sick.' It's him.

'Go away.'

I hear the tap being turned on in the sink, then off.

'Really, Ben, please go away.' Shaking, I sit down on the rim of the toilet. He's the last person I want to see me like this.

'Come out, Gemma, you can't stay in there all night.'

'Can't I?' My voice sounds like it's coming from someone very far away.

'Well, maybe near a toilet, but not actually *in* a toilet.'

I want to stay in there for ever. But he's right. I can't. I unlock the door and am greeted firstly by Weasel with a towel that he's soaked in cold water, and then by my reflection. I'm white and pasty and my eyes are huge.

'Oh shit, you look terrible.'

'Thanks,' I mumble, leaning over the sink and splashing cold water on my face, which feels so hot that you could cook a big breakfast on it. The thought of breakfast makes me almost gag. I dry retch into the sink but nothing comes out. Weasel puts the compress on my neck and it feels wonderful.

'I need to sit down.' My knees feel like jelly and I suddenly have no energy at all.

'Wait, I'll take you to your room.' Weasel ducks his head under my arm.

'No, no, I can do it myself,' I say, thinking, *I've got this. I can do it.*

'Let me help.'

'I'll probably vomit on you.'

'That's okay, I'll have a shower.' Before I can say anything else, he opens the door, grabs me and lifts me off the floor. My legs fold easily over his left arm. He grips the train of my dress, and twists it in his hand, so tightly and securely, I feel like a ventriloquist's doll.

I lean my head against his right shoulder. All I smell is him, sharp, sweet, and refreshing, wood and earth on a cold day, which strangely settles my stomach. He strides across the foyer. The entire room is spinning like I've had fourteen rounds of tequila shots.

Someone comes over and asks if I'm okay, and I can't see who it is because the room is spinning, and I hear Weasel tell everyone, 'She's fine.'

It seems to take for ever to get to my room. My eyes lose focus. I am extremely hot, then shivering and cold. Inside the room I fall onto the bed. Something is tugging at my feet. I think it's a shark. 'Is there a shark?' I ask.

'Shoes,' I hear a voice say. Something heavy and warm is on my head. 'You're burning up.'

In the spinning room and through the waves of nausea, I say, 'I have to work. Tony's edits.'

'Later.'

'Have to. Promised.' But the waves of tiredness, of fever wash over me. 'Please, can you get my laptop.' I point towards what I think is the corner of my room. 'Password is Shakespeare.' I try to keep my heavy eyelids open, and manage to murmur, 'In the writing folder... Edits... Don't open the other one ... under any circumstances ... not the one called Stars, Food, Love. Don't go snooping. Can you just pass it to me...?' I yawn and shiver as the fever turns cold. I can feel my eyelids getting heavy.

Instead of a laptop, there's a glass of water in my hand and someone helps me take a sip. My mouth tastes like hot acid. Then there's a cold towel and it's beautiful and then it's too cold and I shiver and a blanket, soft and heavy, rests on top of me. And there's a hand – warm, reassuring – on my arm, and when it leaves, I reach for it, and it's back.

Chapter Nineteen

M idnight. My entire body is drenched in sweat. When I sit up, the room spins in a strange way, like I'm on a merry-go-round and I can't get off.

I don't know what's happening. My throat is thick. My head hurts. My eyes have floating spots, like tiny little fireworks going off wherever I look. I am underneath what feels like a mountain of blankets, like I'm drowning. I'm not wearing my usual silk pyjamas. Instead, I'm in the bra and lace underwear I've worn to the dinner, and my bed looks like it's been in a tornado, all the sheets are strewn up, and…

THERE IS A MAN IN MY BED.

I jump up.

'Relax, Gemma, it's just me.' Weasel is sitting against the headboard, his computer resting on his lap. He's still wearing his pressed pants from the dinner, and they're completely perfect, as is his shirt. He's taken his shoes off, and his white socks – brilliant white, not a spot on them –

are folded at the bottom of the bed. Ugh, he's perfect, always.

I do a quick step towards the couch where the hotel bathrobe is folded, and swiftly wrap myself in it.

'Where's my dress?'

'You sweated through your clothes.' He shrug. 'I had them sent down to laundry.'

'Oh, um, thank you.' He undressed me?

I don't know where to look. I suddenly realise I'm extra thirsty, and down a glass of water in one gulp. My phone flashes. There are ten missed calls from Adam. 'I should probably … uh, return these calls. Get some clothes on.'

He snaps the laptop shut. 'I'll go down and get something for you, for the fever, I just didn't want to leave you alone while you were sleeping.'

Although I still feel sweaty and nauseous, I say nonchalantly, 'I'm fine, thank you.'

He grabs my hotel swipe card, says, 'Two minutes', and disappears quickly out the door.

I glug another glass of water as I sweat in rivulets. Seconds later, a shiver comes over me. I duck into the bathroom, aghast to see my red blotchy face, my smeared mascara, my eyes dull and half closed. Leaning my heavy head forward, I splash water on my neck and face, and it's so wonderfully cool I almost imagine my skin sizzle. While I'm still alone, I call Adam, and thankfully this time he answers.

'I'm sick.' As I say it, I start to cry a bit, because suddenly I just desperately want to be at home. In my bed. With my real boyfriend. Not continuing with this charade. I walk to the furthest end of the room, towards the window, because I'm very aware Weasel could come back at any moment and see me crying again.

'Oh baby.'

I sink into a chair and close my eyes. 'I vomited in front of my entire family.'

Adam laughs, but then quickly clears his throat and says in a more serious tone. 'Oh shit, Gemma. Is there someone to take care of you?'

I think about Weasel. 'Kinda.'

'Well, that's good, you really need to rest, baby. Take a Panadol. Hey, someone's knocking on the door, think it's my dinner. I got the beef tortellini with that red sauce we love.'

My stomach churned just thinking about it. 'Oh um, nice.'

'Call me in the morning, I want to tell you something big, okay? I think you're going to love it. Hope you feel better. Love you.'

He hangs up so I end up saying, 'Love you too' to the silence and try not to feel deflated. But I can't help it, a few tears run down my face. *Why do I feel so alone in this world? Have I cursed a god somewhere?*

The door quietly opens and closes. Weasel stares at me, a little aghast he's caught me crying again.

'Well, this is embarrassing.' I quickly wipe the tears away. 'It's just because I'm sick.'

'Right.' He's nice enough to go along with my theory, but we both *know*.

I sniff. 'I know I need to be less emotional, less reactive.'

'Says who?' Weasel looks at me with those aqua eyes, those eyes that seem to reach into me.

'You know. All that detachment stuff. Letting go.' I don't really know much about that stuff, but Adam says it all the time.

'Detaching what?' He raises his eyebrows.

'Detach from uh … feeling.'

Weasel laughs. 'What robot said that?'

My brain can barely make a word let alone an argument, and the room is still spinning. 'I just heard it somewhere.'

'Well, unless you're an android, I don't think that's possible or that that's what you should do. You just have to feel what you do, until it stops.'

Now I'm truly confused. I have Adam telling me to not feel anything, and now I have faux-Adam telling me to feel everything. Which one is right?

Shutting it out, I tie my bathrobe around me as tightly as I can, as Weasel unloads his shopping bags – which seem to contain an entire pharmacy – on the table. He's bought one of everything – a thermometer, some Panadol, some things in Italian I can't decipher, bottles of water, bed socks (WHY!), then a washcloth (supposedly for the fever), and even an assortment of herbal teas.

'You shouldn't have…' I feel incredibly uncomfortable that he has done this.

He points to each pile. 'Gastro. Fever. Those are for sleeping or jetlag, I don't know which because it's in Italian so we just have to trust them. Water. Thermometer. In fact we should probably use that now. And then socks, in case you get cold.' I can see the clench of his jaw. He likely hates this weird niceness between us as much as I do.

'Aren't you worried about catching something?'

'Nah, I'm pretty good in a medical crisis.' A shadow flicks over his face.

I resist the urge to ask why.

'Let's see.' He walks over to me and practically shoves the thermometer under my tongue. He pushes some limp, sweaty hair off my forehead.

I try to make sense of what's happening. Weasel is *taking care* of me. My awful colleague is taking my temperature. I must be high as a kite with this fever. But does he keep his hand on my face longer than he should?

'Thith feelth weird,' I say, aware my entire body is shivering, and then, just as quickly, sweating with fever.

The thermometer beeps. He looks at the end and his eyes widens. 'Thirty-eight point five. That's too high.' Then he's popping pills like a doctor and pushing them into my hand with a bottle of water.

'Take those. And do you want a cool shower?'

I raise my eyebrows.

He says quietly. 'No, Gemma, I'm not helping you with that.'

'Thank goodness,' I say quickly, hoping he doesn't see me blush at the thought of him naked in the shower.

———

The shower is glorious. The sweat slick runs off me. Two minutes in, I shiver and turn the water to almost scalding.

As I'm feeling the water regulate my temperature I realise how strange it is to be completely naked, in a hotel room, with Weasel just a few metres away. I keep my eye on the door. *I did lock it, didn't I?*

One minute I'm worried about the lock and the next I'm having a flashback. Weasel lifting me up as if I were a feather. Weasel striding through the ballroom, his rugged blond hair perfectly in place. Weasel protecting me. Gorgeous Weasel, with large biceps, big enough to snap a shark in two. I can feel the tell-tale tingle of my body, my stomach, wanting desperately for him to just burst in here and shove me against a wall, kissing me passionately. I open my eyes and try to scrub the images away. *Damn fever.*

After the shower, I feel dizzy as I bend down to towel my legs. For a minute, I sit on the edge of the toilet trying to control the relentless spinning of the room. Everything hurts. I pull on the bathrobe, double-knotting it for safety.

I crack the door open a bit. He's tried to clean my hotel room, the jumbled sheets now nicely back in place on the bed and the medication waiting in a weird little row, and he's opened all the windows so the warm, balmy night washes in. A candle is lit, and the smell of gardenias wafts through the room. If this was anyone else, any other time, it would almost be – I swallow – *lovely*.

He looks up immediately as I exit the bathroom. 'Okay?'

'Yep.'

'Sit down.' He's in charge.

Honestly, I have no fight left in me as I sit on the edge of the bed. He gives me a glass of cold water and then makes me a ginger lemon tea. My head is still heavy, and my cheeks are hot. I look at him while he's making tea in the kitchenette and if I squint a little he looks like George Clooney, who has dark hair and is way shorter, so I must still be really out of it.

When he brings me the tea, I feel stumped. 'Why are you being so nice to me?'

'Why not?'

'Because we hate each other.'

He tilts his head, with a small smile playing at the edge of his lips, as if considering it. 'We don't *hate* each other. Do we?'

Yes, we do. We hate the fucking pants off each other.

I nod. 'Course we do.'

'And now?'

Fever fuels me and I can't stop myself. 'Now I'm confused. You like cheese. And books.'

He laughs and drops something into my glass of water that starts to fizz. 'Maybe delirium has set in.'

I flop back on the hotel bed, wondering why the room has started to spin again. My stomach clenches. 'God, I'm going to be sick.'

I run to the toilet and vomit again, then lay my head on the cool tiles for a while. There's a soft knock on the door. 'It's open,' I murmur.

This time his hands pick up my horrible, sweaty hair and drape a cold washcloth around my neck.

'That's nice,' I mumble.

His hands are soft on my neck, then carefully they move to my forehead, checking my temperature again. Something unfolds in me that I can't quite describe. He disappears for a second and I can't stop myself calling out feebly, 'Where are you?'

I hate myself right now. I may as well dig my own grave and just lay in it. I am feeling small, soft and vulnerable like a starfish's underbelly. Because I just called out for Weasel. *I obviously have Stockholm Syndrome.*

He doesn't joke or smirk about it though, meaning he must have a modicum of sensitivity towards a fevered girl. Instead, he crouches beside me, both of us huddled near the toilet. 'I'm here.' Again the thermometer is back under my tongue.

'Shit. Thirty-nine.'

My eyes are blurry, and it's hard to make out much, but he looks concerned. Really concerned.

My mind goes into overdrive. *Girl found in bed, unresponsive. End of life for pasta lover. British-born Aussie dead celebrating sister's Italian wedding.*

'Are you sad I'm going to die?' I say miserably, my head resting on the lid of the toilet.

He laughs at that. 'You're not going to die. So dramatic.'

Am I?

I continue without a filter. 'I think I'd be sad if *you* died. Not before. But now, maybe a little.'

'Right.' Weasel's arms are around me again, lifting me up and guiding me back to bed. He hands me a glass of water and another tablet. I take it with shaky hands.

He waits for me to lie down, then pulls the blanket up around me. My eyes close but the pressure in my head is intense, pounding no matter which way I turn. I hear him back in the bathroom washing another cloth for my neck.

By the time he puts it on, I'm burning up, and it feels wonderful.

I open my left eye slightly. He's sitting up on the bed next to me. Close enough that I can smell the faint cedary-ness of him. He keeps his hand on the cloth on my neck, the weight a reassurance I didn't know I needed.

'You're being very nice and ... it's ... it's ... lovely actually.'

His lips twitch. 'Really. A compliment? Finally?'

'I'm confused. Are you nice? Or are you not? You confuse me a *lot*.' Then I add, 'Not that I think about it. Because I don't.'

'You don't?' I can see a small smile dancing on his lips.

God, fevers are truth serums and I hate them. 'Well ... a bit. I do think about it a bit. Sometimes more than a bit.'

He laughs. 'Is that so?'

Immediately, I know I've exposed myself too much. Even in my fevered state, I try to re-balance it. Gain back some power.

'I mean, I think about a lot of things too. Like why snails leave trails behind them. Whether I look weird when I lift weights at the gym, cos I scrunch my nose.'

'Right.' He puts his hand on my forehead, checking for fever, but then he keeps it there for longer than he should. Even with my fever, I feel it. He wants to comfort me.

I allow myself to look at him, and he's smiling at me, as though he can see right through me.

My phone vibrates. He passes it to me. I'm hoping for a text from Adam, but it's Han.

Okay, give me the goss. And if shit goes weird, just straighten that crown, because you are a queen!

I love her. I write back a response I think makes sense, about Weasel and being sick, and it won't be until tomorrow that I discover I'm writing: *in bed with a stranger. Am queen. Have washcloth…*

I lie back on the bed, on my right side, facing Weasel, exhausted but smiling. Han is a godsend. It feels so good and reassuring to remember how much we are there for each other. It's always been like this for us. There's something about her support that makes me feel bold. Maybe it's Han's message or the last bit of fever, but I need to know.

Once the room stops spinning, I contemplate what I'm about to say a full two seconds before I blurt out, 'Can I ask you something?'

'Yes.' He lies back on the bed, shifting so he rests against the backboard. He removes his hands from my forehead and the lightness feels almost unbearable. *Put them back. Please.* When I'm sick I want to be wrapped up and held.

'Do you think I'm a…' I stop. I can't say it.

'Yes, Gemma?'

Before I can stop myself, I say quietly, 'Do you think I can't do my job?'

'What are you talking about?' He looks mystified. If he's an actor, he's a superb one.

He regards me silently for a moment. 'Honestly, if you must know, you're a good editor, a great one even. You can turn the sludgiest, verbose stuff into … well, an excellent read.'

This is a lot to process. How Weasel sees me. Coming from him, it's glowing. But then, none of this makes sense.

'So you wouldn't want my career to end?'

He seems genuinely shocked. 'God no, never. Why would you say that?'

I narrow my eyes, still suspicious, and try to ignore the pounding in my head. 'How do I know that you're honest? You could be lying.'

I can tell I've hit a nerve because his eyes darken for a second. He shifts uncomfortably. 'Because that's just the way I am. Radical honesty.'

'*Radical* honesty? Sounds like a dance fad where you wear Eighties fluoro.'

'Well, I always think the truth is best. Why lie?'

'How can anyone NEVER lie? It's … it's … *impossible*.'

'For you.' He has a smirk on his face that annoys me, as if to say, *we all know you lie your pants off, Gemma Evans, just to please everyone and keep the peace.*

Still, I'm intrigued. 'Do you bend the truth?'

He shakes his head. 'Nope.'

'Little white lie?'

'Never.'

'What about a "Does my atrocious pantsuit look good?" kinda lie?'

He laughs. 'Absolutely not. Do you own a pantsuit?'

'No.' I vow to buy one.

'Well, that's a moot point then.'

'Sooooo anything I ask, you'll answer truthfully.'

'Yeah. Try me.' He opens his bottle of water, and stares at me like it's a challenge.

For a moment I'm stumped. What do I want to ask him? So many things. Why is he a horrid human sometimes? Did he feel something the other day, when we kissed? What did he think when he undressed me? Is he being nice because that's just part of the act? I'm still not sure this isn't just part of some giant ruse to play with me. I've heard him say those words, *It's over*, plain as day through the bathroom. I have the horrible idea that as soon as I let down my defences, he would just know he was *in*, and he'd use something I said against me.

So, instead, putting my walls back up, I retort, 'What makes you think I want to know anything about you?'

Almost immediately, I realise how rude that sounded.

He raises his eyebrow, as if to say, *Really, Gemma*? and looking at his face, there's a tinge of something in his eyes, and it makes me feel incredibly guilty, so I quickly add, 'Sorry, I don't know why I said that, after you looked after me all night.'

'Pulled your hair back when you were sick.'

'Saw me vomit into a pot plant.'

'Put a cold compress on your neck.'

'Helped me when I was sweaty and gross.'

'Undressed you…'

We both stop. His eyes meet mine… *Undressed you.* Tension and heat gather between us. It's palpable. I look down so he won't see my face is on fire. He's seen things. What things?

I roll over onto my back to break the tension, and rub

my temples as if I could scrub the night away. Weasel and I will go back to being enemies because it's easier that way. He scoots so he's lying on the bed, and folds his arms beneath his head, his elbow so close to me, I can feel the heat from his skin. We both lie there, staring at the ceiling.

'Tired?'

'Yep,' I say, even though I'm not sure I could sleep. In my mind, I'm imaging Weasel striding through the foyer with me crumpled in his arms, putting washcloths on my neck, buying me the entire chemists'. And I'm wondering, what would Adam have done, had he been here? 'Not sure I can sleep though. Room keeps spinning.'

'Put one foot on the ground.'

'What?'

'Do it. It helps.'

I half think he is making fun of me, but I bend my knee and let my big toe be the anchor onto the floor. And what do you know, he's right. The room isn't as spinny. I can close my eyes without thinking I'm going to fall off some universal merry-go-round.

'What the hell.'

'Works, huh.'

'Is this magic?'

'No.'

'Voodoo? I could see you with feathers and chickens.'

'Uh, no.'

'How did you know?'

'I know some things.' *Unfortunately he's right. He knows lots of things and it makes him more interesting than most guys. He's not just a pretty head on a gym body.*

'How?'

'Drunk nights out and other stuff.'

I want to know about other stuff. 'Like?'

'Some time spent in hospitals.'

Oh. This seems like an off-limits subject.

He adds quickly, 'Not me. Anyway, it's just something that works because of how the brain works, but I don't think you're up for a science lesson right now.'

'I forget what you just said. Too many words.'

I hate that he's so knowledgeable about everything because it's almost a good enough reason for him to be so cocky. *Truthfully, I love it. I want him to tell me more, I'm insatiable for weird facts. I wonder if we'd do well at pub quizzes. I'm great at English and geography, could he do science?* My mind is twirling again, fever loops, and I beg it to stop.

'Okay, no brain facts.'

'Thank goodness. Maybe you can stop showing off. Like that first day I met you. Parading about like you owned the place. All suave in your dark blue Dolce three-piece whatever.'

He laughs. 'Hugo Boss. It took me a year to save up for that. And it wasn't the first day we met.'

My fever has confused me, but I know I'm right. 'Yes, it was. Because Bec the receptionist practically had a fainting fit at how handsome you were in that dark blue with tan shoes, and you looked like you belonged on a film set.'

'Actually, Gemma, want to know something?' I can feel his eyes linger on me, and I'm not sure I do.

My breath catches in my throat. 'Okay.'

He faces the ceiling again. 'We met before then.'

'No, we didn't.'

'We did. What I told your family was the truth – we met at the awards night. The Finch Memoir Prize. You don't remember me. I think it's because you were busy trying to talk to a guy – Dean, I think.'

Confused, I think back to that time. I remember Dean, the writer I wanted to sign. But how could I forget meeting Weasel? 'I don't remember meeting you. Surely I'd remember you?'

'We said hello. You thought I was someone's secretary.'

My poor tired brain is hunting through memories 'Did I? Oh, that's it!' Suddenly it clicks. 'Jason Hussein, Taylor's editor, had mentioned he'd recently gotten a new male secretary. I guess, I must have thought … you must be him.' Still, I don't remember talking to Weasel at all.

'That's why I thought it was quite funny to return the favour, calling you my secretary that first day. Which seemed to tank.'

'I thought you were being a misogynistic prick.'

He laughs and his eyes linger on me. 'Obviously. But I felt you were playing along, like we had this banter going. And so, when you mentioned a coffee, I gave you a bit of stick about it.'

I roll my feverish eyes, even though they hurt. 'You told everyone I wanted to date you.'

'Did I?' He smiles at the memory, like he remembers how charming he was, and doesn't apologise, because sorry doesn't seem to be in his vocabulary. 'I thought it was just banter. I can get carried away sometimes, especially with you.'

'Me?'

He grins. 'Yes, you're very easy to get into a banter battle with; it's part of what I enjoy most about working at Peacock.'

This is news to me.

I feel a shiver coming on, and he drops the smile immediately, looking concerned. He pulls the blanket back over me, keeping his hand reassuringly on my back, which he rubs a few times.

He traces my neck feeling for the temperature, the pads of his fingers gentle. 'Can I ask you something?'

'I guess.'

'Did you move to Australia to get away from your family?'

I don't know what to say.

'You don't have to tell me,' he says quickly.

I shakes my head. The fever seems to have loosened my tongue and without a second thought the story spills out.

'Ummm, it's okay. I can tell you. You can probably see it right in front of you anyway. But I'm going to do it not facing you.'

To his credit, he doesn't say a word about how weird it is that I need to be on my side, facing away from him.

'When I was about seven, my dad went away for a business trip. He met Marla. And then he just ... left us. Me and Mum. He didn't even say goodbye, just one day I woke up and he wasn't there.' I pause.

'He was gone for a while, and my mum forgot to do things. Sometimes it was buying groceries, and sometimes it was paying our electricity bill. She was just absent-minded, and she got really nervous. Always worried she was having a stroke, or had cancer or some illness. I guess now I think about it, she was just hurting and anxious.'

I think about it. 'I never wanted to burden her, so I just tried to help around the house, tried to cook dinners, and clean and…'

'Be the parent?'

'No, I … well … I guess. Maybe.' I shiver again.

'Did your mum realise?'

'Ummm, no, I don't think she can remember much about back then. We largely just pretended it didn't happen. Swept it under the rug. Well, that's until Lulu and Marla and my dad showed up on our door, and we all had to live together.'

I feel him move slightly on the bed. 'Jesus. Really?'

'Yep. Happy families. And my mum took over everything; she became Mum extraordinaire. And I was so worried that she was going to go back to how she was before that I just tried to be the happiest girl ever, the nicest, even if I didn't feel that way.'

'Wow. It all makes sense now. I get why you're nice all the time: it's because you're pretending you're okay. Because it would be worse to tell your family you're not okay and run the risk of no one caring.'

Fuck. He banged that needle so hard on the head, it hurts. My heart actually *hurts*. I feel winded. But, at the same time, something in me unfolds painfully. I've never felt so seen. I roll over to look at him. His eyes pierce me like the azure blue of the Antarctic, like ice under water. I feel my heart beat double time.

'That's why the other day, when you told me I always do the nicest thing, even if it's a lie, it hit a nerve.'

He breathes out heavily. He rubs his hands over his eyes. 'I'm sorry. I didn't know.'

I swallow hard. 'I've never told anyone but my friend Hannah that.' *And I don't know why I'm telling you. I really don't. You could make this hell for me; you could share it far and wide.*

As if he could read my mind, he says, 'Your secret is safe with me.'

My entire body flushes. For a moment I think it's with relief, but then my stomach cramps. 'Shit. I'm going to vomit.'

I'd never seen anyone leap so fast across the room. Before I can even get off the bed, a bowl is in front of me. A plastic fruit bowl, and then I am gagging into it, but since I've not eaten there's nothing left, except the sourness and saliva. Disgusting. Even so, Weasel is holding the bowl and my hair back at the same time.

When I finish, he tips it straight into the toilet, without complaint, and washes it.

I wipe my mouth. 'Sorry. That's disgusting. So now you I've told you everything about me. And then in a final embarrassment to myself, I vomited.'

'You're a pest,' he says with a wry smile on his face as he helps me back into bed.

I must have fallen asleep straightaway, and then slept for an hour or two.

When I wake up, it's still dark outside, and he's asleep too. I watch his pretty face, eyes closed. It's strange, being alone, here, with this man.

'Stop staring.' He opens one eye.

'I ... I'm not...' I blush. 'But seriously, are you a vampire? I thought you were asleep.'

'I'm on boyfriend duties, and my girlfriend is sick.'

'Faux,' I remind him, but my stomach flipped when he said that. *My girlfriend.*

I trudge into the bathroom and brush my teeth, loving the minty-ness making a fresh forest out of my mouth rather than a rancid bog. My fever seems to have broken somewhat, but he's still waiting outside with pills and more water.

'Now you're the pest.'

'Being strictly accurate, you thought I was a wanker,' he says, laughing.

'True.'

Then he paused. 'Are you regretting this? Me being here?'

Yes. No. Yes. No.

I stare at him across the bed. He isn't smirky and vampiric anymore; he's the person that pulls my hair back; he is fun and bantering; he is laughing with me. I remember how it feels to wake up and have him there: *safe*. 'I guess not.'

He gives me that satisfied smile, showing his perfect teeth and a small dimple I'd never noticed before, on the right. So faint you wouldn't know unless you stared at him. 'Good.'

And that makes my stomach flip for some utterly nonsensical reason. I get back into bed and snuggle under the sheets, and make one last attempt at building the wall between us back up, just in case I wake up in the morning regretting everything I've said tonight. 'When we wake up, we can go back to hating each other.'

'Sure, okay.' His voice tells me that's never going to happen. 'Go to sleep.'

'Yes, sleep,' I say, snuggling down into the pillow. I'll wake up fresh tomorrow.

Before I slide into inky blackness, I think I remember him saying, 'Just rest.'

Then more quietly, but I heard him, 'And the answer is yes, I'd be sad if you died.'

Chapter Twenty

E ight a.m. in Tuscany is bright and beautiful, like it should be. The sun shines on the beautiful hills, only a few clotted clouds dot the sky, the lake is glittering. From the lower hills, the citrus smell of lemon and orange trees wafts up towards my window, past the toast-coloured houses. A chef somewhere in the hotel is making some sweetly crafted bread. My mouth waters.

The entire night is a big fuzzy blur. I look around the room and I see Weasel's hoodie on the bed, folded perfectly. Before I think better of it, I pick it up and smell it. Cold Christmas. I smell the pillow next to me, and it smells like him too. Did he sleep here?

I hear the stream of a tap from the bathroom. Moments later, the door opens, and Weasel in a T-shirt and boxers (God, he's a boxers guy) saunters out as if this is the most natural thing in the world. His legs are muscular, tanned; his boxers are navy, tight. Too tight. I refuse to look.

The only tell-tale sign he's slept at all is his hair, which is slightly more ruffled. Which means we've slept next to each other for at least some of the night.

In the stark morning, without the comfort of night or my fever, this is absolutely, positively bizarre. I pull the sheets up around my chin.

'Relax, little viper.' He laughs and stretch.

I put my face into the pillow and groan. 'Please put some clothes on. It's so weird, waking up to you here.'

'*You* put some clothes on. That's if you didn't sweat through everything. Speaking of…' Before I can say another word he leans across and feels my forehead with his hand. 'Better.'

I can feel where his large warm hand has been, even after he gets back up and grabs the thermometer. 'Once more.'

I groan but inside I almost enjoy how much he's taking care of me. When it beeps, he nods. 'Thirty-seven. Better.'

He hands me a chamomile tea and I take a sip. I keep thinking back to last night. What am I forgetting? I look at him.

'Oh crap. The edits!' I exclaim.

'Done.'

'What do you mean, done?'

'I emailed Tony and said you'd do them when you get back.'

'No, no, no, no, no, no.' I cover my face with my hands and shake my face. 'Tony is going to be so annoyed.'

Oh God, was this his plan?

'For saying no?' He pops a blueberry from the fruit bowl in his mouth. 'I think it takes more than that.'

'I've never let him down. God, I'll be fired.' Suddenly I realise what's happening, this is how Weasel planned to get me fired. *It's over.* 'Which you'll probably love.'

He looks confused. 'Why would I love that?'

'What *exactly* did you say to him?'

'I said we were at a wedding, and you were busy, and you'd look at it when you got home.'

'*We.* God, so now Tony thinks we are a *we.* And I'm refusing to do work, and I can't even be bothered to tell him that myself.'

'Well, it's true, Gemma, you shouldn't have to work while on holiday, no matter how awful that holiday is. Even if the company is rather great.' He winks.

'Ugh.'

'Besides, Tony responded straightaway.'

I braced myself. 'And?'

'He said, "Sure."'

'"Sure" like he was okay?'

He gets his phone out. 'His exact words were' – he looks at me – 'because I know you're going to ask: "Sure, sounds good, Ben, have fun."' He looks at me. 'See? The world hasn't ended because you said no.'

'Well, technically *you* said it,' I say, sounding doubtful.

'Crisis averted.' He leans over and hands me a blueberry which I sniff first before popping it in my mouth, in case my stomach revolts, or he's poisoned it.

'By the way, I did some of the edits. Just in case…' He says it casually, as if it's no big deal.

I stare at him mid-chew. Part of me is happy that they were started, but the other part doesn't like it at all, Ben doing my work for me. His '*It's over*' comment still weighs in my head. I'm annoyed, but also thankful.

'Hmmm, okay.'

'Actually, Gem, in the spirit of honesty, I did something else too, and—'

I put my hands up. 'Enough, my nervous system can't handle any more surprises.' I suppose he's done something like cleaning up my towels or my clothes and wants to gloat. Or he's heard me snore and recorded it.

There's a knock on my door. We stare at each other, neither of us expecting anyone.

'Don't look at me,' I say, getting out of bed, feeling all sorts of insecure.

'Too late. Last night, remember?'

'Delete it from your memory.'

I grab the bathrobe and pad to the door, opening it a crack. It's Mum.

'Good morning.' She pulls Dad into the doorframe and leans into my room, then wrinkles her nose. 'Oh honey, it smells a bit in here.'

'Of what?'

'Sweat. Maybe vomit.'

'God. Sorry.'

'Don't be sorry, we'll ask them to send the cleaners up once you're out.'

I smile sheepishly. 'Thanks, Mum.'

'Got to look after you.' I know it sounds silly, but I like that she said that. I feel an unfamiliar warmth spread over me, and a rare fondness for my family.

Dad looks at me with concern. 'Sweetie, are you still thinking of coming on the boat cruise?'

'Yeah.' *If I must.*

'Well, ummm...' They look at each other. 'Lulu was quite um ... stompy last night, after you were sick.'

'Stompy?'

'Yes, well, stroppy. She even asked the hotel receptionist to spray everything with a disinfectant, but then the entire place smelled like mosquito spray so people went to bed pretty soon after that.'

I take a deep breath. Another thing I'll likely get the blame for. 'Maybe it's best that I stay under the radar. I could stow away in the hull of the boat?' I joke.

Mum smiles. 'She did mention she needed help with the name tags. That could be a good way to make it up to her.'

And there it is. *I* have to make it up to *her*. And I feel the weight of guilt in the pit of my stomach, like I've done something wrong and have to make it right. I swallow hard and try to remember it's only another two days, and then I'll be back on that plane and headed home.

'Sure, name tags I can do.'

'That's my girl,' Dad says.

'Good. I hate it when you two fight,' Mum says as though Lulu is her daughter. She bends down and gives me a large, heavy bag, and I already know before I look that it'll be full of name tags. They assumed I would say yes, and that irks me.

Suddenly, Weasel appears behind me. Thankfully, he's at least put pants on and smoothed down his hair.

'Morning, you two young lovebirds,' Weasel greets my

parents, and I watch Mum flush red, and Dad puff out his chest. What is it with Weasel? People seem to genuinely *like* him.

'Adam, you were a trooper last night.'

'Really, it was easy.' Weasel shrugs and looks at me. 'I mean it wasn't. She's demanding and feisty. She thought sharks were eating her feet.'

'Oh, Gemma, really.' My mum tsks and again I feel a sliver of shame, for just being myself.

'But she amuses me.' Weasel watches me for a moment. I look up at him and he seems completely honest. He has a genuine smile on his face and again I feel a warm glow in my chest.

Dad puts his arm round Mum. 'Go on, love. Tell them what you planned.'

'Oh yes!' My mum smiles broadly. 'For *you* lovebirds, we've left you a little treat.'

'Treat?' My stomach drops. I imagine a romantic dinner, or lunch. 'I can't eat anything too rich.'

Dad nudges Mum, who giggles. 'No, not eating. Uhh, rather doing. Part of our package was a couples body mask and spa, and it's not really our thing.'

'Couples *spa*?' Suddenly, I feel like I've just been invited on a murder spree, rather than a relaxing spa day. It's one thing for us to be nice to each other; it would be another entirely to get disrobed on a bed together. What if he has a stray hand? What if I do? What if we had to be nude like little mole rats? Terrible, horrible, worst idea ever.

'Yes, we know you two will love it. Two p.m. today is

the only time they could fit it in, which means you won't be able to make the cruise. But you'll still be in time to be on the lawn by five p.m. for Lulu's surprise. So, enjoy.' My mum smiles and winks. 'And we don't want to know a word about it.'

As they wave and walk down the hallway, I sigh. '*I* don't want to know a word about it.'

'I think you do, since you could do with a bit of a wash.'

I choose to ignore his comment and close the hotel door. Weasel is standing there fully dressed. *Right, of course.* He's leaving, course he is, back to his lair. I can hardly expect him to hang around with me, like an *actual* couple.

'So, looks like I have name tags to do.' I roll my eyes. 'Thank you for uh … everything last night.'

He looks down at me with those blue eyes, honest and open. 'I can help you out with the name tags.'

'Really?' I'm almost stunned into silence.

He nods.

'Okay, well, first I should clean up this smelly room. There was a strange man in here last night. And before you say anything, I'm sorry about all of it.'

He gives me a gorgeous grin, one of those stupid heart-melting ones, running his hands through his wavy blond hair. 'Okay, I need some proper coffee first anyway, so I'll see you soon.'

Opening the door to his hotel room, he calls out, 'Soy cappuccino?' as if we were together, and it feels really strange, because I expected I would want to say something snarky back, but after a few beats I just call, 'Perfect'.

A small warm tingle spreads across my body, and something in me seems to shift. I truly don't hate him anymore.

Chapter Twenty-One

G loriously alone for the first time since I arrived, I take a long, hot shower , and snuggle into a fresh bathrobe, knowing I don't have to be anywhere this morning. *This* is what a holiday is meant to feel like. I stand by the window and breathe in the delicious smell of summer jasmine, and it reminds me of Australian Christmases, hot, humid and flowery. Outside is just sky and earth, meadows and vineyards, all shades of green and brown. I stroke the window, imagining a country life, time to breathe, to make bread, to *write*. What an endless source of delight it would be to live here.

An hour later Weasel is back at my door with two large coffees and a brown bag that smells delicious, like pastries and butter. My starving stomach grumbles.

'Welcome. I think it still smells in here, so I won't feel offended if you just leave the food and go.'

'This? This isn't for you.'

I feel the embarrassment light up my cheeks. 'It isn't? I just thought...'

He grins. 'I'm joking. Stop apologising, Gem. It's for *us*. And it smells better in here than it did last night.'

So many thoughts swirl around my head. How did it smell last night? And *Gem*. And breakfast, like we were an *us*.

Just in case, as Weasel pulls out plates for the pastries, I slip into the bathroom, pick up my perfume, and spray aqua watermelon scent, wafting it with my hand. When I come out, I can tell he knows exactly what I'm doing.

'That's not going to do a thing.' He looks at me, amused, a smile still playing on his lips. 'But I like that you tried. It's cute.'

Cute. I don't know how to respond to that, so I busy myself picking up all the towels and sheets and then bundle them up and shove them into the corner of the room. Weasel cranks the rest of the windows open, the ones I couldn't reach, which needs some force, and I watch his muscles flex as he does it with such confidence. He then calls down to room service and asks if they could come up and do a deep clean. This man who brought breakfast. Who held me when I was sick last night. Who cleaned my room. Who *is* this guy?

He pulls out what looks like a small *crostoli*, a crispy fried pastry, dusted with sugar. I shake my head.

'Perhaps you want a plain bagel after last night?'

'Maybe.' I take the bagel and chew a piece thoughtfully, willing my stomach to accept the fluffy carbs coming its way.

The coffee is glorious, strong and hot, and the name tags only take half an hour, thanks to Weasel, who seem to have perfect handwriting. What can't he do? What fazes him? Nothing, it seems.

Weasel is sitting on my sheetless bed, his tanned muscular legs in white shorts, his eyebrows drawn together in contemplation. I steal glances at him, the curve of his cheek, the strong line of his jaw, the fullness of his lips, a small hint of stubble, meaning he hasn't shaved – of course he hasn't, because he's been with me all morning.

I'm bunched up on the small chaise, in denim shorts and a white singlet top, doing an awful job. I bite the end of my pen, cursing silently. My little attempts are wobbly, like I've done them with my left hand, and I know Lulu would rip them up, and then snap at me like a viper.

'It's the S's I just can't get right. I shall have to seat Sarah Simpson and tell her, her name is now Arah Impon. Or that her nametag was eaten by the crocodiles in the moat or flying monkeys.'

'Very *Wizard of Oz*.'

'Which makes me Dorothy.'

'With Lulu as the Wicked Witch?'

'Or Marla. Tough call. Which clearly means you're the Tin Man.'

'What? I'm not. I'm at least the Lion.'

'Tin. Creaking,' I say in a tinny, robotic voice. 'Need heart.'

'A *heart*?' He slightly moves his eyes, sizing me up. I can't tell if he's about to blow a fuse. I kinda want him to, lose it because I can't imagine that, but on the other hand, he did look after me last night.

'I'm sorry?' I say coyly before he can get mad.

He tips his head back and laughs.

'No. Keep going. I really like this version of you.'

'Version? I'm not a computer game.'

'I mean this *side* of you.'

I try not to smile, but my mouth twitches, and a warmth spreads under my skin.

He rolls his eyes in a teasing way. 'God, Gemma, so pedantic. You're exactly like Hermione, you know that?' He puts on a high-pitched, annoying voice. 'It's not wingardium levioosa. It's wingardium leviosaaaa.'

I'm quite chuffed with that analogy. 'Without Hermione, Ron and Harry would have been screwed. Their corpses would be somewhere deep below in the dungeon with the Basilisk. And poor JK would not be a billionaire.'

He laughs. 'True.'

'Also, words are important because I'm an editor. And so, *apparently*, are you.'

'Chief editor, actually.'

I roll my eyes. 'Insufferable. I believe I deserve an award for hanging out with you in a room so long, without considering murder.'

'Considering?' he grins. 'Surely, once or twice.'

I almost laugh. 'Okay, without substantial planning and plotting.'

He looks around the room. 'The cushion?'

'Too obvious. It's got to be slow and painful.'

'The butter knife in the kitchenette.'

'Perfect, only make sure it's in the bathroom. Could be messy after many stabs.'

'Wow. Okay, the award of creepy serial killer ingenuity goes to Gemma.'

I stand up, grabbing my hairbrush, and, holding it aloft like an award, say, 'I shall accept this half-compliment award with a bow, and thanks to Toto my little dog.'

'If only you were like this in front of your family.'

Ouch. It feels like a dig, but when I look at him, it doesn't seem to be. I can see he's bantering with me, not challenging me. It kinda feels like something has shifted in him too.

'I could also demand that you be nice to everyone, but we all know that Rome was not built in a day.'

'I'm nice to your family. They love me. And it was built in one thousand two hundred and twenty-nine years.'

'You're acting. There's a difference. Oh, and I'm in no need of a history lesson.'

'Am I acting?' he says, as though butter wouldn't melt.

'*Aren't* you?'

I feel a flush spread quickly around my chest. Isn't he? But I don't want to open that Pandora's box. Before he can answer, I quickly add, 'Stop interrupting me, *Weasel*. I have to concentrate.'

'Got it, little viper.' And he winks, because apparently I also have a nickname now.

I go back to the name tags, but no matter how hard I try, I keep on screwing them up. 'Seriously, how do you do the S's?'

He waves me over to where he's sitting on the bed. In

order not to watch him upside down, I have to sit next to him. His muscles flex as he picks up the pen. I lean over his shoulder, careful to keep a polite distance. He draws a perfect S, with little careful calligraphy strokes at either end.

'Easy.'

Somehow, I think not.

'Your turn.' He hands me the pen. Intently I write an S, hoping it wows.

'Looks like it's being murdered,' Weasel says, laughing.

'Perfection is over-rated, calligraphy nerd,' I say as I slap him lightly on the arm, as though this is who we are: jokesters, friends. My hand hits a wall of muscle, biceps and triceps, and I can't help but notice his T-shirt is soft cotton, and stretches across his tanned arms. I look away because I've never cared about muscles, ever, *until now*.

'Can I…' He holds out his hand, letting it hover over mine. I give a slight nod, which says okay. His broad shoulders brush mine as he inches closer. I can feel his warmth right next to me. I can make out the rise and fall of his chest. He needs to shift a bit to get his hand in the right position on top of mine, and it's warm, and heavy, and solid and secure.

I let his hand guide mine, and I feel the warmth, as he – we – draw an almost perfect S. I also hold my breath the entire time, half because I'm nervous, and half because I don't want my breath to smell like bagel.

'And that's how S's are made.' He winks. 'Looks like we're done.'

He runs his hand through his blond hair and it goes

back perfectly into a soft wave. This mission needs to be aborted because if I stare at this guy any longer, I'll think about his lips again and how he kissed me that first day, softly, tentatively, then more intimate, with hunger. This guy is so handsome, it *hurts*.

'So, what's our plan? Do we go on enjoying the wedding festivities? Or grab our suitcases and head for Rome? Milan? I hear Naples do a good pizza.'

In the last few hours, I've managed to forget about the entire flock of people who've been introduced to Gem-man. And now I have to face them. Pretend I'm okay, say, no worries, and chuckle or smile as we all have a good laugh at Gem-man. But what's the alternative? Tell them I felt hurt, that it was horrible?

I know if I said anything, Mum would be disappointed, as she hates any sign of tension, and Dad would pretend nothing has happened, and Lulu would declare I've ruined the entire wedding. And where would that leave me then?

'I'll just pretend nothing ever happened.' I know how it's going to go: I'm going to face everyone and smile. Back in Sydney, after this entire shitshow was over, I can collapse into my bed and cry a tornado, and then maybe I'll prick my hand on a loom and sleep for ever.

'What are you thinking about right now?'

God, nothing gets past him.

'A loom, if you must know.'

'Well, Sleeping Beauty, afraid you can't sleep for a hundred years. Maybe you'd feel better if you told Mia and Lulu how you felt—'

I sigh and give him a pointed look and, to his credit, he stops talking.

'So how about this boat cruise? Are we going?'

'Everyone on a tiny little ship in the middle of a harbour talking about how funny last night was? I'd be forced to jump off the side and swim for land.'

'Even if it's shark-infested?'

I laugh. 'I don't think anything would stop me.'

'I'd have to stop you then.'

I feel a warmth spread to my cheeks, images of him holding me back with his broad arms. For a split second I glance at him, and I can see his eyes locked on me. A moment of tension seems to simmer between us. Quickly, I look away.

He finally adds, 'Because if you drowned, who else would check the wedding centrepieces for floating dead fish?'

'Well, there'll be *doves* at the wedding.'

'Doves then.'

'I hope you're not suggesting that there will be *dead* doves; such a bad omen. Lulu will roll in her bridezilla casket.' I roll my eyes and we both laugh.

I hadn't thought that there was much chance that Weasel and I would get along. Or laugh together. Until now. It feels really nice.

I try and keep my voice steady. 'I guess it's the couples spa or we can just do our own thing.'

'I guess it's the spa,' Weasel says. 'Can't let down your mum and dad.'

Again I think about the fact that the spa requires us to be dressed in next to nothing. That makes me wonder what he might look like in his swimmers. Would he wear boardies? Or a Speedo? I hoped boardies. Budgie smugglers are just too, too ... *out in the open*. As if they announced, Here's my penis. With a thin bit of material on the top. What you going to do about it?

Not look, I tell myself, *definitely not look*.

He has a small smirk on his face. 'What are you Gemma-dreaming about right now? Because your cheeks are pink. I could swear ... are you blushing?'

'No,' I add hotly. 'Sick. Fever. Remember?'

He shoots me a look to say, *Yeah, right*, but thankfully lets it go.

He heads to the bathroom. The tap goes on as he washes his hands, and I hear him clear his throat. 'Uh, so this note in here...'

Oh bloody hell. The Adam List. My stomach drops.

'Is this...' He pokes his head out the bathroom door. 'Something we should talk about?' That cheeky little smile is back.

I'm blushing with embarrassment. 'It is not. Don't pry. No one likes a pryer.'

His smile is charming. 'Shall I just leave it there then?'

I stride into the bathroom, past him, grab the list off the mirror, and crumple it, putting it in the bin at the end of my bed. 'It was just a reminder of my very wonderful boyfriend, but I don't need the reminder, do you know why?'

'Because he's not that wonderful? Otherwise he'd be here.'

Ugh. That takes the wind out of my sails a bit. 'No, because it's in here.' I double-tap my heart for impact, but then realise how silly that feels, and how … I'm not sure it's true. He hasn't really been on my mind much in the last day.

Weasel raises his eyebrows. 'Is this the guy who told you emotions are just annoying things that get in the way?'

'I … uh…'

'And you say I don't have a heart…'

'Well, maybe … sometimes … it appears…'

'Like…'

I lie back on the bed. 'Fine. Like last night. I appreciate you looking after me. I am grateful.'

He grins. 'Good, because I was starting to think your plane behaviour was normal.'

I started to laugh. 'Whatever do you mean? I was the perfect companion.'

He raises his eyebrows once more. 'You wore pyjamas in the business class lounge with a gummy bear in your hair. I thought you were going to get deported.'

I pretend to be gutted. 'Shunned from all fashionable events for ever. Whatever would one do on race day?'

'Please, you'd never be invited in the first place.'

'Because they'd seen me hanging out with you?'

I have to admit, this banter makes me fizz from the inside, like parts of me I didn't know existed have come alive.

'I put your brazenly awful behaviour down to the fact

you had zero sleep and you gorged on too much red wine and pudding.'

'Wait, how do you know about the pudding?'

'I know everything.' Weasel grins.

'Stalker.'

'Pyjama-wearer.'

'Well, if we're talking about bad behaviour, can I just say the last four months, at work, well … it hasn't been the ultimate work experience.'

'Not a platinum VIP Chief Editing experience?'

'Not even bronze. Actually, going to work with you is like receiving a lump of coal for Christmas.'

He laughs and I catch him looking over at me, those arctic blue eyes searing into my soul.

'You tired, little viper?'

'Yeah. Maybe.' *No, not with you beside me so close.*

He rolls towards me and perches on his elbow. And now he's even closer, and I can hardly breathe. I refuse to look at him. He pushes a lock of hair off my forehead, and I hate that he's done that, because now I've felt his fingers on me, warm and soft, large and protective. I will replay it later, even though I don't want to. 'And now?'

'Now.' I can only repeat what he's said because my brain is mush.

'What are we doing?'

I don't know if he means at eleven in the morning, or *What are we doing, us laying here?* So all I can do is shrug. His eyes linger on my eyes, my lips, my hips.

I have to dig deep, from the deepest parts of me, some sort of willpower, because frankly, I have a boyfriend waiting for me at home, and our life is … well, it's *perfectly fine*. I refuse to get caught up in the whirlwind of weddings and cocktails and a handsome man.

'I don't know. Pretending to be a couple. Going to a wedding tomorrow.' It's the right thing to say, but it leaves me feeling confused.

I can't read his expression. 'You know, I thought, after last night, we could call a truce.'

'A truce?'

'Yeah, maybe it's time for us to start to actually get along. Be friends. Stop fighting or play-fighting. And actually enjoy our time in Italy. We could even have fun with this fake relationship, give Aunty Janice and your family what they want, proper The One stuff.'

I make a motion of slitting my throat. 'You're one to talk about The One. That's so not you.'

'You're right, it's not me.' He grins.

'Thank God.'

'But I do know how to be a great boyfriend. Promise. I'm not emotionless.'

It's a dig at Adam, and I know it. The temperature cools between us. I take the chance to slide off the bed and grab a can of Coke from the mini fridge.

'So you actually can have feelings for people despite not having a heart? What a medical miracle.'

He laughs and sits up on the bed. 'You'll be amazed at what I can do.'

There it is again. The womaniser in him, the flirt. But that stuff doesn't work on me, and he knows it.

I suppose it wouldn't hurt my ego if Weasel, this

handsome man, were to pretend to love me. I would have second thoughts, if he wasn't a player, but I'm sure he probably does this all the time, so it's not as though this will end up being tense or weird. I was going to ask him, but think better of it. I don't need to know his sordid history or body count, which is likely to be in the hundreds.

Taking my silence for hesitation, Weasel picks up the side of the white sheet and waves it a bit.

'A-ha, so you're surrendering?'

'Not exactly, just making your bed.' He winks. 'Say the word, Gemma.'

'The word?'

'Truce.'

I pause as one last part of me hesitates, still not sure I should give in. My brain quickly analyses the last twenty-four hours. He started the edits and looked after me. He was probably up half the night at least. And maybe he doesn't want my career to be over, given that he seemed genuinely offended I even suggested that.

'Gemma, c'mon. We could just enjoy the next two days: a bit of wine, great cheese, some wonderful Italian vineyards... We could even take part in one of those Gemma daydreams you seem to have ... which is probably you on a Vespa, imagining you're Audrey Hepburn in Italy in the Fifties.'

Damn, he's good.

'You forgot the scarf.'

He smiles. 'So? Let's be the best couple, better than any other couple in any book we've read.'

'Better than Henry and Claire in *The Time Traveller's Wife*?'

'A thousand times. We'll blow them out of the water.'

I feel part of me relenting; I have to admit it has appeal. 'I suppose it would be easier. But NO kissing or … bits. I am, after all, in a committed, *real* relationship.'

'No kissing,' he readily agrees. 'Believe me, Gem, that's not difficult.'

I don't know why, but that statement slightly bothered me. 'Fine, truce.'

'We can't really go around saying truce. Maybe we need a code word?'

'How about "Weasel"?'

'A hard no on that one. C'mon, we're editors, this should be easy.'

'Pineapple,' I said, thinking of my favourite pizza topping. 'Besides, I think I read somewhere it's the safe word a lot of people use in sex dungeons.'

He laughs. 'Pineapple it is.'

He smiles at me, then looks down at his cup of instant coffee. 'Right, well, I'm going to hit the gym. Do you want to come?'

Him saying that feels … *nice*. A warmth spreads across my chest and I gather myself. 'Why would I want that?' I tease.

'Now, now, Gemma. Testing the truce boundaries so soon?' he says with a large, gorgeous grin on his face. My new … *friend*.

'Fine, fine,' I say, smiling but pretending to grumble as he walks towards my hotel door. 'I take it back.'

He pauses at the door, a teasing look on his face. 'Say it, Gemma.'

'Pineapple,' I shout. There's no response, so I call out, 'Your turn!'

'Pineapple,' he calls back before the door slams shut, and I can hear him laughing to himself and that makes me smile.

Chapter Twenty-Two

As soon as Ben leaves, I go downstairs to the hotel's small bistro, La Tavola. Painted on the walls are the most majestic scenes of rural Italy: murals of lavender tufts, and small cottages and the hills of Tuscany. I close my eyes and inhale the scent of fresh garlic frying in the pan. I order red wine, which comes in a long-stemmed glass. It's not even midday, but I don't care. Soon my food arrives piping hot, big billowy gnocchi dumplings, with lashings of pesto oil and parmesan. Two slices of crusty oven-baked bread. The food is heaven after not eating properly for a day, and I find myself eating way more than I should. It's comforting and grounding in exactly the way I needed it to be.

After lunch, I go outside for a stroll, following the tree-lined driveway down to the rolling vineyards. The vines are in full bloom, little white flowers marking each row. Over on the next hill, there are cute lines of olive trees. I imagine myself buying a house here overlooking the hills, a little shack even. How much would it cost? Could I renovate something, breathe life back into it, eat olives at night under the stars, have breakfast on the terrace every morning, and just write?

With only two days left in Italy, every moment counts to relax. I take a deep breath, slip my shoes off and sink my feet deep into the earth, which is warm like oven-baked bread. My phone vibrates. Hannah.

'I'm *dying* to know how it's going!' she almost screams.

I fill her in on the Gem-man debacle and she has a very Hannah response.

'That is horrible. I hope someone told them to fuck right off. I would have if I were there.'

When I tell her about Ben suggesting I say something and then offering to do it himself, Hannah has a very non-Hannah response.

'Hmmm…'

'Hmm what?'

'I like him.'

'*What*?'

'I like his vibe. Radical honesty. I'm gonna try that.'

I laugh so hard I almost snort. 'You already do.'

'Do I?' she says wryly. 'Well, this is certainly very different from the guys you're normally with.'

Here she goes. 'You mean Adam.'

'I do. He wouldn't say a thing for you. If a dinosaur came up and started growling like it was going to tear you apart, he'd say something like "Fear is just a state of mind".'

I laugh. 'It's not that bad.'

'Well, I like this Ben. Tell me more about him.'

I can't bring myself to tell her that I'm having thoughts

about him that I shouldn't be having, considering I have a boyfriend. Surely it's just a silly crush. Like when actors pretend to be in love, sometimes they get confused, and start to actually think they are. Instead, I tell Han about how he looked after me when I was sick, and helped with the name tags.

'We've called a truce, but still, I can't shake the feeling he was talking about me when he said it's over.'

'You don't know that for sure until you ask him what he meant. And since he's been promoted, what would he gain from that?'

I ponder that, and pause at the top of a row of vines, extending my fingers to trace a fresh green leaf. 'Maybe...'

'Definitely. Just tell him you overheard him and ask him exactly what he meant. And then you can know for sure where you stand.'

When I put down the phone, I think about what she's just said. Could I tell him I've heard those exact words? Just ask him openly? And would he give me the truth, even if it meant telling me that yes, he said that?

I don't want to think about it, and there's something else niggling me, heavy on my heart like guilt. So I call Adam and confess about Weasel faux-kissing me. Radical fucking honesty.

He laughs. 'That's fine, Gem.'

'It *is*?' I ask in disbelief, because if the shoe had been on the other foot, I doubt I would have been so generous.

'It means nothing, so of course it's okay.'

I'm flummoxed. Not even a shred of worry.

'Okay, well ... that's great.'

For a while we chat about his ceiling (he's chuffed how clean it is) and his excitement about his new job, and he asks me about property prices in Italy because he's read they are going down.

I feel a swell of hope. 'Oh! Are you thinking a holiday villa in the hills with a large outdoor courtyard?' Already I'm picturing us exploring sweet secret towns and eating a mound of cheese a day.

'Not at all. Too many repairs. I was thinking we could start to invest in a small unit when the time is right. Build our property portfolio *internationally*.'

He's right. I got carried away. But still, it's a fabulous feeling, that I could one day *live* here.

When we hang up, I call Ruby as I walk back to my hotel room.

'ANNNNND?' Ruby squeals down the phone. 'HOW IS IT?'

'It's weird.'

'I'm so happy to hear from you. And that you're still talking to me.'

I couldn't be mad at her, not even for a second. 'It seems so.'

'I was beside myself wondering what you'd think.'

'Well, I do want to know why on earth you chose him.'

'Ben overheard me on the phone, trying to convince Craig, and he asked what was going on. So I just confessed. He has this way of looking intensely at you.'

Don't I know *that* look. Just thinking about it makes my body shiver a bit and break out in goosebumps.

'And he seemed interested in going to Italy. Kept talking

about an author he was keen to sign. How cool is that? An Italian author. Oh, and he did say something about the money.'

I feel strange about that, that maybe he was only here for the five hundred I'd offered. For some reason my heart drops.

'But isn't he lovely?' She giggles. 'So maybe it was weird initially but a good plan in the end?'

'Good is a stretch. I still don't know. I don't trust him yet, but we've called a truce, so at least we are being polite to each other.'

'I've been pulling out tarot cards, and you'll never guess what I got. Ace of Cups. New beginnings. And Two of Cups. Lovers' meeting! Cups means EMOTIONS,' she tells me as though I should know already.

I don't feel so sure. 'I hardly think that.'

Ruby's voice takes a more serious tone. 'But he is quite funny. I know you've never taken to him, but the rest of us think he's actually lovely.'

'You do?' I'm amazed. 'Even Gavin who he can't remember how many kids he has?'

Ruby sighs slightly. 'Yeah, I admit he can come across a bit blunt and direct, like he doesn't care, but he shows he does in other ways. Like the time he helped Gavin get all his edits in by pulling an all-nighter.'

'He did?' My mouth drops open.

'Yep. And what about the time he found your files and put them on your desk, the ones you looked for for ages and no one else helped you with?'

I collapse onto the hotel bed. '*He* did?'

'He did.' I can almost hear her nodding emphatically.

'I thought that was you.'

'Nope. Him.'

'Then why did I think he was such a … monster?'

'Because he's competitive, because he's successful, because he's kinda your rival. You're both really good at your job. And he banters, and maybe you don't like his sense of humour because it seems mean. But really he's all bark, no bite.'

My world is spinning. I feel giddy. It's true. Weasel is lovely. Weasel helps people. Weasel is all bark, no bite.

Ruby continues. 'From what I know, he thinks just like you do. He loves books. He loves words. He has ambitions.'

'And supermodels,' I say, trying to think of anything that would bring him down a peg or two.

'He hangs around with them a bit, sure. But he's just a person who likes, uhh … pretty things.'

I wrinkle my nose in disgust. 'You mean superficial.'

'Not exactly. Just … I'm sure no man would complain if his social group was full of supermodels.'

'I prefer men with brains. Nerdy, intelligent brains. Anyway, I don't know why we're talking about this. I have Adam. It's not like this is *anything*.'

'Are you sure? I mean … TWO OF CUPS.'

'A fluke,' I say. 'I'm not actually going to start believing the cards now.'

'Hold on.' Suddenly she gasps. 'Oh God, I just asked about your current situation and turned over the Ten of Cups.'

'And?' I say, leaning forward and cupping my hand

around the phone so I can hear her more clearly. 'This means?'

'God, I hate to say it, it sounds so cliché.'

'But?'

'It means happily ever after.'

'Ohhh, I get it. With me and Adam clearly. We're serious, and considering buying a house.' *The Adam List*, I think fondly.

'Okay, sure.' Ruby doesn't sound convinced at all. 'I could pull a card for you and Adam specifically…'

'No, that's fine.' I don't want to know.

Then I look at the clock, almost two p.m. 'Rubes, I have to go. Have some massage spa thing.'

'Oh, sounds amazing.'

I put down the phone and think about what I've just discovered, which is making my head spin. Weasel is lovely. Weasel helped out. Weasel isn't a weasel, apparently, at all. I feel like someone has just told me the earth is flat, and not a sphere, and everything I've ever known was a lie.

My mind is reeling, and I want to digest everything, but I have to go. Spa time.

Chapter Twenty-Three

The giant wooden door swings open. Inside, the smooth polished sandstone walls give relief from the summer heat gathering outside.

Down the long corridor is a large window showcasing a gorgeous view of the vineyards. The spa smells delightfully like green mint and cucumber. Soft piano and panpipes sound across the grand reception area, and in the middle a majestic stone fountain is trickling. Another minute in here and I'll need to pee. In a corner is a white alabaster woman's breast, a perfect Renaissance statue.

Ivy hangs from the eaves, as though Greek goddesses were about to come out and anoint my forehead, and I'm inching close enough to see if the ivy is real, when I'm greeted by a tall Amazonian blonde woman. Talia leads me down the white stone corridor to a large circular domed area with a spa pool. I breathe a sigh of relief. We'll be with other people. In swimming costumes. Thank goodness. She offers me a champagne and excitedly I take a large sip.

Right behind me the doors swing open and Weasel walks through. 'Well, hello.' He nods as Talia offers him a glass of champagne. 'Is this where the damage gets done?'

I look at him, shocked. Damage? 'Keep it together, Thomas Ben. I don't think violence is the answer.'

He whispers, 'I meant the damage of us seeing each other in bathing suits. It's kinda like a point of no return, isn't it?'

I find myself looking away and concentrating on the fountain, trying desperately not to think of him half-naked. Talia peers at us strangely, but continues her spiel. 'We have five emotional showers, a thermal pool and a series of couples treatment rooms.'

Weasel raises his eyebrows. 'I'm sorry, emotional showers?'

'Yes, to balance. Standing in them is a magical moment that frees the mind and brings together the five senses in a "water jet", with different colours, smells and sounds that cuddle and wrap around the body, while instilling a strong vitality.'

She gives us a warm smile. 'But first, the mud!'

She wheels in a giant terracotta pot of mud. 'We leave you here, to prepare.'

I look at her and then the mud. What type of preparation is needed?

Sensing my confusion, she adds, 'Be free. Naked. This is a place for the couple to just enjoy each other, no clothes.'

God, the Europeans are always so free. She's literally leaving us in here, with a 'go ahead, have sex' approach.

My face flushes red. She winks and leaves us. Now

we're alone. Properly. Without most of our clothes. I don't look at him and that is an achievement. Instead, I look at the big vat of mud between us.

'So, you first?' Weasel looks at me.

'I'm doing this in my swimmers!'

'If you want.'

I clear my throat. 'Well. Yes. I want.'

I take off my bathrobe and hang it on a hook. He takes off his too, and wow, the guy really is *yoked*. His shoulders are well defined – okay, they're like rocks that some Italian sculptor has chiselled – and his chest is so smooth, I immediately want to run my hands over it, down to where his muscles dip in that familiar sixpack, a mountain of muscle that falls away into his boardshorts. He seems to be staring at me too, in my black bikini. It's string, but still conservative enough. I may be slightly skinny in my legs, but I'm aware my hips widen, and then my stomach curves in, something past boyfriends always seemed to love.

I feel a bit nervy thinking about this giant vat of mud. 'We could just do it ourselves, like mud ourselves up?'

'We could.' Weasel winks. 'Or…'

I try to slow the hammering of my heart. Keep my voice even. 'Yep, let's just do it ourselves. Then we can help each other with hard-to-reach places, like our backs.'

'Right.' His voice is hoarse. Huskier.

He nods and then bends down to pick up some mud, and puts it on his feet. I try to bend down and pick up a handful, but the thing is, the mud is heavy and clay-like, and it needs two hands, but bending over makes it slippery and it seems like an accident waiting to happen. I drop the mud back in the vat.

He waits until my eyes met his. 'This would probably be easier if we helped each other.'

'Riiiight.'

'In a very respectful pineapple way of course.'

We both laugh, which eases some of the tension.

'Okay then. A pineapple non-romantic, friends-helping-friends mud-up kinda way.'

He steps towards the big vat. 'I'll go first.' He takes a handful of mud, and then looks at it, and then me, as if he's unsure where to start. 'Feet?'

'Yes! Good idea!' I say as the colour blooms on my cheeks. Feet are safe. Feet are ugly. I'm suddenly glad I haven't shaved that little patch of hair that demands to be known on each of my big toes. Perhaps that will dispel any strange feelings, which is *exactly* the plan here.

Weasel practically dumps two big handfuls of mud on my feet. It's warm and wet and oozy. It feels delicious and gross at the same time. 'Moist,' I say, laughing, because who likes that word?

Next he crouches down and slips another handful of mud on my shins and calves. The warm sloppiness is like a giant hug, and it feels lovely. I take a deep breath in and relax a bit. Next, he does the knees then he suddenly skips the thighs, and he puts a glob on my stomach, almost throwing it at me.

'Ouch! Unnecessary!'

'Sorry, I just didn't know if I should be … you know.'

'I'm sorry, has Mr Radical Honesty lost his ability?'

'I just don't know if the lady would like the gentleman to get too near her nether regions.'

'Disgusting. I wish you had lost your ability to find those words.'

'So?' He's standing there with a pile of mud in his hands. 'Am I?'

I'm suddenly a bit shy, even if this is just us helping each other out. 'Do whatever you feel is…'

'No, Gemma. I want you to say the truth. What do you want?'

I cringe a bit inside, then shut my eyes, so I don't have to see his response, and I mutter, 'Okay, put it everywhere.'

Suddenly I feel the warmth of his breath on my knee. We've gone from friends to … to *this*. Everything slows down. He gathers more mud and slides it up both legs. My heart flutters. He reaches my thighs, his fingers slowing to a crawl as he reaches the outline of my bikini bottoms.

God.

My breath catches in my throat. My heart skips a beat. I look down at his hands and wonder what it's like to be one of those supermodels who hold his wide, masculine hands. I wonder what they talk about. I wonder if he massages them like *this*.

This is all going too far, too fast. But I couldn't stop it even if I wanted to. Every single muscle wants to be touched, to be massaged, to melt.

I close my eyes again, my heart in my throat. Slowly, lightly, he covers my bikini bottoms, his fingers confident. My body shivers in a chill. He senses my goosebumps, rubs a spot on my hip with his thumb.

His fingers brush slowly up my skin and my stomach flips. Hard. Twice. So much so I'm sure he can see it. *Stop giving meaning to this*, I tell myself, *it's just a massage between, um*, friends.

His strong, warm hands move up and down the curves between my ribs and hip.

My heart hammers. God, the man is kneading just under my bikini top like I'm dough. His fingers graze the bottom layer of string and I feel an urgent desire to lean into his hard rock wall of muscle. As if he can tell I'm about to overheat, he steps back.

I can hear him getting more mud from the vat before his hands continue to softly massage the mud across my arms and shoulders, and it gives me chills.

'You can open your eyes now,' he tells me, and when I do he's standing above me. We lock gazes. His eyes are crystal blue, but his pupils are larger. A muscle flinches in his square jaw.

'I need more permission.' Was his voice always this deep?

And I know he means can he cover my breasts in mud, and *who am I kidding*, I wouldn't mind it. In fact, a shiver runs across my body.

A corner of his lips tugs. 'Normally I take control, but now...'

It's the word *control* that does it.

Yes. Bottom line, I don't want this to stop. I squeeze my toes. A little shiver runs across my stomach. As soon as I say, 'Okay' he looks at me with a sense of heat.

'Really?' He lays it down like a challenge, and there's a

primal sense about him I've never seen before. His body tightens. A pulse. Electric.

'*Really*. In a pineapple way.'

His hands smear more warm mud up my arms again, then down my stomach, everywhere but my breasts. My eyelids drift shut. I'm being lulled into relaxing and I feel like rubber.

Then he waits. He waits like a painter staring at a canvas. He gathers more mud. He's teasing me and I know it.

Everything slows down. He takes a small amount with his right hand and starts smoothing it over my neck, then downwards, until he reaches the line of my bikini top, two small triangle pieces. My heart is pounding because never did I think this would happen, and it feels ... *good*.

He hesitates for a second, and I think he's lost his nerve. But when I open my eyes, he looks completely confident, and with one finger he trails slowly over each collarbone, like he's painting.

'That's an S,' he said tracing it again, lightly. Each time the shape gets bigger, and further down towards the top of my bikini.

One of his fingers accidentally catches the side of my string bikini at the neck. And for a second a small part of my white breast is exposed to the warm air. I expect him to be apologetic, or embarrassed, or at least make a 'shit, sorry' face, but he doesn't. Weasel is all confidence. The tension between us skyrockets. My entire body tingles. A surge of heat shoots inside me. My pulse skyrockets. My heart is pounding. My nipples are hard points. In short, my body seems to know more than I do, because I can barely register what's happening.

Just then the door swings open and Talia strides in, and part of me is glad, and another wants to shout OUT.

She looks at Weasel. 'But you're not even mudded up?' She looks down at the vat and then at me, as if I've failed mud duties.

'Uh…' Because right now my words aren't working. My pulse still skitters in my ears. 'Could you help?'

I need some time to get my breathing back to normal because my skin is still sensitive, aroused, and I can barely look at Ben. I manage just a quick glance, as Talia slops the mud onto him in the most unromantic way, giving me time to take a deep breath, and cool my goddamn jets.

Thankfully, we're directed into two separate shower rooms for the emotional shower. There are soft lights flashing and five shower heads against my body and it's lovely and warm. As the mud drips off I slowly regulate myself back to normal.

Talia pops her head in. 'Okay, bikini off, we will wash for you.'

'Oh, okay.' I slip it off and hand it to her in the barely lit room and cover myself with a towel.

'Now, steam! Open the pores and the chakras.'

God, she sounds like Ruby. She beckons for me to follow her into a side room, and I'm thankful no one else is there because she instructs me to hang up the towel and go inside completely naked.

When I open the glass door, the entire room is filled with

the sizzle of steam, the smell of lemon and honey. I look at Talia, feeling a little unsure.

'I come and get you in twenty minutes. Relax and enjoy.'

I nod and step in. The floor is completely moist, and hot. I let the door close gently behind me. I can't see a thing through the thick fog. I stretch out my hands hoping to find something, but I haven't a clue how this room is set up, how big it is, or if there are seats.

'Hello?' I say gently, but there's no response.

From the door – the only thing that I can see – I trace with my hands around the right side, until my legs bump into what feels like a tiled seat. I ease myself down onto it, and hear the gloop! slap! of my thighs as they stick to the wet tiles. For a second I feel a little rigid. I'm naked, and alone. But the heat feels nice. After a few breaths, I find myself relaxing, leaning back and tilting my head up, no longer worried that I can barely see my hands in front of my face.

I start to focus on breathing in and out. I listen to the drip, drip of the condensation falling from the roof, loud as footsteps. Giant drops, landing in water puddles.

Finally, a moment to myself. I take a deep breath and sink further back onto the warm tiles and let the faint scent of sweet honey open up my pores ... or whatever it does. Weasel and I had a quick faux kiss. Then some stupid mud stuff. That's all. Weasel is a smoking hot handsome man; of course any girl in this position would have a stomach flip and briefly feel things that they don't *actually* feel.

I was just caught up in the moment. I take a long deep breath of honey-lemon air. Then I try one of those little oms or humming-chanting that people do to relax, and find it does actually relax me even more. As I'm finishing up an om, I hear a click.

'Hello?' I ask into the fog. But there's no response.

But there's something else I can hear, other than the constant drip, drip of the water. A slooshing sound of sorts, as if water is coming in from somewhere. I stand up and step cautiously towards the opposite corner where the sound is coming from. I hit something wet and slippery and hard. I know what it is. Almost immediately.

It's another person's body. A naked body. A naked male's body, slippery, and warm.

As soon as we both realise this, it all happens so quickly. We both jerk away, we turn, then we're falling.

I land on warm skin. My body smooshed against theirs. *Everything* is touching, our feet entwined.

The stranger exhales, winded from smacking against the tiles. 'Jesus.'

And I know in an instant, it's Ben.

I quickly try and untangle myself, but without sight it's hard. We both try and twist our bodies to the same side and that just makes more of us slide together. My legs straddle him. I can feel *everything*.

'I'm going to the right! The right!' he says urgently.

'Ohhhh God!' I say, trying to scramble to my left. 'Your right? I don't even know where that is.'

'Gemma?' Suddenly he stops urgently trying to move me. He takes a deep breath. 'Just stay where you are.'

His warm fingers brush down each side of my body, and I get chills. His strong hands, now on both my hips, give a small push to lift me up. I let out a gasp of surprise and try to use my feet to find the floor, but they slip on the puddles, which means I overbalance and fall back onto his body.

He groans softly. 'Don't…' It sounds like a warning.

We pause for a second. I try and keep my full weight from lying on him, so I hold myself rigid, but even then, my body, honestly, is responding in ways that confuse me and I have a growing desire to stay right here.

I can't move, or think.

Finally, I grip his shoulders with my hands and lift my chest up a little, so he can't feel my breasts on him. I blush, and I'm glad he can't see my face right now. I suck in several deep breaths and try to keep calm.

He confidently finds the back of my head with his hand, and I think he's going to pull me in and kiss me.

Instead, he whispers in that self-assured tone. 'So … hey, if you wanted to get close to me you just had to ask.'

Jesus. I suck in a breath. Everything about this feels dangerous. Even in the thick steam, where I still can't see a thing, I'm painfully aware that my lips are inches, maybe less, from his.

'Do you want to get up?' I can hear the teasing in his tone.

I don't know what I want.

Instead, I say in the steadiest voice I can manage, 'Yes, obviously.'

'Just relax,' he says confidently. He lifts me up, this time easily, his hands on my hips until I can push myself back into a strange downward dog. And then I walk backwards on my hands and feet, until I'm clear.

I can barely think. Can't speak. My heart is pounding. Ben covering me in mud, and now this... I don't know how to stop these things that my body wants to do.

I quickly jump away from Ben and find my way to the glass doors, which I yank open. 'Enjoy the steam,' I say. And before I second-guess myself, I walk towards the showers and turn one on, as cold as it will go.

Chapter Twenty-Four

Cold showers. That is the answer to all of these ridiculous feelings and thoughts inside my head. I try not to think about what just happened and instead retreat to my hotel room, forgoing the couples massage.

I pace up and down asking the same question over and over: what just happened?

I really have no fucking idea. And no amount of flashbacks, over-analysis, or Venn diagramming is going to help me decipher this strange afternoon.

We'll have to talk about this, yes? Or do we just both ignore it, and continue to act normal? God, it's a freak-show kinda world.

Just in case, I choose the frumpiest maroon dress I can find in my suitcase. Very librarian. Wait, is librarian sexy? I think it is, so instead I select the nightie dress, and even consider leaving a roller in my hair. Does this erase the fact that just an hour ago, my naked breasts were on his chest and it made my body tingle?

By the time I'm ready, it's almost four-thirty p.m. and we have to be in the bar, on strict Lulu orders, at least ten minutes before five p.m. for this big reveal, whatever it is. I, myself, need a lot of alcohol, because I just felt Ben's penis against my right thigh, and it was *not* small.

STOP IT.

Inside the hotel's classy wine bar, a small crowd of the wedding party and family is gathering. The pyramid of champagne glasses is tempting. Big armfuls of stunning blue hydrangeas, picked fresh from the garden, line the room.

Next to the bar, Chip and Lulu look almost identical in their nautical luxury clothes. If I tried to pull off that outfit, I'd look like a tennis coach, not someone who should be laid out on a sundeck asking for more champagne with their caviar.

As I wave, Lulu gives a look of disgust. She goes to the trouble of looping the silk scarf from her neck around her nose and mouth, as though just being in the same room as me could make her sick.

Despite her makeshift mask, I can still tell she's scowling as her eyes flash me daggers. Still, I have to get this over with, so I take a deep breath and walk towards them. *Remember, brides get like this. Just apologise and move on.*

'I'm sorry,' I say with a tentative smile, and even though something in me is itching to say, *Are you sorry too?* I shove that inner voice down, and smile harder.

But Lulu just squints slightly and I know underneath the scarf her mouth is scowling. 'Gemma, it was so inappropriate, and so embarrassing.'

'I know.'

'I had to apologise to the mayor. I think you should too.'

'I will. I didn't plan on getting sick. It just happened.' And then I feel like I'm grovelling, yet again, and I hate myself for a second. 'Let me go and find the mayor, make my amends.'

I find the mayor, and I am charming Nelly Nicepants, before slipping in a 'Did you see that girl last night getting sick in the pot plant?', and when she says she did, I confess it was me. I apologise, fall on my own sword and say I'd had a twenty-four-hour stomach bug, but it has passed. But then she looks at me as though I were still contagious, backs away and says she needs another drink, even though her vodka on the rocks is still three quarters full.

Speaking of drinks, I need one too. I take a quick glance around the room but Weasel isn't here. Thank God. I scull an entire coupe of champagne, and manage a good go at another before a deep, suggestive voice resonates right behind me.

'Gemma.'

I inhale the smell of him, cedar and warmth. He steps around so he's at my side, facing me. This close he towers over me. I'm already slightly tipsy, but seeing him again is stone-cold sobering. His hair is perfect, waving and with volume that comes without the need for hairspray or gel. He hasn't shaved and the darker stubble accentuates his jawline. He's so goddamn hot. He's wearing a white polo and navy shorts, and I wonder if his clothes are brand-new. Everything about him always seems so polished.

'Good to see you ... clothed.' A small hint of a smile plays at the corners of his smooth, full lips.

I feel my pulse quicken and my cheeks already blushing. Not knowing how to respond to the reminder of being naked and pressed against him, I take a long gulp of champagne, and put the glass on the table.

When I fail to respond, I feel his eyes watch my cheeks redden. 'Are you thinking about our little rendezvous earlier?'

Thankfully, just then Marla saunters past. 'Oh Ahhhdam,' she coos. 'I heard you did the name tags? How thoughtful.'

'It was mostly Gemma.' Weasel glances at me.

She turns as if seeing me for the first time. 'Oh, Gemma. You came. How...' She doesn't finish the sentence because I can see her eyes trail across Weasel's smooth chest and perfect abdomen. She is undressing him with her eyes and purposefully leaning forward as if offering Weasel a glimpse of her cleavage. A strong wave of nausea flows through me.

Even Lulu, walking towards us, glares at Marla like she's out of her mind. Lulu catches my eye, and for a second, she gives a mini shrug, as if to say, *Mothers*.

For a glorious moment, I think, *Yes, there's hope!* I want to turn around and say to Weasel, 'See, there is *good* in everyone; we can all *connect*. We are sisters.'

But then Lulu sniffs as she waits for the waiter to pop open a new bottle of champagne, and looks at me, and I can tell what's coming next is going to be something nasty. She always does this when she sends little barbs my way, and my toes curl in trepidation inside my two-inch heels. 'You know, you guys seem … perfect together.'

My heart skips a beat. 'We *do*?'

She tilts her head to the side. 'I never thought I could picture it at first. But there's definitely something there.'

I'm stunned into silence.

I hear Weasel say breezily, 'You're right. There is.' And I can't tell if he's being facetious. Casually, he drapes his arm around me, so it rests on my hip, warm and heavy, and pulls me into him, so close our entire bodies are touching. The way he looks at me, adoring, is exactly the way a loving boyfriend should. His act is so convincing, I feel a buzzing underneath my skin. I can't hide the feel-good factor that flutters in my chest.

Help me.

Lulu turns to me and says with a slight hint of confusion, 'I like him.' As if she'd been sure until that moment she wouldn't like anything to do with me.

'Yep, good,' I manage to say, because my brain is racing and Weasel's hand is still resting hotly on my hip. He squeezes me quickly, a sly grin on his face, and I try not to yelp. I take my drink and almost down it in one large gulp.

Lulu grabs Chip's arm and is about to head over to her girlfriends when she turns around to add, 'I hope you're not thinking about coming to the wedding rehearsal tonight? I can't imagine how it would look if everyone was talking about you getting sick in a plant, rather than focusing on the preparation. But then, I suppose it won't matter as you're not in the bridal party anyway. We can find someone else to do the music.'

God. Is that what my role was tonight? Delegated DJ? I could say so many things, but I choose to keep the peace, like any big sister would. I close my eyes, take a quick deep breath or two and go to my happy place. For a second I feel I have nailed life because I feel infinitely better, but it also could just be the chilled champagne in my hand. 'Sure, okay.'

'But you do have to come to the lawn for the big surprise.' Lulu squeezes Chip's arm, and they smile triumphantly at each other. 'A very big surprise.' Lulu turns and says to Weasel, 'You can come too' in a tone that suggests she's just given him access to the most prestigious club.

'Well, thanks.' He seems amused at her offer, but thankfully she doesn't notice.

Marla leaves in a shroud of musky perfume, and Lulu and Chip descend onto the lawn to prep for the big surprise.

Once they've left, Weasel gives me a mystified look. 'Um, excuse me?'

'You're excused, Satan.'

Weasel turns to face me. 'Seriously, you've got to be kidding.'

I look at him wide-eyed. 'The lawn surprise?'

'Not that. What Lulu just said.'

'Well, yeah, but she's a bride and it's her wedding—' I shrug.

He cuts me off. 'That's what you are? Bunting and music?'

'I may also be a side act too; I can do a mean trapeze

show. We did it once for a Christmas event at work. I even attempted a somersault dismount, I'll have you know. Didn't go well. Landed weirdly on my shoulder in the net, but still.'

But he doesn't smile. 'She didn't even apologise for last night. Did you want me to say something?'

I laugh. 'Are you feeling swoony? Protective? Getting on your horse to come and save the day?'

'No, I just… Why don't you say something?'

He doesn't get it. 'You think the worst of everyone, don't you?'

'And you always think the best of everyone. So, you find yourself in situations like this. Not saying anything, when you should. And the Gem I've gotten to know here is so much more than that.'

He leaves that last sentence hanging in the air. I'm not sure how to respond. But I'm in no mood to be intrigued.

'Well, *you* keep people at a distance. And that means you'll probably end up alone and sad, like a little … crab … a hard shell to crack.'

He gives a wry smile. 'A *crab*?'

I shrug. It wasn't my best. 'I'm still suffering from post-fever brain delirium.'

'Well, I think you shouldn't always think the best of people. People can be shitty. Exhibit A.' He points towards the ballroom. 'You have to be cautious. And you can't always keep the peace.'

'Ha.' The thought of him teaching me something feels ludicrous. In fact, it irritates me.

'Just … say something. Stick up for yourself.'

I step away from him. 'Well, maybe *you* could learn some things too, like this concept of being considerate, and compassionate. Besides, I like everything to be peaceful. This whole thing will blow over soon, and I want them to be happy.'

'At the cost of your own happiness?'

I go to open my mouth but I don't know what to say. He has a point. This nutter has a goddamn point.

'I don't need your help,' I announce proudly. Good sisters stay in their lane. They support, they cajole, they do what is asked, what's expected. But how could I expect him to know this? He's not a girl, not a sister, and not at his family's wedding.

'Well, I can, you know, say something. You can even blame it on me.'

'This princess, is fine.' I winked at him. 'Abort that horse mission.'

Twenty minutes later, the concierge ushers the families outside for the big reveal.

Lulu has pulled out all the stops, but this one is another level of crazy.

On the bottom lawn, near a long path (which I now understand is an airstrip), is a small plane about to take the Evans and Montague families on a scenic flight.

We're about to experience Italy by the skies, and God love her, she's even managed to get the pilot to come out and meet us, carrying a *Lulu and Chip's Wedding* banner.

I'm almost convinced she thinks she's the President of the United States. Mr Montague claps everyone on the back – that's the kinda guy he is, a tall, silver-haired gentleman, who swills whiskey and stands in libraries and claps people on the back. I bet he even calls them 'old boy'.

He claps Weasel on the back, and for once cool-as-hell Weasel splutters.

'You all right son?' Mr Montague's voice booms out, so everyone looks at Weasel.

'Fine.' Weasel nods quickly.

'He does look a little pale.' That's Lulu, and if one should know pale, it's her.

'No, he's just a vampire,' I joke, and then think about him nibbling my neck and I have to scurry my thoughts somewhere else.

'Hi, Mr Montague, we haven't officially met. I'm Gemma,' I said, feeling like I'm back at school.

'Philip,' he booms before moving on, and I think, *He should be American*. And have paddocks, or an acreage down in Texas.

Weasel is peering at me. 'You have the look again. What are you thinking about?'

I'm trying not to directly look at his smooth lips, chiselled jaw, perfect face...

'He's an oil baron down in Texas,' I muse, tilting my head and looking at Mr Montague. 'One loaded shotgun and a world to take revenge against.'

Weasel gives a small laugh. 'I'm rather enjoying these Gemma daydreams.'

'It's how my mind works. Sometimes there's an entire movie in there.'

'Have you ever written them down?'

I'm about to say, *I do, I have, I did. I wrote about Italy once, about how food brings people together. No one liked it.* But this doesn't seem like the time to bring this up.

Everyone lines up to get onto the plane. Lulu saying dismally, 'God, it's much smaller than it looked in the photos.' I assume she'd pictured a private jet with champagne and here we are in a little twelve-seater with plastic arm rests.

Before I climb on, I lean in and apologise for my sister, but the pilot just smiles. Either he can't understand me, or they've paid through the nose for this. Both is my guess.

Weasel sits next to me, on the window side. We haven't been this close to each other since a few fateful hours ago during MudGate. Apparently armrests between seats aren't a thing in Italy, so he's almost touching me ankle to thigh, while completely pressed against me hip to arm. I do my best to ignore it, but his entire energy is like a heartbeat pounding next to me.

I'm about to break the ice, say something about being squished together as we die, when I turn towards him and realise he looks extremely uncomfortable. And pale. Much paler than he did outside.

Suddenly, he isn't at all like the suave guy he is in the boardroom, or the first night here on the plane, or in the ballroom. In fact, he's was looking positively nauseous.

'I don't feel great.' He's right; he doesn't look great either. He's sweating a lot on his forehead.

'I didn't realise being so close to me would make you so sick,' I joke.

'No, it's not that, it's…' He looks around. 'I'm just going to close my eyes for a second.'

He's almost shaking. 'What's going on?'

'I … I…'

I've never seen him like this. 'Do you have what I had the other night?'

He shakes his head.

'Then, what is it?'

Finally, he says in a small voice, 'I hate tiny planes.'

Oh.

I look around. This plane is indeed tiny, far from the airbus we flew in from Australia. This one is rickety with a tiny wheeze of an engine.

So, we have found something the infallible Weasel can't do. I want to feel smug about this. I want to feel smug as hell, because I love tiny planes. I love the excitement. The thrill when it gets a little bumpy, the feeling of the air rushing around us, dipping with the currents, but I can't.

I can't because Weasel isn't just work Weasel anymore. He's the guy who helped me when I was sick. And now it's my turn.

'Tiny planes are okay, and if we plummet to death, at least we're together.'

He gives me a pained look.

'No? Not funny?'

His face has a green tinge. 'Why can we see the pilot? There isn't even a door!'

'Okay, wait.' I dig around in my handbag and pull out

the two little bottles of white wine that I stashed in there, just in case. 'Scull them.'

This is a great time to joke about me being the Mary Poppins of alcohol but he doesn't. He looks panicked. His face is ghostly, a sheer white.

'You can do this.' I open the twist tops for him, and he takes the first one, then the second one, downing them in seconds.

Aunty Janice leans through the seats from behind us like a stealth ninja murderer and says, 'What a wonderful way to see Italy at night. We're apparently going to get so close to the Duomo we could land on it!'

'Great!' I'm excited but Weasel looks like he's going to pass out.

As the plane makes a tiny whirring start-up sound, Weasel looks as if he's forgotten how to swallow. He's lost all ability to be confident or charming. He breathes heavily, his chest going up and down. Part of me wants to put my hand on his chest, and reassure him, *It's okay, calm down.*

But I definitely don't do that.

The plane jets down the runway, and he clenches the plastic seat on either side. This is a proper phobia, and I've never seen someone so scared. As the plane lifts into the air, rattling a bit, he jams himself back in the seat, his eyes tightly shut.

Finally, when we level out, I look at him. 'Better?'

His eyes remain shut. 'Not until we land.'

'Why did you even come?'

He says quietly, 'Because you were.'

'I don't always need a chaperone, even amongst these lunatics.'

'No, because…' He can't finish it.

I say jokingly, 'Because you wanted to be *entertained*? Or because then I'll owe you? Hmm, which one…'

He takes a deep sigh. 'No. Maybe because you told me I shouldn't care just about myself, something about being nice, caring… Lame, right?' He focuses on breathing like he's at a Lamaze class.

My eyes widen. *He did this for me?* From the look on his face I suspect, despite his radical honesty, he really hadn't wanted to tell me that. I feel like putting my hand on his, but I stop myself.

'Well, I wish I could say I feel smug, but…'

He's not even listening to me much. He peers out the window. 'Can you hear the sound of the engine? Does that sound right to you?'

'It sounds normal, I guess. Never flown Lulu and Chip Airlines before.' I laugh and expect him to crack a smile at least, but he doesn't.

He's petrified. He can't spend the rest of the forty minutes like this. He's so wound up I'm scared he's about to have a heart attack.

I finally give in and reach out and hold his hand. I guess it's an act of mercy. He opens his eyes and looks grateful. It's warm between our hands. He loops his strong thumb on top of my hand, as if to say, *Don't move.* He has nice hands and I can't help but see how strong his fingers are, how wide his palm is. I could see these hands on tractors and mowers, covered in grease and oil, and saving people from fires in houses or something, and—

We lurch suddenly to the right, banking quite hard as the plane turns, and he squeezes the life right out of my hand like a python.

'Ouch. Trying to break a few bones?'

'Sorry.'

The plane rights itself.

'Better?

He nods, but remains a white shade of mozzarella pale. I know he needs something quite dramatic to take his mind off this. Meanwhile, everyone else is nattering over each other, and I keep hearing Lulu say, 'Can you take another one of me, Chip? This time, with the dome in the left of the background.'

'There it is, the Dooo-oh-mooo!' my mum exclaims, pointing out the left window.

'Duomo.' Lulu sighs as if she were suddenly fluent in Italian.

Over Weasel's incredibly tense shoulder, there it is. A majestic sphere rising out of the city, pointing towards the night sky. In the background the last of the sunset is gleaming, the rays bouncing off the red tiles making them shine like a crimson gold.

'Wow.' I lean over to see out of the excruciatingly small window. I forget about personal space; I forget I'm pressed against him, still holding his hand. That my face is inches from his neck. That he smells more and more like a piney, cold Christmas up this close.

It's funny, but instead of leaning forward, he seems to lean into me. 'Can you see okay?'

I nod. 'Mmm.'

We watch in silence as we soar around the Duomo, and he squeezes my hand every time when we bank hard, but gradually less and less tightly. Until finally he leans back in his chair, and pulls me forwards so I'm leaning against his chest, and we stare out of the window together at this gorgeous city lit up by the most spectacular orange sunset. I can feel his body starting to lose tension.

'I love Italy,' I say breathily, because I'm overcome with a sudden urge to write, the words seeming to tumble down into me, inspired by everything around me. 'I want to write about it.'

I wonder momentarily if I'm going to regret this candour tomorrow morning, since I'm floating on a three-glasses-of-champagne cloud.

'You should. You could. Why don't you?'

I feel considerable relief when he says that. He's about to open his mouth and say something else, but I silence him with a look. I like that he knows what that look says. It says, *We're up in the sky above in Florence, let's just enjoy it.*

'Better now?' I look up at him, but I couldn't have said it at a worse time because the plane hits a patch of turbulence and we lurch up and down, and jerk in our seats like rag dolls.

'Oh my!' Aunty Janice says as if she's about to strap in for a rodeo ride.

'Fuck.' He's pale again and looks like he's about to faint. I'm so close to him I can see the fear in his blue eyes. He looks miserable and I'm racking my brain to think what we can do to get his mind off this flight because there's at least another fifteen minutes to go. Without thinking, I lick his cheek in a bid to get him to laugh.

'WHAT?'

'No? Not a fan of the cheek lick?' I can taste him on my tongue, sea salt and clove.

He wipes his cheek with the edge of his jumper. 'If I wanted you to put your tongue on me that's not the spot I'd have chosen.'

Tiny fires in my heart. *Where does he want my tongue?*

As the plane starts to bank again, his knuckles are clenched so tightly they're white. He shuts his eyes and presses back into me so hard I can feel his muscles through his soft jumper. There's an undeniable warmth that tingles up and down my body. I'm so close to him now, his cheek is an inch from my face.

I lean forward, just slightly, pressing my lips to his warm cheek. Just quickly. No lingering. It's not a kiss, but rather a reassuring *You got this*. Things I don't know how to say in words.

He seems surprised at first, but then, something softens in him. For the first time on this plane, he relaxes, and gives me a half smile. 'That was almost worth the horror of this ride.'

'Just helping out a poor stranger on the plane,' I say teasingly.

'I hope you don't do that with all strangers.'

We bank again as we head away from the city and back to the hills of Tuscany. He winces. I can appreciate how much this sucks for him, so I squeeze his hand as tight as I can.

When we level out, he turns to me.

'No kiss this time?'

'That wasn't a kiss.'

He raises his eyebrows. 'It wasn't?'

'No, it was a cheek linger. Because when I kiss someone, they'd know I mean it.'

He gazes at me so intently I can feel my heart starting to race. He unhooks his hand from mine, and turns so we're facing each other.

'Really?'

Against my better judgement, I nod.

'Really,' he repeats, like a warning. He puts his warm hand on my cheek. I can smell him everywhere and my heart races. He's looking at me intently. There's a feeling of electricity zapping between us. Oh, the tension. I should sit back. I *should*. But…

He leans in further, his lips so close to mine. He pauses. My whole body quivers. My heart bashes against my chest. I'm sure he can hear it. With a smile, he grazes up and down my cheek with his finger and I can hear him saying it again. '*Really*.'

I'll never know if it was the force of the plane, or if it was it him, but he slides towards me. My eyes shut. And then his mouth is on mine.

Softly at first. Warm pressure. My lips tingle. I want more. He wants more. His lips part. My lips part. His tongue finds mine. I put my hands through his hair, and it's like silk. He tastes incredible, like warmth and faintly like white wine. I hear him groan softly. I pull him into me. Our kiss grows deeper.

It's a kiss that makes me see things, colours all around me, even though my eyes are closed. A tiny firework goes off in my chest.

I like him. God, I *really* like this man, who came on this plane just for me.

But then I'm hit with the realisation of what I'm doing. *We can't.* I pull away, breathless.

'Wahoo!!' Aunty Janice claps loudly in the row behind us. 'Now THAT was a kiss.'

Chapter Twenty-Five

I 'm a harlot. A cheater. A scorned woman who should be
made to carry the letter A.

I'm rapidly pacing in my hotel room, where I've hidden
myself to decompress.

Giant mistake. I've made a Giant Mistake. I just kissed
Weasel. Weasel, who is my colleague. My arch nemesis – or
at least he *was*. This is all so weird. I feel my chest constrict
and it's hard to breathe.

I lecture myself. *Nice people don't do this. Nice people don't
kiss men that aren't their boyfriends, and* like *it*.

I pick up a bottle of water and take a slow drink. How
did this even happen? I try to trail back to the beginning,
and I'm certain this started when I agreed to take a stupid
plus one to the wedding with me, but part of me keeps
going. And once I unwind one strand, there's another, and I
see how they're all intimately connected like some giant
fucked-up web.

I feel I've been running around this entire wedding – my

entire life – appeasing people. Trying to be helpful. In order to be sweet, nice, kind.

But maybe Weasel's right: if I'm nice to everyone then I get in situations like this. I get Tony wanting me to do work while I'm supposed to be on vacation. And Lulu demanding I do name tags and dead fish like an employee rather than a sister. And Mia embarrassing me with stories about Gem-man, while I sit there and take it, not saying a peep. And Adam not really caring about how this wedding is going or the fact that his refusal to come has led to my *kissing Weasel*.

I pace up and down the small hotel room.

Fuck's sake. Let's be honest, I've been blindly going through most of my adult life saying, 'Yes! I can! Yes!' Being the Good Girl. The one who always has an answer and a smile. Because I hate the guilt that comes when I say no. The anxiety and the fear that everything will just fall apart if I'm not there to piece and glue it together. But doing everything for everyone demands my time and my energy, and I'm *exhausted*.

And now I've hurt people: the real Adam at home; myself; possibly even Weasel, by kissing him, confusing everything. I feel bone-crushingly bad. Embarrassment and shame rush through my body.

Fuck, it's horrible. *I'm horrible.*

All I know is this: I must undo the mistake. Particularly because I'm meant to be the kind one, the caring one, the nice one.

The realisation dawns on me and I feel a bit ill. Was Weasel right all along? Was I really a doormat? Was I so nice that it all just bottled up and now I've exploded and done something so out of character as a result?

I pick up the phone and hurriedly dial Ruby.

'Strange question, Ruby. How would you describe me?'

'Oh, um … sweet, lovely…'

'Am I a doormat?' I wince as I said it out loud.

'I mean … I wouldn't say "doormat". But you are … lenient.'

I bite my lip. 'Okay. How?'

'You help everyone out when they need it, which is great! But some people have come to expect it of you. Tony quite a bit. Remember that day he gave you some of his receptionist tasks because Susan wasn't there?'

The truth settles in my stomach like a cold stone. His EA was away so I had to answer his phones and take his messages. I had so many urgent deadlines of my own that I had to work really late to meet them. And I did it all graciously, but then I got sick with a cold and even then I worked from home, whilst I should have been sleeping. I whisper, 'Yeah I do.'

'It's just, I think you being so willing not to think of yourself means no one else does either.'

'Oh God.' Everything is falling into place. 'Do you think that's why I didn't get the promotion?'

'Could be. I really don't know.'

I take a deep breath in, then let out a long sigh. 'I don't want to be known as the editor who will do your admin, or go to events to butter up other authors for other editors. I don't want to be the girl that everyone thinks will be okay spending time re-doing name tags.'

'Wait, what? You lost me on the name tags thing.'

'That's okay. Thanks for listening and helping, Ruby.'

'Should I pull a card?'

'No, now I'm clear what I need to do.'

Crystal clear.

This doormat life is not only casting me as an afterthought in people's minds, it's potentially ruining my career.

After thirty-something years of embracing kindness, tolerance, people-pleasing and forgiveness, I've finally had enough.

I can feel the blood pumping in my ears. I needed some yang to my yin, some spark, some pep, some spiciness. I needed to remember the girl I was before everything happened with my family, before the affair, the girl who spoke up, the girl Han constantly tries to remind me of.

I shove back my shoulders and feel a surge of energy in my stomach. Well, she's back now, and there's only one thing to do.

I have to make this entire situation right. And tell the *truth*.

Chapter Twenty-Six

I can hear the music of the wedding rehearsal coming from the ballroom. Giving a silent prayer of thanks that I don't have to be there, I take my time in getting ready. Weasel texts.

> *I'm downstairs. Garden. Drink then 8 p.m. dinner? Made reservations at La Tavola.*

Like a perfect boyfriend. *Shit.*

My stomach lurches. I have to tell him. I spend another few minutes trying to figure out what I'm going to say. I think he likes me – I mean, he did get on a plane he thought was destined to plunge from the sky. For me.

I swallow hard. But that doesn't necessarily wipe away the time I've had with Adam. I have a boyfriend and he is my priority. My future.

By the time I get downstairs, dressed in white pants and a silver glittery camisole, Ben has grabbed a chilled bottle of local Sauvignon Blanc and two glasses. *Like we're celebrating. Yikes.* I gulp. Luckily I've had a shot of tequila, otherwise this would have my anxiety skyrocketing.

Out in the garden, the tiny fairy lights twinkle like stars, and the muted sounds of a string quartet flow across from the ballroom.

He pours me a glass. 'Wow, Gemma, you look…'

'Yes?'

I think he's going to say 'beautiful' – and God, I hope he doesn't – but instead he chews his lip, before he says, 'Almost relaxed.'

'I'll have you know I am very relaxed at times, when my chief editor isn't following me to Italy. Or thinking he's going to die in a small plane.'

'We should clink glasses before we start sparring, and someone needs to say pineapple.' He grins and holds up his glass.

The sun flashes its last rays, everything painted in pink and red as they streak across the sky. The cicadas start up like a choir, a distant hum. Everything smells like honey and jasmine, and the most perfect smell of all: a pizza crust baking.

I'm about to say something; I'm just finding the right words, the right time. Where do I start? With that kiss on the plane? With this entire holiday?

'Another glass?' he asks.

I shrug. I've lost my nerve a bit already, seeing him here. The good girl in me is trying to take over the new boldness. But I can't lose my resolve, not now. He pours me a half glass and I take a sip.

I have to do it. 'I have to be honest, about earlier…'

'Yes…'

'You know, on the plane. I need to apologise…'

'There's no need.'

Just say it. 'I have a boyfriend and I shouldn't have kissed you on the plane.'

'And I shouldn't have … uh … put mud on you in the spa,' he says lightly, but I can tell his tone is serious.

I give a small, strangled laugh, but then I remember what I've done on the plane and feel overwhelmed again. The weight on my conscience is heavy, like an anvil dragging me down.

'I don't know what I'm thinking about over here. I don't know why I did any of that. I seem to have temporarily lost my mind.'

'I get it. You have a boyfriend. I'm a great stand-in. Say no more.'

I cast my eyes over his face and try to read his expression but can't.

'Right,' I say flatly, wishing there wasn't an ache beneath my breastbone.

'Right.' He nods a little too much.

'Right,' I say again, the lead ball in my stomach getting larger. I swallow and try to ignore the strange sense of sadness about what will happen in a few days when this Italian bubble bursts.

I try to look away, but everywhere around me are fairy lights, and twinkling stars and music and wine, and God, it's just so bloody *romantic*.

'I can't break up with him,' I say quickly, trying to explain.

'Did I ask you to?' He raises both shoulders as if to say, *How much has this girl been drinking?*

He's right, he didn't, but it stings to hear him say the words.

I take a gulp of wine and we silently stand there and watch the night. Off in the distance, at the rehearsal dinner, the string quartet starts a new tune.

'I like this one—'

'Pachelbel's Canon,' I say humming along.

'I know what's it's called, Gemma. You may need to school others, but not me. And as I was saying – before I was rudely interrupted – I like this one, but I'm rather a Beethoven cello sonata guy myself.' He gives me a little smile.

'Arrogant music twat.'

He's laughing now. And I'm relieved that I get the sense that everything is going to be okay, and maybe we'll be friends when we get back, and go for coffee, and talk about books or music.

'When we get back can we go for coffee?' I ask impulsively.

'Yeah, of course.' His voice is warm and he looks happy I've asked that. 'As long as you don't wear those grey pyjamas again. That's something I think we need not repeat.' He has a glimmer in his eye.

Okay, friends. I can do this. I've got this. *Friends,* I think, nodding to myself.

'Another glass?'

Why not. I hold up my glass, and he fills it up.

'Cheese? ' He points at the charcuterie board. 'I asked them to put together something to snack on. We don't want you getting hangry.' He smiles and passes me a large chunk of brie. 'You like brie, right? By knife this time, not fingers.'

I can't help but laugh. 'You're quite good at this faux boyfriend thing. I suppose you've had a lot of practice.'

He laughs. 'You have a lot of assumptions about me.'

'Do I?'

'You know you do.' A hint of amusement flashes across his eyes. 'But you're so wrong, it's embarrassing.'

He fills my glass with a splash of crisp white wine. I can't help but bite. 'All right then, go ahead.'

'Let's start off easy. I'm Ben Thomas McDonald. Favourite colour is blue. Favourite author we have is Annie Wilcox. Favourite book is her Ode on Light poems.'

'*What*? You, vampire Weasel, like nature poems?'

'I do.'

'Sure it's not James McMahon?'

'No, definitely not the walking sexual harassment case that is James McMahon. Christ, that guy.'

'So you noticed.'

'Noticed? How could I not? When he … pawed you. We all saw it.'

I was morbidly curious now. 'So why didn't you do anything?'

'You've said plenty of times that you don't need saving.'

I look up at him. 'I don't. But if I'm doing radical honesty' – I pause – 'sometimes I may like to know that someone cares about me. Not saving. Caring. There's a *difference*.'

He grins. 'Okay, I think we're getting somewhere here. Should we have a little sign maybe, when you do need protecting or saving? Like maybe tugging on your earlobe?'

'I do that when I think. How about a little bear paw.'

'It may look like you're swatting mozzies.'

'Exactly! I need saving from them!' We both laugh. And it makes me feel warm.

'Okay, your turn.'

But do I even want dirt on Weasel? Do I even *want* to know anything about him? Wouldn't that make it harder when we get back to real life?

Instead I say, 'The other night … I've been wondering. How come you didn't worry about catching what I had? And how did you even figure out how to move me around whilst I was a comatose lump?'

'I've had experience.'

Oh, I think, all the models and supermodels he's dated. Getting themselves too drunk, and he's made himself an expert at shimmying them out of dresses. *What a chauvinistic little…*

He sees the look on my face and quickly adds, 'Not with girlfriends.'

I feel horrified. 'Then who? With *strangers*?'

'No, I uh, looked after my brother for a bit. He needed help getting in and out of…' He peters out. 'Not dresses.'

He looks so soft and vulnerable right now, it can't be a lie. Suddenly, every part of me feels like iron filings and he's a giant magnet, and I have to fight with every ounce of my being not to lean over and hug him. What's happening? I want to *hold* Weasel?

I try to think fast. Change the subject. 'Okay, well ... since you're here with my family, how about you tell me about your parents. Are they as crazy as mine?'

He turns away for a second. 'I don't, um, know them.'

'What do you mean?'

'They had me, then my brother Lucas, when they were young – just teenagers – and they couldn't cope. We were shipped off to different foster families, changing homes often.'

He sighs and runs a hand through his hair as he frowns. 'I mucked up a lot, and so families would get sick of me and want me out. Then our parents came back and said they'd changed their minds. I was about ten – Lucas would have been eight – and I was so excited. Lucas and I packed our bags and waited out the front. We waited until past midnight, but they never came. After that we vowed never ever to lie, to each other or to anyone. It's much better to just tell the truth.'

'I didn't know. I'm sorry.' I'm crushed for him.

It all makes so much more sense now. How independent he is. How he can't care about others because no one has ever *taught* him how.

'I'm just telling you because that's the reason why I'm so ambitious. I want to set Lucas and me up so we never need to worry.' He actually looks as if telling me has lifted a weight off him somehow.

I nod. I know the best thing I can do right now is to just listen.

'And Lucas. He, uh…' He looks down at his hands and is quiet for a while. 'He had a brain injury a few years ago, and it was pretty serious. Life and death stuff. He's doing pretty well now, with rehab, but the aim is for me to work hard enough so I can give him whatever he needs.'

I hate to admit it, but for a second, I wonder if he's lying. 'Wait, is that … true?'

He looks at me with those pure blue eyes, and his voice drops an octave, gets gravelly. 'I would never lie about something like that.'

'God, sorry, of course.'

He pulls out his phone. 'You can call him if you want.'

'I don't think…'

He gives me a wry smile. 'I was joking, Gemma, he can't speak that well.'

Oh God, now I feel a million times worse. 'I'm so sorry. About everything.'

'That's okay. I think he'd think it was funny too. He's always had a dark sense of humour.'

'God, you're a guy who looks after his brother.' I shake my head feeling stunned. 'This is the *last* thing I expected. So it's just the two of you?'

'Three. There's also Bella.'

For some reason my heart drops a little. Maybe she was a sister?

'Bella is the third leg of our tripod. She's not related to us, but I love her with all my heart.'

'Oh.' I can feel myself deflate as a strange sense of anxious disappointment spreads across my chest. So there's a non-sister someone. A Bella someone. I always thought of

Weasel as not having someone at home. But maybe he does. 'Is she, uh, nice?'

'She's a good licker.'

'*What*?'

'She's a dog, Gemma. A rescued border collie.' He opens his phone and scrolls to a photo of a cute, fluffy black collie, sitting on a large beige couch next to a man staring off in the distance, like he's trying to look at the camera, but his eyes won't focus. Lucas.

'You're pulling at all the bloody heartstrings.'

'Am I?' he says with that heart-breaking grin.

'You are, and you know it.'

'Well, that's everything. My soft crab insides.' He shrugs and runs his hand through his tousled blond hair. 'It's the reason why I'm sometimes a cynical … what did you call me? Wanker?'

I nod as a soft bloom of fondness rises in me. Fostered. Sick brother. Rescue dog. Anyone with a past like his would act the way he does.

I have to turn away. Suddenly it's becoming all too real. He can quote Shakespeare so perfectly that my heart beats like a jackhammer and he's literally the most beautiful human I've seen, but it's beyond sexual now. It's emotional, and that is dangerous territory. If I stay here, I know what will happen. I'll end up wanting to make out with his pretty face all night. And it won't stop there. Why did I even agree to this silly drink anyway? Still, I can't help but suddenly want to know everything about him. 'Did you ever meet them? Your birth parents?'

'Nope, my turn.' He moves away from me. 'What would you do if you weren't an editor?'

The question hangs heavy in the air. I consider not answering it truthfully, but no, that's what got me into this entire mess in the first place: not being honest.

He beats me to it. 'Have you ever thought of being a writer?'

Ugh, another topic I wanted to steer clear of. Why does it feel like every conversation with him is littered with landmines? 'I don't.'

'Really?'

'Well, I used to think about it, but…'

He raises his eyebrows. 'But?'

'I thought about it, but it … went nowhere. So now here we are.' I give him a quick glance. 'And before you say it, I wouldn't write a romcom.'

He holds his hands up. 'I didn't say a word.' He pauses. 'But you did *write* something?'

'I did. Once. But…' I take a deep breath. 'I don't think it was good enough.'

'Why?'

'It didn't go anywhere.'

He shrugs. 'You know, I was thinking…'

'Oh? It thinks?'

He ignores me. 'Maybe, now you're here, you could stay on a few days, spend some time writing about Italy. Away from all this hotel and wedding stuff. The real Italy, the heart of it.'

The way he phrases it seems strange. It's as if he knows I have already written about Italy.

'Maybe spend some time in the Tuscan hills. You know, soaking in the culture.'

It's as if he's reading an overview of my book. A strange eeriness comes over me. Does he know? But he couldn't possibly. No one has read that. No one knows except Tony, and he couldn't get rid of it fast enough. So why do I suddenly feel so uncomfortable, and like I just want to leave? 'I'm quite tired…'

He stares at me for a second. 'Is that the truth?'

There are two responses in me. One is a Nelly Nicepants: *Oh yep, promise I am, still jet-lagged, just beat.* And the other is the truth: *You scare me; this conversation scares me. If we're not almost kissing each other, we're talking about the softest part of me and it's overwhelming.*

'Actually no. It's not.'

'Say it then.'

'The truth is … I don't like to talk about me and writing.'

'Okay, fine. How about some more cheese? Wine?'

I shake my head. I know where more wine would get us. Non social distanced, that's where. 'I think it's best that I remove myself and don't insert myself into any more of these situations.'

'What about if we sit further apart? You sit over there, and I sit here.'

Every part of me screams, YES, LET'S DO THAT, but I know it won't help. I need to leave and leave right this second.

'I should go. But this was … *nice.*'

'Sure.' He stares at me and I can't read his expression at all.

I grab my bag, then pause. There's something still niggling me. And now that I have the warmth of wine in my veins and I'm no longer Nelly Nicepants, I want to get it off my chest.

'You know, there is one thing I wanted to ask you about…'

'Shoot.'

'I heard a conversation the night of James McMahon's drinks. You and Tony. Something that sounded like it was about me. And I'm sure I heard you say something like "*It's over*". You told me you didn't want my career to be over, so what was that about?'

His face flushes. 'I…'

I expected him to say it wasn't about me. But he can't. He can't even look at me, and I know then, it *was* about me.

'It's true? You want me to leave Peacock?'

'It's not that… It wasn't … uh…'. He's struggling. I wait as his mouth opens and his jaw flexes as he tries to find the right words. He swallows, quickly looks at me, then looks away.

So it's true. He wants me out. I feel suddenly cold, covered in goosebumps. So much for radical honesty. He can't even bring himself to admit it.

'I'm going,' I say crisply, suddenly wishing I hadn't pulled down my walls, hadn't trusted him, had never kissed him.

'Wait, Gemma.'

'Yes?'

His face is white, strained. 'There is something I do need to tell you.'

I nod as if to say, *Okay, go ahead*. And I brace myself for what he's going to say.

'I edited your book.'

I take a large inward sucking sigh. I can feel my heartbeat in my ears. 'You *what*?'

'The other night when you gave me the password to your laptop, I thought… I saved it as another version, but I thought, well … I was trying to help.' He looks at me hopefully, as if I'm about to bow in gratefulness.

My body stiffens. My fists clench. My blood is pumping in my ears. I'm so mad I can't think straight.

'You had no right to do that.' My voice is wobbly, shaking. I bite my lip to stop myself from getting really supernova angry. But my blood is boiling.

What the actual fuck?

'I was trying to show you what it could be. It needed—'

I want to cut him.

'I really, really wish you hadn't done that.'

'I'm sorry. I just thought—'

'No, you didn't think. That's the thing. You just went ahead and did what you wanted to do. Like always.'

He looks at me as if this is not the reaction he was expecting.

I can't see straight. It's my writing. My *baby*. My most precious creation. And now it's got his paws all over it because he wanted to show off what a good editor he is. Chief editor. He did the one thing I asked him not to.

I feel sick. And shaky. Old Gemma – Nelly Nicepants Gemma – would have said, *Oh that's great*, and then I would have gone to bed and cried. But this is the last straw. And

I'm sick of being the doormat, in life. In everything. And it has to stop now.

'Maybe you did teach me one thing.'

'Yeah?' He looks nervous.

'About telling the truth. Well, here it is: it's probably best that you leave and don't come to the wedding.'

Before he can respond, I walk away, feeling angry and hurt. It should feel satisfying, telling him to leave, it *should*. But nothing feels good about it.

Chapter Twenty-Seven

I n my hotel room, fury roars through my body. I pace up and down wringing my hands, wanting to shout, or cry, or scream, or hit a pillow, or something. I don't even know.

Then, finally, I can't help myself. I grab my laptop and enter the password. See his traitorous file on my desktop. He's saved it as *Ben's edits*. I'm livid. My heart is thumping. My head is spinning.

When it opens, there's marks all over it. Comments galore. Rage grips me. My body is molten lava, and I'm going to explode.

Breathing heavily, I drag the file to the recycle bin and dump it, then empty it. When it says 'delete forever?' I click 'yes'. Yes, yes, yes, yes, a million times. I snap the lid shut.

I'm shaking. I pace up and down the room, taking short sharp breaths, feeling the red hot anger twist inside me. It's wave after wave of fury. It's like the floodgates have opened.

I'm angry at Weasel for hearing me say no, don't open

my book, and doing it anyway. Angry at everyone for treating me how they want to. Angry at myself for allowing it.

It's not just Weasel who is arousing this resentment. It's everyone. I'm angry at everything. I feel like I can't breathe, I'm so angry. Underneath that, I can feel the bubbling up of something else that makes me want to cry. My mind is running a million miles an hour.

How did I not see this before?

Lulu simply smiles and I do things for her. Mum is anxious and I aquiesce. Dad is nonchalant and humorous and gets away with ripping apart the family. Marla makes passive jabs at me and I stay silent. Tony calls me 'sport' and gets his way. Editors ask me to help them with their work, but end up dumping it on my desk, and I work till ten p.m. and call it collaboration.

Adam … God, *Adam*. He wants me to change, be less emotional, be more like him. And what do I do? Instead of standing my ground, I tried to be more detached.

The stark realisation hits: I give pretty much all the time. No one is ever thinking about what I want or need, including me. No wonder I'm angry. And exhausted. And sick.

I fall onto the bed in an exhausted heap, and feel warm tears running down my cheeks. Han is right, I've lost my way. I never speak my mind; I say yes to people even when I want to say no; I do whatever it takes to please them; I play the game; I'm the nice girl, the good girl, the kind girl, aka the one without boundaries, the one you don't respect. *Ugh*. That hits hard.

In this moment, I make myself a promise: I won't be a doormat anymore. I'll say what I truly feel in every moment.

As if the universe is testing me already, an email notification pops up on my phone with a loud BING. Tony. Nervously, I open it. He's asking if I've managed to have a look at the edits, despite the fact Weasel has told him I was a) on vacation, and b) deathly ill. Little monster.

My face flushes with anger. *He can go and...* But then I stop. I won't get angry at him, and then apologise for getting angry and say, *Yes sure, whatever you want.* Weasel has shown me one thing at least. There's another way. Say no.

Yep, that's what I'll do. I'll tell Tony no. A flat, please-respect-this no. I raise my fingers ready to type. But I don't know how to start. My insides turn. Gosh, for a people-pleaser that little two-letter word is hard. If someone offered me the chance to either climb Everest right now or say no to Tony, I'd be strapping my ice boots on.

I take a deep breath and quickly type before I can overthink.

Sorry, Tony, I'm at a wedding. Will look at it when I'm back in the office.

After reading it for the tenth time, I decide to delete the word 'Sorry', and replace it with 'Hi'. Because I'm *not* sorry for being on this holiday ... if you can even call it a holiday. I'm not sorry. *Not sorry,* I repeat to myself as I press send.

Almost instantly, I get a response. My stomach drops. Cringing a little, I read it.

Have a good time, Gemma.

Holy shit. It worked. This truth thing. This boundary thing. My body is literally vibrating with happiness and surprise. I suddenly really like being the Girl with Good Boundaries. The No Fucks Given Girl.

But then I realise there's a larger test. Adam. It's one thing pretending Weasel is my boyfriend, and quite another explaining this silly pantomime to everyone.

I get into bed feeling miserable and wondering how I, who doesn't want to hurt a fly, have managed to put myself in a situation where I'm about to hurt many people. For a second, I feel the looming weight of what I've done.

I hear Weasel's voice in my head. *Just tell the truth.*

Ugh, get out of my head, I think.

I switch off the light and stare at my ceiling.

Now, I need to figure out how to tell my family. Because I'll need to explain why Ben has packed his bags and gone home, and that will include explaining that Ben isn't Adam. I've told lies and now I need to come clean. And I need to do it all on the day of Lulu's wedding.

Chapter Twenty-Eight

T he wedding is glorious. Of course it is. Lulu is gorgeous in a floor-length 1920s-inspired ivory silk and French lace dress, with small capped sleeves. Her hair is pinned up in a soft chignon, with small wispy waves framing her face, and on her ears are slim diamond drop earrings. If ever a girl stepped off the cover of British *Vogue*…

The ceremony is surprisingly short, followed by an incredibly long photo shoot against another flower wall, this one covered in small pink rosebuds.

Meanwhile, I'm completely at a loose end. I really need to keep myself occupied, because anything is better than thinking about Ben, in the hamster wheel that's my mind at present. Ben, who's probably already in the sky, zooming back to Sydney. I try hard not to think about it because every time I do I feel guilt and then an immense sadness.

Thankfully, everyone is swept up in wedding fever and they don't have the time to realise Ben isn't there until after all the formalities are over and the cocktail hour has started. Mum and Dad finally notice I'm standing by myself, and when they ask, instead of making up some lie, I suck in a breath and say, 'Let's talk about it later.'

I thoroughly enjoy the brilliant Italian food, and have positioned myself near the kitchen to get first dig at the delicious mushroom and goat's cheese arancini balls that keep appearing.

A waiter walks past and I'm about to say, 'Are there any more risotto balls?' when Chip makes a beeline for me, with a worried look. 'Have you seen Lulu?'

I shake my head, thinking I'm the last person who would know where she was. 'Not since the reception started.'

'Would you mind helping me look for her?'

I swallow the urge to say, 'Have you checked in front of all the mirrors?' Instead, I manage to say, 'Are you sure she's not just off chatting somewhere with the guests?'

Chip bites his lip. 'We … ah … had a bit of a fight. And I thought you may know where she'd go.'

Fat chance. I don't know Lulu at all, but I'm not about to admit that to Chip, who looks rather like he's lost a puppy.

'Okay.' I shrug. 'Let me try.'

I check the bathrooms first, as they have all the mirrors, but only find two women having a conversation about plucking versus waxing, which I don't want to stick around for. Outside, everyone is getting tipsier and tipsier. Even Aunty Janice is on the real vodkas, and seems to be hugging the grand curtains and saying to no one, 'Shall I buy some like this for the lounge?'

I knock on Lulu's hotel room door, check the front garden, and finally I sneak out to the side bar where no one is sitting. Just in case, I do a small walk up to the entry of the vineyard, and I'm about to turn around and give up, when I catch a flash of ivory pearl silk, and the glimmer of lace.

I tiptoe around the stone wall, and there she is: Lulu is lying, eyes closed, on the grass, as though she'd collapsed.

'You'll get grass stains.'

She sits up. 'Will I?'

'But you know that.'

'Maybe.' She pushes her creamy white stiletto heels off, revealing perfectly manicured pink toenails. 'I just needed a moment.'

I raise my eyebrows. *Lulu* needed a moment?

'*You*?'

'I guess so.'

'Um … are you okay?'

'Chip and I had a moment.'

I'm not sure what she's trying to tell me; it's entirely cryptic.

'Chip and Mia. They also had a moment.'

What? I don't know what to say. 'What moments are we talking—'

She cuts me off. 'You'll probably think it's nothing. It was just a kiss. Years ago. Before Chip and I even met.'

Wow.

She picks at the hem of her dress. 'But still, this morning, while I was getting ready, that's what I thought about. Them. Kissing one night because they both got drunk. Then

293

that thought grew and I found myself thinking, maybe that's who should be walking down the aisle.'

I'm so surprised by this show of vulnerability from Lulu that I'm struck silent for a second before I manage, 'That's awful. Of course you're thinking about it; it completely makes sense.'

She turns to me with wide eyes. 'Does it?'

'Yes. It's part of the process: getting cold feet, questioning things. I mean, it's a big day, one of the biggest. I think it's normal to do it. And I'm sorry that happened.'

She shrugs. 'He's sorry too, but I can't stop thinking about it.' She picks a few blades of grass. 'What if all this isn't real? What if we don't make it?'

'The way Chip looks at you,' I reassure her, sitting down beside her, 'it's clear how much he loves you. He adores you.'

She seems uncertain and I realise I've never seen her look like this, ever.

'I've probably been horrible to everyone, a real Bridezilla, but it's just because I wanted it all to be perfect. Because if it's perfect, then doesn't that mean we'll make it?'

'Perfect is a tough bar to reach.'

She looks over at me. 'You seem to be reaching it. Everything in your life seems—'

'*Perfect*? Are you *kidding* me?' I take a deep breath.

She shakes her head and her chin starts to wobble, and I think she might actually cry. And I don't want her to spoil her make-up. Usually I'd just say whatever I thought she wanted to hear, but instead, I try telling her the truth for once.

'You know, I always thought you were like the sun, Lulu, and everyone just rotated around you. And I hated that, and I think that's why we're not close. You always seemed the perfect one to me. Perfect job. Perfect looks. Perfect husband now.'

Her chin wobbles even more, and she lets out a half-sob, half laugh. 'I don't feel that way at all. Look at you, you're off living halfway around the world, doing all these wonderful things, and Dad can't stop talking about you: how nice you are, how you care so much about everyone. People flock to you. If anyone's the sun, it's you.'

I laugh incredulously. 'Hardly. I always thought I was Pluto.'

'Pluto? That's not even a planet anymore.'

'*Exactly.*'

She shrugs. 'Well, people think I've got it together, but I don't. *I don't.*'

'Neither do I.'

'But Adam, your job, everything…'

'Yeah, actually, about that…' I take a deep breath and feel like I'm going to faint. My hands shake because this could ruin everything. 'He's … he's not my boyfriend.'

Her eyes get wide. '*What?*'

I feel exhausted and embarrassed saying this out loud. 'The real Adam is at home because he's working, and so I … brought a stand-in.' I feel a wave of guilt. My stomach churns.

'But … *why?*'

'Because I thought you'd all say stuff about me being

295

single if I came alone. Gem-man can't get a man, or something.'

Lulu bites her lip and looks at me. 'I'm sorry about that, the whole thing. That was the only time you came to my birthday and it felt like we were really *sisters*, so I talk about it, even if we weren't nice to you at all.'

'Really?' I let this sink in. '*That's* why?'

She nods. 'And then the other night, with Mia telling that entire story to everyone. I wasn't expecting that.' She shrugs. 'Sometimes she's just a bit…' She can't finish the sentence.

Normally I would have brushed it under the rug, and said, 'Oh that? That old thing. It didn't bother me at all.' But Weasel's words stay in my head. *At the cost of your own happiness? Stand up for yourself, because sometimes no one else will.*

'It really hurt me, and it was very embarrassing.'

She nods. 'I'm sorry. I really am.'

I take a deep breath. 'And while I'm being honest, I didn't want to do your name tags. Or your music. Or bunting. I just wanted to be here as your sister.'

Her eyes well up and she nods. 'I'm so sorry, Gemma. Can you forgive me?'

'Yes.' I nod and look at her. 'Can you forgive me for bringing a stand-in to your wedding, who is actually a colleague that I despise?'

'Despise? I'm not sure that's the word I would have used.' She gives me a small smile. 'Where is that colleague now?'

'Well … we had a bit of a fight, so I told him to go home. Ben, by the way, that's his name.'

Lulu laughs. 'So you're not perfect.'

I laugh too. 'And you're not perfect.'

'Maybe no one really has it together.'

I smile wryly. 'Look at us, sitting here on the grass because we both tried so hard to be perfect, and we finally had to admit we just aren't. No one is.'

She reaches out and puts a manicured hand on mine. It's cool, and slender, and I grab it. We smile at each other. And it feels nice. Neither of us is the sun, just both big chunks of space granite hurtling around this vast universe, trying to find a place to fit.

She squeezes my hand and I grin. It's such a relief to just be us. Sisters. Just the way we are.

'And Lulu, I'm sorry for what happened with Chip, but he loves you. And you're actually a really, really good couple.'

She smiles and the warmth radiates off her. 'I needed to hear that.'

'He's going to make a great addition to the family.'

In the spirit of generosity she says, 'If it helps, I pluck my grey hairs too. Been getting them since I was twenty. I shouldn't have pointed yours out. I was just being bitchy.'

'Bitchy Bridezilla.'

She laughs and I laugh, and for a moment all the years drain away.

I give her a smile. 'Now, are you ready to get back in there? Dance the night away?'

She grabs my hand. 'Yes.'

And as we enter the ballroom, Chip sees her and immediately beelines for her. Before he gets here though, she leans in and whispers in my ear, 'That guy, Ben or fake Adam or whoever he is, I think he likes you too, you know. The way he looks at you… I can tell.'

I'm about to say, *Of course he doesn't*, but her words catch in my mind.

The way he looks at you.

And there's a shiver up my spine because I know the look she's talking about. It's the one Ben gave me after we kissed. But he's gone. And that makes me feel incredibly sad.

Chapter Twenty-Nine

I try and shake off the sadness the best way I know how: with champagne. I swig half a glass, and decide I don't want to see Ben. He's an idiot. So it's a good thing he's on a plane.

The bubbles fizz about in my head, the way champers does, and when a great tune comes on I sashay to the dance floor like someone who's just shaken off the weight of the entire world, or Pluto, from her shoulders.

I shake the moneymaker. I do the YMCA, even though the music isn't YMCA at all, because that is far from cool. I don't care. I am not cool, never have been cool, and I'm good with that. Cool is too much effort.

Out of the corner of my eye, I see my mum and dad looking a bit tense, and out of habit I think, *Shit, no, I need to go and sort this out.* I'm about to walk towards them, but I stop.

They're adults. They can look after themselves.

Ugh. Ben's probably a million miles away, and still I can

hear his silly words in my head. Instantly, I feel sad again, thinking about him leaving, I miss him. I miss bantering with him, laughing at him. But I'm still mad at him. Livid. Editing my book... I stop thinking about it. I have to. *Enjoy the night.*

I walk off the dance floor to grab another champagne because I'm thirsty and I need it. I push through the crowd, who are all getting drunker by the second, and I spot Lulu hugging Chip. All is well. She winks at me, and I wink back, and it warms my heart.

Suddenly I smell a hint of fresh forest in the air. I stop in my tracks and look around. But I can't see him. God, am I making this up now? *Ridiculous.*

A slightly tipsy man sidles up to me, 'Gemma, is it?' He's got a bit of a paunch, but I can't fault that because I have no curves, so he has enough for both of us. His face is warm and red, a largish nose that's definitely Scottish, and he reminds me a bit of Santa Claus, and this is exactly why I didn't want to come to this wedding alone.

I try not to sigh. 'Yep.'

'I'm Gary, by the way.'

I sip my champagne and hope he'll get the point: I'm not interested.

'Do you want to dance?'

Not at all, Gary. I'm about to let him down gently when he points across the ballroom where an older woman is watching us excitedly, clearly his mother. 'Maybe just one dance?'

Oh, I get it. I feel an instant pang of sympathy for him.

I nod and let him lead the way out onto the dance floor.

As luck would have it, the DJ puts on a slow track. I hate slow dances, but it's too late to back out now. They're just so cheesy. *Dear lord.*

Gary, like a gentleman, puts one hand on my lower back, stiffly, and the other he holds out for me to grab. I do, but his hand is cold, and his palm is slightly clammy, so I try not to let them touch too much.

'So you live in Australia?'

'Yep. You?'

'Oh, um, England. Yes. Midlands. Work in finance.'

'Right.'

'Single for about four years. Wife left me.'

Jesus, Gary, that's a bit much for a first dance, I think.

'Sorry to hear that.'

While nattering on about dating apps, Gary tries to break the stiff side-to-side shuffle by twirling me around, and when I finish turning I'm facing the bar.

My heart stops. There he is. Weasel. Ben. Dressed in a tuxedo, and it does not disappoint. The crisp white shirt is open at the neck so I can see his tanned beautiful chest, his wall of muscle. His jacket is open, showcasing black pants that hug his legs. Black leather loafers, no socks. God, he's even put on glasses. Glasses with black frames, like he's a sexed-up Harry Potter. Or an Abercrombie and Fitch model. He looks glorious.

He's holding up a whiskey and he takes a sip, looking directly at me. He winks (cocky little bugger). He puts down the whiskey slowly, and then starts pushing through the crowd. I'm so happy I want to cry. There are pieces of me that like him. So many pieces. Pieces that are invested.

And I'm mad at him, but I'm also happy. I'm so fucking happy that he didn't leave, I feel tears in my eyes.

He taps Gary on the shoulder, and Gary looks around and freezes for a second before realising what's happening. When Gary gets it, he backs away, leaving Ben and me staring at each other. His blue eyes are bright, his skin looks tanned from the Italian sun, and his lips have never looked more inviting. I refuse to dance with him, so we just stand looking at each other on the dance floor.

'Wow.'

'Wow, what?'

'So you *can* dress. You look … gorgeous.'

I won't blush, I won't give him the satisfaction. I try to say with a hint of nonchalance, even though my heart is beating out of my chest, 'What makes you think I'm talking to you?'

'Possibly the fact that you're talking to me.'

Damn his arrogance.

'I want to explain everything, if you'll just give me a chance?'

'You have two minutes.'

'Before you say it, I know what all of this looks like.'

I look around, my eyebrows raised. 'Um, it looks like a dance floor that we're standing on while not dancing.'

'No, the book. And then coming back here now. But I wanted to apologise in person. I am your plus one after all, right?'

'*Were.*' I can't make it easy for him. It goes against everything in my being, which right now is screaming that I should apologise too, sweep it under the rug, like I always do.

He grimaces. 'Finally, Evans, you're making this hard.'

I nod. 'Guess so.'

He pushes his hand through his hair nervously. 'I royally fucked up. I'm really sorry about making you feel uncomfortable.'

'Right. Is that it?'

'And editing your work. I shouldn't have done that. You said no. It's just … I wanted to help. I was out of line, and I'm sorry.'

'Okay.' I give nothing away, but inside, parts of my ice queen façade are melting.

'And I wouldn't come back for most people. In fact, I wouldn't have come back for anyone else. But I would for you, so I'm here, and I want to make this right.'

'How?' I can feel myself relenting.

'By telling you my edits were terrible, and you should throw them in the bin, and pretend this never happened?'

'Hmmm.'

'Are you a little bit happy to see me?'

I try not to smile. 'No.'

'Would you like me to get Gary back?'

'No!'

He smiles ruefully. 'So maybe we could just have fun together at this wedding? As a plus one, a friend. And then when we get on the plane you can swear to never talk to me again.'

I don't want to never talk to you again.

'Well, I guess this is what it's come to then,' he says with a shrug as I remain silent. 'I'm invoking the law of pineapple.'

I try not to giggle. 'It's a law now?'

He looks at me very seriously. 'Yes, they passed the bill just recently. Which means Gemma Evans has to give at least one pineapple truce to Benjamin McDonald for being an idiot, since he held her hair back when she was sick.'

I narrow my eyes teasingly. 'Well, if it's the law... I wouldn't want to go to prison.'

'So we're okay?'

'I guess we are.'

'You do really look gorgeous.'

I go very still. And check his face for any signs of insincerity. But find none. 'Thank you, faux boyfriend.'

He rakes his hand through his fantastic hair. 'Any time, faux girlfriend.'

He's about to say something further when the DJ stops the track. 'And now it's time to go out on the lawn, and enjoy the releasing of the doves,' he croons in a low voice.

'Dove time?' Ben repeats. 'Are you on dove duty?'

'Nope, thank goodness. So much has changed since you left.'

He gives me a *yeah? tell me* face, but before I can, we are ushered with the rest of the wedding crowd to the front gardens. I eye up the place where the taxi left me just a few days ago, and think about how different everything feels now.

Above, the sun is setting, and the fairy lights twinkle. There's an almost full moon. On the lawn, Lulu and Chip stand together, staring into each other's eyes again, very much in love. To the right, Mia is gorgeous in a long aquamarine slip dress, and eyeing up Ben like he's a snacky prawn cracker.

'You can mingle, you know.'

'I'm happy here.'

A warmth flushes through me.

I look out at the front lawn where the cages are being set up. 'Do you ever wonder if those doves really get set free? Or are they just recaptured again? What a life.'

He gives me a wry smile 'Are we about to stow away twelve doves in our suitcase?'

I nod. 'Adventures of the—'

'Terrible Twosome.'

'That's awful. We're editors! We can do better than that. Terrific Tales of the—'

'Tortured Tautologists.'

I groan. 'Don't give up your day job. Or actually, do,' I tease. 'Perhaps it would be Gemjamin. Or Benma. Terrible.'

'Did you just say our couple names?'

'Oh, no, not couple. Just um … putting our names … like combining … a moniker…'

'Right.' He gives me a sneaky smile, and my stomach twitches.

Once the doves are released, we are led to a makeshift dance floor set up outside, and the DJ plays a few last tunes whilst the six-piece orchestra waits to play. Of course.

It's all very Lulu. I wouldn't be surprised if she left via helicopter. Or a gigantic blimp. The things we do to try and be perfect. Just thinking about it makes me smile.

Ben offers, 'Are we dancing?'

'We can, I suppose.'

'Don't know where those hands have been though…'

'Just saving doves.'

He laughs and I follow him onto the dance floor. It's an upbeat song, and we start dancing next to Mum and Dad, who both have left feet and keep going in the wrong direction, but look like they're having a lot of fun.

'By the way, Lucas asked me to say hi.'

My eyebrows rise, as if to say, *You were talking about me.*

'Yes, Gemma, I did mention the unpredictable quirky girl I happened to be holidaying with, who kinda sent me home.'

'But I thought he couldn't speak.'

'Video chat. He can make some hand movements. But I'm sure he smiled when he heard about you. He's not an easy win either.'

Suddenly the music cuts to a slower number. I'm about to leave the dance floor when Ben whispers, 'Shall we?'

My stomach flips and I feel faint. I'm nervous because it's Ben … and I really want to dance with him. For some reason I want his warm hands on me and I don't want to walk away.

I step towards him. Unlike that first night, I'm closer now. His hand on the small of my back. His jaw twitches as I lean in. A loose lock of hair falls across my face, and he pushes it back gently. I can smell him everywhere around me. Delicious and warm.

He pulls me towards him, strongly, carefully, until I'm pressed against his chest. God, he smells good. I turn my face to the side, and I can hear his heartbeat and it's going so fast, like crazy.

He whispers into my ear, 'I missed you. I missed fighting with you. I missed talking to you.'

I gulp. I missed the same things.

Finally, I lean back and look at him. 'I took your advice and told the truth.'

'And?'

'I told Tony no. And I told Lulu how I felt. And it kinda worked out.'

'Ah, so that's why I saw you and Lulu walk in holding hands. So the day went well?'

I grin at him. 'Really damn well.'

'You look happy.'

I tilt my head. 'I am. Really happy.'

'Good.' A slow smile spreads across his face. 'It's funny, I took some of your advice too.'

'You did?'

'Yep. Several things. I sent Lulu some good-luck flowers, and told her her sister is amazing and a great support.'

I feel the world disappear under my feet, and I'm floating. 'You did?'

He nod. 'And I had to call the office and speak with Gavin, so I made sure to ask him how he was doing, and how his *four* kids were.'

I'm surprised. 'Unironically?'

'Unironically. And … it kinda worked out. He seemed happy that I'd asked. And after he told me that his kids had drawn all over his wall in permanent marker, he told me about an author he thinks we could get for the new luxury brand, and it's pretty exciting.'

'See.' My eyes glimmer.

'See.' His eyes glimmer. 'So, we're okay then?' he says, a smile playing across his warm lips.

I grin at him. 'I guess we are.'

'Good, I'm glad.'

He rests his chin on my head, and it feels so natural that I lean into his chest. I can hear his heart beat. Feel the smoothness of his chest. We rock back and forth gently and I close my eyes and breathe in his deep woodsy Christmas wonder smell, which I've grown to love.

'This is nice,' I say into his chest.

'Hmm?'

I look up at him, into his piercing eyes. 'I never would have thought you and I would be doing this.'

'I'm glad we are.'

My small lace purse starts vibrating. 'Sorry.' I look down at the phone and see it's Adam calling. Not now. I haven't even considered what I'm going to say to him. I press decline.

My bag vibrates again. 'Shit, sorry.' I look down at my phone, and a pang of guilt erupts inside me. I need to talk to Adam; I had thought of waiting until I was back at home, but maybe it's something I have to deal with now.

I step away from Ben. 'You know, I should really get this.'

Chapter Thirty

I walk quickly off the dance floor, my phone buzzing in my hand.

I step towards the garden, where just a few days ago, I rocked up in a taxi wearing old Qantas pyjamas. I smile ruefully. *How things have changed.*

I find a small, cloistered spot away from the wedding party, and answer Adam's call.

'Gemma! Where have you been?'

'Um, at the wedding.'

'I just thought you were going to call in the morning, your morning, when you were feeling better.'

Oh crap, I meant to but then I woke up and there were croissants, then coffee, then hair, and I completely forgot. 'Oh shit, it's been—'

'Are you okay, baby?'

'Yes, great. But actually—'

'How was the wedding?'

'Yep, also great. Flawless. Lulu looked beautiful. Mum

and Dad both cried. Marla spied her next husband. You know. A typical Evans kinda outing.'

'So, I've been a busy boy.'

Boy? I cringe. It's amazing how when you realise something isn't right you suddenly get the ick.

'You have?'

'I've been talking to the new executive team at Lincoln. There's a lot of great initiatives they're involved in. Charities. But also community weekends away, that sort of thing. Spouses too. It's for all the managers and executives.'

'Oh, um, great.' *Why is he talking about this?*

'And the team that go, they're all married, and with kids, most of them. I don't think girlfriends make the grade. And that was just a catalyst, and with you being at a wedding it dawned on me. Why not?'

'Why not?'

'Maybe we do it too.'

'Do it?'

'Get married soon. You and I.'

'Oh?' I laugh nervously.

His voice shifts a gear. 'You don't want to?'

'Well … I…'

'It's a simple yes or no.'

My heart starts to beat fast. 'Is this, like, a *proposal*?'

'Well, it would make a lot of sense, especially since we'll be buying a place soon. We've already discussed it, so we can just do it a bit quicker than we had planned. We can do the formalities when you get home, but yes, let's do this thing.'

This thing. I think quickly about the ways I've dreamed

to be proposed to: in a bookstore, during a walk through autumn leaves… Not over the phone, like it was a business deal, or part of a goal-setting plan. And definitely not when, just moments earlier, I'd been slow dancing with someone else.

'Gemma?' He sounds concerned. 'You okay?'

'Just … shocked. And Adam, I need to—'

'You just wait. I'll get a great ring. I'll send you the photo as soon as we hang up. You'll love it. I think I have nailed exactly what you like. Flower style.'

He's right, I do like flower rings. But this just feels … *wrong*.

'Let me know when you're coming home. I'll pick you up at the airport and we can talk about this. This is good, really good. Love you.'

I'm left with the sound of silence. He's gone, just like that. I think about the Adam List that I crumpled up and put in the bin. *It's not enough*, I think.

Here's a truth: I know Adam and I are not that good. I think I've known for some time, that I told myself it was easy, but it isn't. I've edited myself in this relationship. I was trying so hard to be someone I'm not. I'm emotional, and I will never be a robot. And I can't keep apologising for that. In fact, I don't *want* to apologise for that.

Another truth: for a small part of this trip, before he was a douche, I knew I'd rather be kissing Ben, and if you're thinking about kissing someone else when you have a boyfriend, it's not good. I kissed him on the tiny plane because I wanted to. That's the absolute bare truth of it all.

I know already I can't go on like this. And if I go back

and just say yes to Adam, we'll get a house, and a ring, and then it will be just that much harder to undo.

Still amped up on adrenaline, I think, *Now, just do it now.* My brain is running in circles with things to say… How do I start this conversation?

I don't think we should…

I've been doing some thinking and…

I walk back towards the wedding party, where Ben is waiting. 'You okay? You look as if you've seen a ghost.'

Normally, I'd laugh at that. *Normally.* But now I've just been proposed to, and over the phone. *Let's do this thing.*

'Gem?'

I can't feel my toes. My feet. My lips. 'Ben, I think I'm…' I can't finish the sentence, especially not now.

I look at my phone, as if it had the answers. 'Adam just proposed.'

Ben looks over my shoulder and his face goes white.

I look around, and there she is, in full earshot.

Marla.

Chapter Thirty-One

'"Ben"?' Marla is flipping her head between Ben and me like she's at a tennis match. 'Don't you mean "Adam"? What's going on?'

Marla's tone of voice is shrill, and it's already attracted the attention of anyone within a five-foot radius.

'What the hell is going on?' Marla demands, and the scent of musk almost sets me off again. She calls over Lulu and soon Mia and Mum flock around as well. 'I think the bride deserves to know what is going here. At her very own wedding. Like … like treachery! Treason!'

I will not indulge her, because she is an over-reacting monster. I will keep calm. I haven't plotted to remove my half-sister from her throne of matrimony. It's just a little case of mistaken identity.

'This isn't Adam.' Marla's voice has shifted up an octave and a hundred decibels as she declares this to anyone within a hundred yards.

Mum grabs Dad, who happens to be walking past. She

whispers something in his ear and they both look at me, waiting as if I'm about to tell them Marla has made all of it up. But she hasn't. It's me who's lied.

Ben looks down at me. I open my mouth, but no sound comes out. He whispers, 'You don't have to do this. Just call me Adam.'

But he's wrong. I do have to do this. I have to tell them, and why. I always planned to, just never like this.

Finally I say weakly, 'His name is Ben. And he's not my boyfriend.'

Marla gasps. 'You've brought a *stranger* to our WEDDING?'

Mia almost looks gleeful. She turns to Ben. 'I *knew* Gemma could never get someone like you.'

'Is this true, Gemma?' Mum looks like I've broken her heart.

Lulu is staring at me, the hard stare of a bird, but instead of anger, I feel waves of something else coming off her. Protection. She steps towards me and holds my hand. 'I already know. And it's fine. Gemma can have whoever she wants to at this wedding.'

'But I think we deserve an explanation, Lulu,' Marla demands.

My mum looks crestfallen.

'Not really,' Lulu says, still clutching my hand. In this moment, right now, I love her. I feel that for the first time in forever, we're *sisters*. 'Since this is *my* wedding.'

Mia is eyeing Ben up like he's the last morsel on a buffet table and she's about to pounce. 'So you're single?' I hear her saying.

Marla is demanding that I tell them what is going on, and why she is paying for another seat at the table, and who the hell is this guy? And Mum looks like she's about to cry and Dad is asking if I've made it all up.

And God, I feel so guilty, and I don't want to hurt anyone else, and I have nothing to say that will pull me out of this. Yes, I lied. I brought my colleague to a wedding and pretended he was my boyfriend. Yes, I have no idea what is happening with my actual boyfriend. It's all too much.

I feel like I'm going to faint. 'I … uh…'

Instead of dumping me in it, Ben stands strong behind me, and whispers in my ear, 'You have got this.' And my heart starts to beat faster. I open my mouth to say something, but no words come out. I just gob a bit like a fish.

Ben clears his throat. 'What I think Gemma wants to say is how much she loves you all.'

'So much she *lied* to us?' Marla is livid. 'And *on our day*?'

'Well, really it's *our* day,' Chip says and shrugs. Marla glares at him.

Mum clears her throat. 'Gemma, honey, is it true? Did you lie?'

'Well, the truth is…' But I can't continue. God, what a mess. My throat has something stuck in it, something that is stopping me from saying how I truly feel. It's the fear that gave way to Nelly Nicepants. The fear that if I admit the truth, maybe they won't want me around anymore, maybe it will be like that time my dad left, and maybe Mum will leave too this time.

Ben squeezes my hand and tries to speak for me again.

'The truth is my name is Ben… I'm just a colleague, helping out, because the real Adam is back at home, dependable, and secure and setting them up for their future.'

'No. *No*,' I say a little too forcefully. I won't let him say things that I've discovered aren't true. 'Well, yes…'

'Gemma, make it quick, the mayor is just over there,' Marla hisses.

Ben looks at me, and mouths the word 'Basilisk'. It's *exactly* what I'm thinking. 'C'mon, Hermione,' he whispers.

I nod, then turn around to face them all. 'Ben's telling the truth. The real Adam is at home. He couldn't come because he has a new job to focus on. And he is nice. And, well, he's just proposed to me. Over the phone.'

'You're *engaged*?' Mum looks like she doesn't know whether to laugh or cry.

For a moment, I picture my life with Adam for the next ten, twenty, thirty years. Successful. Stable. Easy. We'll be the type of people that have Saturday plans, cycling around Narrabeen Lake, maybe two houses, one a holiday cottage by the beach that we let out. A really nice remodelled kitchen. A stash of expensive red wine. Great coffee. A French press fit for a king.

But that's not what I want anymore.

'No. I, um … no, I'm not.'

I look at Ben, standing beside me like he's protecting me, keeping me safe. Then on the other side is Lulu, holding my other hand. I'm telling the truth and no one is leaving me. In fact, I feel more loved and cared for than I have in my entire life. I feel so choked up I get tears in my eyes and blink them away.

'Anyway, like he said, Ben is my colleague back in Sydney and, despite a rocky start, he was the best pretend boyfriend I could have asked for. He even came on a tiny plane for me even though he thought he was going to die. So everyone, I'd like you to meet Ben. My uh … uh…'

'Your new boyfriend?' Lulu suggests, eyebrows raised as she gives me a small wink.

Mia looks shocked. 'What?'

I shake my head. 'No. But I do like him. A lot. He's actually pretty great. He quotes Shakespeare and he's funny and kind. Actually, I think he's wonderful.'

I look at him. He's guarded. Of course he is. I've just told him I've been proposed to, and now he's standing in front of my family, which feels a bit like facing the firing squad.

'You all deserve the truth.' I look around at them. 'I don't know why I'm admitting this to everyone, but I don't really feel like I fit in here. In this family. I never felt enough. I was always trying to be so nice, to fit in, to not cause a fuss, but it never seemed to work.'

'Oh Gemma.' My mum's eyes mist over.

'And the other night, with the … the Gem-man jokes and then getting sick. It was horrible. And I think I would have left, except for this guy.'

I look over at Ben. 'He looked after me when I cried and while I vomited.'

'Like a walrus,' he adds.

I laugh. 'Apparently like a very ladylike, beautiful walrus. And he helped me stay, rather than pack my bags and leave. And he made me see that I've exhausted myself

317

trying to be nice to everyone else, so I'm not going to anymore. I'm going to tell the truth.'

His eyes tell me that he has been wanting to hear those words for ever. I can see the bottom of his jaw twitching, and his hand clutches mine a little tighter.

'So, truthfully, there are some things that I would like to say.' I can't stop now because I'm on a roll, and I'm nervous but doing it. 'Lulu, I loved our conversation earlier today and I want things to be more like that between us from now on. Mum and Dad, it's weird hearing about your sex stories, but I'm glad you're happy. And Marla, well … so many things. But mainly, no one cares if the fucking mayor is here.'

'Gemma!' Mum looks shocked but also pleased that someone other than her is putting Marla in her place.

'Apologies if any of that came out wrong, but it's going to take me a minute to get used to being vulnerable, and telling you how I really feel.'

'I'm sorry about the Gem-man night. I didn't know how much it bothered you,' Mum says, still looking teary. Dad nods in agreement and Lulu mouths, 'Sorry'.

Mia sniffs as though all of this was so unnecessary.

'And Mia, I don't even know why you're in this little huddle. You're *not* family and I'd rather not discuss this with you. And Ben isn't for you. So I think you'd better give up and move on to someone else.'

Mia huffs and strides off. I feel an urge to call out something to get her to come back, and realise old habits die hard. But I resist. I stand silently and let her sulk away.

Ben grins at me and I can't help but smile. Who *am I*? My inner voice says, *Slay, girl, slay*.

'Lulu, I apologise if I stuffed up your wedding, or took away any of the focus. I really needed to share all of this though.'

'Consider it all forgiven.' She gives me a warm smile. 'Especially if one of you gets me another one of those pink fairy floss things.'

'Done. I'll get you thirty.' I turn to look at Ben. 'Finally, Ben. Ben Thomas, you annoy the crap out of me, but also, you're lovely, a true stand-up guy and so genuine. So thank you.'

Marla sighs. 'Well, this is just a waste of time really. I'm going to see the mayor. *Some* of us do care that she's here.'

Dad and Mum smile at us, and Mum hugs me and tells me she loves me, and that really makes me glow from the inside. Then Lulu winks and says, 'Where's my cocktail?' and we all laugh. But they know to give us some space.

'That can't have been easy.' Ben stands close, and just by being there, it feels like he's absorbed some of my worry. 'But you did the right thing. Ten points to Gryffindor.'

I grins. 'It felt pretty darn good too.'

I see a hint of trepidation in his eyes. 'Since you're on the truth wagon now, tell me, how do you really feel about me doing those edits?'

A flush of residual annoyance runs through me. 'Beyond annoyed. Livid.'

He's not affected. 'I bet you haven't even read them.'

'Correct. I deleted the file.'

'I knew you'd do that. Check your Writing folder.'

I lean back and stare at him. 'You saved two copies?'

'I know you.'

I laugh. 'You make a good faux boyfriend.'

'Yep, if that's what we're doing.'

I want to ask, *What* are *we doing?* but I don't. Because there's still one thing to clear up.

'So, five people down, one to go. Adam.' I give a deep sigh.

'You're going to say no?'

'I need to tell him it's over – *we're* over.' I shake my head. 'We ran the course. I don't hate him, we're just … different.'

I have some things to take care of I should have dealt with a long time ago.

Chapter Thirty-Two

A dam takes the news rather well. I expected him to be at least slightly disappointed and say something like 'I Love You,' or 'We Belong Together', and I had a speech prepared for that. But he doesn't.

He just stays silent and says, 'Well, Gemma, I hope you know what you want, because I'm not going to fight for you.'

I roll my eyes. 'How romantic.'

'I'm going places and you're not going to be able to enjoy all the money or the house we could have bought now I'm Head of Digital Strategy.'

'That's fine. I'm not really into job titles that much anyway.'

'What's got into you? You're normally so much nicer than this.'

'I think you mean I'm normally a doormat. And I've decided not to be one of those anymore.'

'You're like a different person.'

'Thank God.'

'Goodbye, Gemma.' He hangs up.

And that's that. I don't feel the need to apologise, or call him back and see if he's okay. And it feels like an immense relief.

I open my phone and log into the account that connects me to my laptop.

Truth time.

Shaking slightly, I open the folder and can see he's saved the file exactly where he said he did. He's labelled it: 'Take Two: Weasel's version'. I open it up and scroll through all the changes and suggestions.

They're not just good edits and comments. They're incredible. And he's absolutely right, I did dilute things because I was trying to write for every reader … because I was being too nice. Halfway through he's written, *If you write for yourself, with no reader in mind, and you stop giving a crap about what anyone thinks of you, then this book will be one of the best I've ever had a chance to read/edit.*

Afterwards he's written one last comment.

It's four a.m. and you're sleeping and I want to talk to you about this book, because Gemma, it moved me. You write about love and connection and community in a way I'd never seen or thought about. It's made me feel bad for just focusing on myself all this time at work, and maybe being a bit cutthroat. I do help people out now and then, but not enough. I used to think it was just us – Lucas, Bella and me – against the world, but now I think I want to let others in a bit. Well, you, I want to let you in a bit. So it seems … you have rubbed off on me.

I can feel tears in my eyes. He's seen things I hadn't. But also, he was kind. He was amazing. And I can't wait to go and tell him.

I walk back to the dance floor, a smile on my face. Ben is waiting for me.

'Done?'

'Single. And free.' I grin at him. 'And I read the edits too.'

'Just now?'

'Yes, I'm an avid multitasker. P.S., the edits? They're amazing.'

'Are they?' He has a grin the size of Italy on his face.

'They were fantastic.'

'Well, *you* did fantastic. You're a good writer. No, Gem, actually you're great.'

'I thought you said I was the best?'

'Ha, well, it was one of the best books I'd read in a long time.'

I glow. 'It feels so good hearing that. You can tell me as much as you want.'

Ben hands me a glass of champagne. 'And you did so well with your family just now.'

I take a sip. 'This truth-telling is quite freeing really. A bit like I'm travelling at a fast speed, to the stars and back.'

He smiles at me. 'So I was thinking about before, with the basilisk and you being Hermione. Does that make me Harry or Ron?'

'Actually, you're probably Snape.'

'Ouch, she hits and she hurts.'

'Well, you do have a Slytherin vibe.' I grin at him. 'And before you say anything, I'm not a Hufflepuff.'

'You completely are though.'

'Not anymore.'

'No, you're right, something changed earlier. I got a solid Gryffindor vibe.'

'It was bravery.' I puff out my chest like I'm a solider.

'I'll let you have it for now.'

'So, now we're together, what will the office think when you step back from chief editor and give it to me?' I tease him.

'Ha! Not so fast. There could be other plans for you.'

'Other plans? Isn't that what people say when they're firing you?'

He laughs. 'Not at all.'

I pull myself up on the stone wall that rings the front lawn. 'I'm going to sit here for a bit and let everything that's happened settle in. Including the fact that you came back to chase me.'

'I think "chase" is a bit of an exaggeration.'

'How the tables have turned, Benjamin. The stories I'll tell back in the office,' I say loftily.

'You wouldn't.'

'I would.'

When he doesn't respond, I kick him gently from where I'm sitting. It's meant to be playful but my shoe falls off and my toes graze further up than I intend, catching just above his knee.

'Don't.' He smiles, but there's a small warning tone.

So of course I do it again. This time I swing a bit harder,

and connect with his inner thigh. He flinches in a way that suggests he likes it too much.

'Gemma.' His jaw is clenched but he doesn't step away. I feel a shiver come over me, as I realise how close I am to his boxers, his package, his penis. *I bet it's perfect too.*

'More champagne?' he offers.

Not a good idea. It's clearly already gone to my head.

I nod. He grabs two glasses from a passing waiter then walks back. I jump off the stone wall. He's close now, giving me a glass. My hand is inches from his chest. I can almost feel the warmth.

He stays there, staring at me. Those blue eyes piercing me, undoing me. 'So, I'm wondering, Evans, how much would it take to keep you quiet?' His voice is deep and husky.

I tried not to think about his inviting lips, that kiss.

'So much.' I hate myself for playing this game, but I can't stop.

'What would you need me to do for your silence?'

The tension between us is palpable.

'I have no idea.' I whisper.

I have images of him kissing me again, moaning, like a man starved. Like a man devouring me. That's how I'd like to go out of this world. Being devoured.

He steps closer, leans in. We're inches apart. I get light-headed. And dammit, here we are again. There's something about this guy that's addictive. And the closer he gets, the harder it is to... Oh. Now he's tracing my hand lightly up and down. A zing travels immediately up my spine.

'Give me some idea.' He holds my gaze, his stare

hungry. It penetrates me to my core. I feel my knees become butter, about to give out on me. I have to hold myself back. *I won't respond, I won't respond.*

'Like what…' I chew my lip, biting down so hard that it gives me a pulse. Everything is beating hard. 'I don't know what you want.'

'Yes, you do.' He is close now. So close. I can smell his cedar, feel the warmth, from his build. He's so tall and large, he could pick me up right now with one hand.

'What are we doing, Gemma?' It's his eyes and the expression in them that stop me. He's turned on too. He wants me.

'Standing.' It's the only thing I can say.

'Yes. And?'

I know he's asking about us. The tension between us… This is more than just pretending to be together. This is more than just friends, isn't it? His jaw twitches again. I want him, I do. The more I try and think about Ben, the muddier it gets. Are we friends? Colleagues? More?

'We could have a…' I want to say kiss. A fling. But I don't want that from him. I want *more*.

'A one-night stand?'

'How did you know I was going to say that?'

'I guessed.'

I nod. 'We could.'

Already I'm undressing him in my mind, tearing off that beautiful tuxedo. Imagining my hands on his smooth chest, unbuckling his pants, the next day, lying in bed, happy, together. I let myself picture it. Ben in my apartment, us quietly reading books, looking up every now and then to share a great line we've just read. In winter, him getting up out of the warm duvet to make us a carafe of delicious coffee. In summer, an early morning walk on the beach at sunrise, spotting the surfers.

Nothing about it feels like a fling, a one-night thing. I feel my cheeks blush, and a warmth spreads from my stomach, underneath my ribcage, and it's a feeling I know well. I *like* him.

He steps back and something shifts in his expression, as though he's assessing the situation. He said carefully, 'I guess we could.'

'No strings.' Even though suddenly I want the strings. All the strings.

He looks at me, and sighs. 'I mean, my friends would think I'm an idiot saying this. But no.'

Oh.

'I can't do that. Not with you, Gemma.'

Oh.

'I want more. I want you every night.'

My heart beats wildly. 'Every night?'

'Every… single… one. Gemma…'

'Are you…'

'Screwing the no-dating-at-work policy, and asking you to be my real girlfriend? Yes.'

Every little hair stands on end. I'm on fire. Inside. Outside.

'So?'

He leans down, cups my cheek in his hand, and slowly leans in. I tilt my head up. He's so close I can feel the warmth of his breath, his eyes are staring hungrily at me with a look that says, *I want you. Now.*

I didn't realise I was making him wait. Who am I kidding, I'm out of my mind for Benjamin McDonald, and it's about time he knew it.

'Yes, absolutely categorically, a hundred per cent yes.'

'Good, now, little viper, stop talking.'

I'm so breathless because *this is it.* I'm single, and I'm about to be kissed, by him. The most handsome, interesting, wonderful man in the world.

He leans down and for a second he pauses. That delectable second, where you know what's coming, and you want it. *You want it so bad.*

Just before I pass out from the anticipation, he bends towards me. Lowers his head. Suddenly, he presses his mouth against mine. Hot lips. Sweet lips. Softly kissing me, his fingers fluttering over my jaw.

I want more. I want him everywhere. I melt. His mouth opens. Our tongues find each other. He groans. I can smell him everywhere on my lips, my skin, wrapped around me – the scent of pine trees, cedar woods. His body shifts, the hardness of it welcome against mine. I grab his neck and tug him closer. It's building now. The urgency. This isn't the kind of kiss you have at a lovely wedding. This is the kind you have behind closed doors, the kind that involves button-popping and being lifted easily and held against a wall.

As if reading my mind, Ben breaks away. His eyes are melted blue pools.

'Now I'm taking you to my hotel room.' His voice is deep and gravelly.

'Mine.'

'No, yours is a grubby little fever room.'

'And yours is a vampire room, where I think you sleep upside down in the closet.'

He leans down, brushing his lips against mine, biting my bottom lip, teasingly. 'Why don't we go and find out?'

And that's all he needs to say, because I fall into him, and he practically carries me, as if I were weightless, across the lawn and up the stairs, taking them two at a time, saying, 'Lifts take too long.'

Inside his room he pushes me up against the wall. I wrap my legs around him, straddling him. He kisses me, slowly and tenderly at first, like a long ache, but our kisses quickly become deeper, more intimate. He hitches up my dress, grazing his fingers against my thighs. His hand then hard on my ass.

My body responds like it never has before. His hands are everywhere. I melt. I'm on fire every place he touches me. But every now and then he groans, and pushes me back as if it's too much, then pulls me towards him, as if it's not enough.

He pulls down the top of my dress, then my bra and the cold air makes everything tighten. Goosebumps on my arms, and the back of my neck tingles.

He breaks for a second, stares at me, into me. I've never felt so together, so bonded with someone in my entire life.

'God, Gemma.'

I know. I don't want it to stop so I pull him back to me, our mouths frantically finding each other once more.

He kisses my neck as if he couldn't wait to put his hot lips everywhere on my skin. His moans sound deep, wanting, *hungry*. I feel his tongue move down, and run lightly across my breasts. My nipple is in his mouth, he bites gently and I moan loudly. Every hair on my body stands to attention.

'Bed. Now,' he murmurs, carrying me easily.

He throws me onto the bed. Unbuttons his pants, his shirt too, until he's standing there naked, with his perfect body, staring at me as though he's about to devour me.

I want us to stop, to take all the time in the world, and I also want him *now*. If I don't have him, I'll explode. He leans down and his hands grab my ass. He finds the edges of my g-string, curls his fingers around it, and gently tugs it off.

The slowness is agony.

He teases, as he leans over and pulls off my dress, the feeling of silk brushing over me making all the hairs stand on end. Heat rises to the surface of my skin. How can something feel so *right*?

All my senses are overwhelmed as he slides on top of me. Warm skin to skin. His hands, everywhere. Hot little fires. I burn for him. And then he's kissing me, hot and passionate, and I'm losing all sense of time and place as our bodies slide together.

And then he's all the way inside me. A jolt of electricity shoots through my body and I am gripping the edge of the duvet, trying to muffle the many moans coming out of my mouth, and it's magic. It's exactly how I always imagined it would be.

Chapter Thirty-Three

The airport is bustling at this time of day but thankfully we're already seated in Seats 10A and 10C in business class, ready to head home.

Flashbacks of last night run through my mind. I don't realise I'm smiling until Ben looks at me seductively, as if reading my thoughts. He leans over and kisses me softly, and I melt under his touch.

'How different is this, compared to when we arrived?'

'Very,' I say, proudly lifting my feet. 'I'm wearing real shoes.'

Ben reaches out, grabs my hand and squeezes it. 'That's my girlfriend – real classy, this one.'

'Her boyfriend is a wedding escort. Watch out.'

We grin at each other. *This*, I think, *is what it means to be happy.* Bantering with my boyfriend in business class.

The flight attendant arrives and welcomes us with a tray of champagne, and a cute little bowl of nuts.

I sigh happily. 'You know, I could get used to this.'

'What, bowls of nuts being delivered to you?'

'Yes, and maybe you. Here. And business class. I've decided I belong here.' I grin at him.

'Shall I order you four chocolate puddings?'

'Very funny.'

'Just remember that I'm not made of money, not until I sign another bestseller or the next Man Booker prize winner, so enjoy business for now because next time we'll probably be back in cattle class.'

'Sad. Speaking of literary prizes, who was that author you were going to sign? Did you do it? Was it the mayor?'

'Oh, Gemma.'

'Oh right, that was *another* lie. So much for your radical honesty.'

'It wasn't a lie.'

'Then who was it? Don't tell me Lulu has convinced you that she needs a book about her and Chip. Or Mia? Watch out, she'll try and con you into writing it for her.'

'No, I haven't actually pitched to this author yet, but I have a good fourteen hours or so until I get to Dubai.'

'Your writer's in Dubai?'

'Well, technically not at the moment, but they will be.'

I look excitedly around the plane. 'Are they famous? Are they sitting near us?'

He smiles at me. 'What do you say? Shall we get some champagne and talk about it?'

Shivers run up and down my body as my mouth drops open in realisation. My body feels like it's exploding into a million pieces of confetti.

'I… Oh my goodness. *Me?*' My head is spinning.

He has the audacity to laugh. 'Are you only figuring this out now?'

'Wait, what? I'm totally confused.' I immediately want to cry, and before I can think to stop them, there they are, fat blobs running down my cheeks, and I'm not even embarrassed, not a single bit.

'I can see that.' He lovingly wipes them away. 'I assume these are happy tears?'

I nod emphatically. 'So, you want to be my editor?'

'Yep. On my first day Tony gave me your manuscript and said, "Make this work."'

It's starting to make sense. All of it.

'So the people-pleaser comments and the "it's over" conversation I overheard…'

'Tony said if I couldn't get your real author voice to come out, the book was going nowhere.'

'So you…'

'Pushed you. Prodded you. Tried to get to who you really were, so you could write something more real, rather than what you thought everyone wanted to hear.'

'Wow.'

'Sometimes it was fun.' He winks. 'But at times I could see it was hard for you, but I kept going because of your book, so it could be everything it can and should be.'

I feel a total body shiver, and my eyes fill again with tears. 'My book. I'm going to have a real book.'

'I don't think it's going to be just one book, Gemma. I wholeheartedly believe you're going to be the next big thing.'

'You can tell me that as much as you want.' I grin.

'I will, with pleasure.'

The plane starts pummelling down the runway. 'You know, I'm kind of sad this isn't a small plane because I wouldn't mind having an excuse to kiss you the entire way back.'

'Sounds to me like the perfect way to pass the time.' And with that, he puts down his champagne, takes both my cheeks in his hands, and leans in to give me the most perfect kiss of all time.

Acknowledgments

Thank you to my editors – Jennie Rothwell, Bonnie Macleod and the crew at One More Chapter. I'm forever grateful for the many nudges in the right direction and your instinct and precision.

Thank you to the best of friends that make a girl laugh, tell her when she's made a shit decision and don't ever quit having her back. Nancy 'Pants' Belas, Lil Ma Nil Crowley, Barberini Puccini, Zoe Jack and KT Hotson, you are the cheerleaders of my life. Note – I've hidden your names to slightly protect you from having any sliding DMs or a bunch of friend requests, simply because I want to monopolise all your free time for more margarita drinking.

John Casper – I'm forever inspired by the fact that you suggest we dress up like the Backstreet Boys, and although it didn't make it into this book, here's to the next... or perhaps that should be about a friendly ghost-man who had a hen's party?

Thank you to my mum and dad, who support me, and buy and read every one of my books, despite them not being crime thrillers (maybe one day?).

ONE MORE CHAPTER

The author and One More Chapter would like to thank everyone
who contributed to the publication of this story...

Analytics
James Brackin
Abigail Fryer

Audio
Fionnuala Barrett
Ciara Briggs

Contracts
Laura Amos
Laura Evans

Design
Lucy Bennett
Fiona Greenway
Liane Payne
Dean Russell

Digital Sales
Lydia Grainge
Hannah Lismore
Emily Scorer

Editorial
Kara Daniel
Charlotte Ledger
Federica Leonardis
Laura McCallen
Ajebowale Roberts
Jennie Rothwell
Tony Russell

Harper360
Emily Gerbner
Jean Marie Kelly
emma sullivan
Sophia Wilhelm

International Sales
Peter Borcsok
Ruth Burrow
Colleen Simpson

Inventory
Sarah Callaghan
Kirsty Norman

Marketing & Publicity
Chloe Cummings
Grace Edwards
Emma Petfield

Operations
Melissa Okusanya
Hannah Stamp

Production
Denis Manson
Simon Moore
Francesca Tuzzeo

Rights
Helena Font Brillas
Ashton Mucha
Zoe Shine
Aisling Smythe

Trade Marketing
Ben Hurd
Eleanor Slater

**The HarperCollins
Distribution Team**

**The HarperCollins
Finance & Royalties
Team**

**The HarperCollins
Legal Team**

**The HarperCollins
Technology Team**

UK Sales
Isabel Coburn
Jay Cochrane
Sabina Lewis
Holly Martin
Harriet Williams
Leah Woods

eCommerce
Laura Carpenter
Madeline ODonovan
Charlotte Stevens
Christina Storey
Jo Surman
Rachel Ward

**And every other
essential link in the
chain from delivery
drivers to booksellers
to librarians and
beyond!**

YOUR NUMBER ONE STOP
ONE MORE CHAPTER
FOR PAGETURNING BOOKS

One More Chapter is an award-winning global division of HarperCollins.

Subscribe to our newsletter to get our latest eBook deals and stay up to date with all our new releases!

signup.harpercollins.co.uk/ join/signup-omc

Meet the team at www.onemorechapter.com

Follow us!

 @OneMoreChapter_

 @OneMoreChapter

 @onemorechapterhc

 @onemorechapterhc

Do you write unputdownable fiction? We love to hear from new voices. Find out how to submit your novel at www.onemorechapter.com/submissions